BURGLAR OF SOULS

a novel

Brian Ferris

Love is a thief:
A burglar of souls
It steals integrity and faith
And leaves nothing but the truth

***

"When the body is awake the soul is its servant, and is never her own
mistress…But when the body is at rest, the soul, being set in motion
and awake…has cognizance of all things—sees what is visible, hears
what is audible, walks, touches, feels pain, ponders."
Hippocrates of Kos (460-370 BC)
Regimen 4, or Dreams

PROLOGUE

Ballycastle, County Antrim, N.I.
Friday, August 6, 1971

Ballycastle was just as Carol had imagined it: The pretty seaside town with its beaches was picture-perfect—a real-life postcard. On their way here, she and Bill had visited the legendary *Giant's Causeway* and walked the forest trails of *Glenariff*—one of the more magically scenic Glens of Antrim—where Carol decided that fairies and leprechauns simply *had* to live amidst its waterfalls, streams, and ancient forests. She had delighted in the sheer, natural beauty of those places, but as far as Carol was concerned, Ballycastle was the icing on the cake. And here, on the Causeway Coast of Antrim, the "Troubles" currently plaguing this small country seemed a million miles away.

Born in Belfast in 1951, Carol Quinlan emigrated to Canada with her parents while still a toddler, and was raised in south-central Ontario. In 1970, with Northern Ireland deep into its third year of civil unrest (and over her worried parents' objections), she applied to and was accepted at Belfast's, Queen's University. Carol returned to Belfast to live with her aunt and her family, while she worked towards earning a B.A. in archeology.

Bill Flanagan, a Belfast boy born and bred, had vague plans about becoming a teacher and would be starting his third year at Queen's the following month when Carol planned on starting her second. They had met at the university's Christmas dance where Bill was smitten by the beautiful and vivacious Carol. Due to his fervent pursuit of her, they began to date. By the spring, Carol and he had become a veritable couple; each enamoured of the other and delighting in one another's company.

After checking in at Seaview ("It's just *Seaview*—not *the* Seaview," the pretty receptionist insisted), a quaint bed and breakfast nestled into the hill overlooking the harbour, they decided to stroll back into the town proper, and there, amongst the bustling gift shops, and ice cream parlours along the seafront, Bill found the pub he was looking for:

"It hasn't changed a bit!" he said. Looking at his wrist where there was no watch, he licked his lips and added, "I think it must be about that time, don't you?"

The Harbour Bar was typical of Antrim pubs: A large, front door, wedged open, lent access to a foyer and two more doors, both of which were closed. They were wooden doors, but the top half of each sported a pane of frosted glass.; the one on the left had the word BAR in Gothic Old English script etched into its glass while the one on the right was marked LOUNGE. Bill reached for the handle of this door. "Probably a wee bit nicer in here…" he said, "…what do ye think?" Carol nodded her acquiescence, and there, in the purportedly *nicer* lounge, they sat at a table by the window, drank Guinness and beer, and ate "homemade" fish and chips while they planned the rest of their day.

From the back pocket of his jeans, Bill produced the brochure picked up at the bed and breakfast and spread it out on the table between them. He stabbed a finger excitedly at a spot on the pamphlet. "Look," he said, pointing, "Bonamargy! We have to go there. I haven't been there in years, but I remember us going there when I was a kid."

"Is it an old church, or something?" asked Carol.

"No…" said Bill, thoughtfully, then, "…well, mebbe—probably was a church there at one time, but now, it's just an old ruin. I think, once upon a time, it was an abbey…or somethin'."

Carol elbowed him in the ribs, playfully. "It says 'Bonamargy Friary' right there on the map."

"So, is it a ruin, like Dunluce Castle?"

"Well, no. I don't think it's quite as dilapidated as Dunluce…"—here, wringing his hands and rasping his voice, he added—"…but there's a very old graveyard there—ancient—and *that's* where they say *she's* buried…"

Carol rolled her eyes. "Okay, I'll bite. *Who* do *they* say is buried there?"

Bill looked around the near-empty premises theatrically, making sure that no one was listening in, and whispered, "The Black Nun, of course…" This time Carol said nothing. Moments passed as she sat smiling sardonically. "Okay, okay," he said, lifting his hands defensively. "Ye don't haveta get rough; I'll tell ye everything I know…"

Bill proceeded to recount the legend of The Black Nun—or at least, his version of what he remembered it to be, finishing with, "…so, according to local folklore, this nun, Julia McQuillan, was *murdered* by Vikings, or mebbe it was the Normans, or…or, somebody. Anyway, Julia became the legendary Black Nun *of* Bonamargy, and her ghost still haunts the ruins to this very day! It appears every month…on the night of the full moon…at the exact, same spot where she met her gruesome end!" Wringing his hands again, Bill laughed like a theatrical villain, and Carol smirked obligingly, but even though Bill's knowledge of the legend seemed rudimentary, she found the story intriguing.

"Why don't we go there now?" she said.

Bill chuckled. But she was serious. He looked appraisingly at her short, white sundress, and fashionable, but impractical, high-heeled sandals. "Then, mebbe we should go back to the B&B and get ye somethin' a bit more suitable to wear," he said. "Ye're not exactly dressed to go traipsing around dirty, oul ruins, are ye?"

"*Traipsing?*" Carol had snorted. "Listen to you. Who goes *traipsing* nowadays?" Rising, she picked up her purse and pushed the roughly folded brochure into it. "Come on, *Dad!*" she said. "I'll be fine like this. Let's go."

"Listen," said Bill, "Bonamargy*'s* on the road out of town…off the beaten track, so to speak…so why don't we have another pint, and think about it, and—"

"Oh no," said Carol. "I know how this works. We'll just end up sitting here all afternoon, drinking."

"No!" said Bill. "Honestly…we'll have one more drink here, and then we'll go check on some of the other places I used to go to when I was a kid, but I promise I'll take ye to Bonamargy afterwards, okay?"

"Okay," said Carol, "but that's a promise, right? We'll go see Ballymargy before it gets too dark."

"Aye," said Bill, catching the waitress's eye, "I promise. And it's *Bona*margy."

"Whatever," said Carol. "Just as long as we go there. I'd like to know a bit more about her."

"Who?" said Bill, smiling at the waitress who was approaching their table.

"Jesus, Bill!" Carol smacked his shoulder. "The Black Nun, of course. What was her name again?"

"Julia McQuillan," said Bill.

PART ONE

1662-1665

CHAPTER ONE

Ballycastle, County Antrim
Saturday, September 23, 1662

Julia McQuillan dragged her sister from the dark belly of the Harbour Inn into the street and the broad light of day. Máiri, at twenty-six, four years younger than Julia, struggled and screamed, and cursed her to no avail. Donal MacDonnell, following them outside, quickly intervened. Grabbing Máiri by a flailing arm, he wrenched her from her sister's grasp.

"Away with ye now, wumman," he growled. "Away, I tell ye. Leave the girl in peace!"

"*Girl!*" cried Julia. "Manys the year has come and gone since that one was a girl." Turning to her sister she reached out a hand. "Come away now, Máiri," she said. "Leave this divil and come away home with me. Sure, ye know I'll look after ye, love."

MacDonnell, a bear of a man, moved threateningly towards the much smaller woman. "Did ye not hear what I said? Are ye *deef* as well as stupid?" This drew snickers from a gathering crowd of onlookers. "Away on home with ye now," he continued, emboldened, "afore I put my toe in yer arse!"

Julia had cared for her sister since their mother's death twenty years before and stood her ground defiantly. "Oh, ye're the big man aren't ye, Donal MacDonnell?" she said. "Oh, we all know ye're right and handy at kickin' and beatin' up wimmin, but ye scare me none." Again, she turned to her sister. "Please, love, come away home with me." She threw a hand in MacDonnell's direction. "Sure, ye don't need this…this…hellion in yer life."

Máiri moved to MacDonnell's side, wrapped her arms around his waist, and laid her head against his wide chest. "Donal's my man," she sneered. "Ye're just jealous cause y' don't have a man of yer own."

"*Man!*" Julia snorted. "There's more to bein' a man than havin' balls an' whiskers, Máiri. Can ye not see what he's tryin' to do to ye, love? He's tryin' to turn ye into a trollop. Sure, he's nothin' but a whoremaster!" MacDonnell, moving unexpectedly fast for such a big man, closed the space between them and backhanded Julia across the mouth. The blow was hard enough to split her lip and knock her to the ground. Julia landed heavily on her back and lay stunned and helpless at the big man's feet.

MacDonnell was unconcerned. "You watch yer mouth, wumman," he said. "Now, I'm warnin' ye, for the last time. Take yerself off!" Laughing then, he spread his legs and stood over her prostrate form, grabbing lewdly at the front of his britches. "Y' know," he said, turning to the spectators, "mebbe Máiri's right. Mebbe all this one needs is a bit o' this."

Everyone laughed, and Julia, looking into their faces, was dismayed to see little sympathy for her. A darker fury overtook her when she saw Máiri laughing right along with them. Taking her weight on her elbows, she aimed a kick at MacDonnell's crotch, but he expecting as much, blocked the blow easily, catching her ankle in his big fist. The crowd laughed and egged him on, and whooped harder when he started to drag Julia this way and that, over the dusty cobbles in front of the inn.

Julia's skirts rode high on her thighs, and she was fighting furiously to keep her modesty when suddenly, MacDonnell stopped. The jeers and laughter turned to cheers mixed with boos when the town constable strode onto the scene alongside the innkeeper who had gone to fetch him.

Joseph Briggs was a heavily built man himself—a town official—but, like most of the menfolk of Ballycastle, he kowtowed to big Donal MacDonnell.

"What seems to be the problem here, Donal?" he said, eyeing Julia and her dishevelled state with inflated distaste. "Fix yerself, you!"

McDonnell pulled himself to his full height and expanded his chest. "This *bitch* called me a whoremaster!" he said, brimming with indignance. He gestured at the crowd. "And she said it right here...*didn't* she?" There were several, "she dids" and "that's rights" from the spectators.

Briggs, tutting, shook his head slowly in disappointment. "Ye're under arrest wumman," he said. "Ye'll be comin' with me, and comin' *peaceably*, mind ye!"

No one moved to help Julia as she struggled to her feet. She spat blood and drew her arm carelessly across her mouth. "And just what would ye be chargin' me with...constable?" At once, Briggs grabbed her left bicep and squeezed, hard. Julia grimaced but would let no sound escape her damaged lips.

"Ye'll be finding that out soon enough, won't ye?" said Briggs.

CHAPTER TWO

1

Julia was born in Ballycastle on 28 September 1632—seven years after the completion of the stone castle that gave the town its name. She was Sean and Caitlín McQuillan's firstborn. From the moment she first looked into her infant's questioning, dark brown eyes, her mother knew her baby was a "strange wee bein'."

Julia was a happy baby; playing with her toes, giggling and burbling incoherently, like most infants her age, but Caitlín's uneasiness heightened as Julia grew to be a quiet, watchful toddler, happier in her own company than in others'. Still, if that was to be the extent of her daughter's "strangeness," Caitlín could live with that.

One night, deep in the middle of Julia's third winter, unbeknownst to her mother, the child awoke to find an old woman standing beside her cot, smiling at her benignly. Julia, unperturbed, wondered why the old woman's mouth did not move in time with her words.

"Do y' know that you and me have the same name, m' wee love?" she said. Julia missed the question and started when the old woman laughed—a laugh that became a cackle, then a cough which rattled wetly in her chest. Catching her breath, she wiped her mouth and rheumy eyes with a piece of flannel cloth before speaking again. "I'm so glad that ye can see me, darlin'," she said, "D' ye know who I am?"

Julia shook her head. She was more interested in knowing why the old woman had no teeth. The woman smiled and answered the child's unspoken question. "Because I am very old, love, that's why I've no teeth."

"Where—" Julia started, but the old woman shushed her, so she lowered her voice to a whisper. "Where do ye live?"

"Here," she said.

"Here?" Julia repeated.

"Aye," the old woman replied. "Sure, I've always lived here. I'm yer granny, love. Do ye know what that means? It means that I'm yer mammy's mammy. D' ye understand, love?" Once again, she smiled her gummy smile at her granddaughter's confusion. "Sure, it doesn't matter, darlin'. Now listen, I need ye t' give yer mammy a wee message fer me—will ye do that fer yer oul granny, love?" Without waiting for an answer, she continued, "Tell her that she has to *pray* fer her mammy. Tell her that she's forgot to pray fer me, and that I'm sufferin'. I'm tired out, and want t' rest. Now, ye won't forget will ye, love? It's important. Cat *has t'* pray fer her mammy's immortal soul. Tell her…" Julia's grandmother—her mammy's mammy—was still talking as she became one with the darkness…

It wasn't until Caitlín was tucking her in the next evening that Julia, catching a glimpse of the old lady's likeness in her mother's tired features, was suddenly reminded of the events of the previous night.

"Mammy," she said, "I 'member I have t' tell ye somethin'—it's *important*!"

"Well," said Caitlín, "tell it to me quick, then. Yer mammy's dead tired. What is so important?"

"M' granny says that the cat has t' pray for her mammy's 'mortal soul."

"What…? Who said…? What about the cat?"

"M' granny—*your* mammy!" said Julia, impatiently. "She said that the cat has t' pray for her mammy's 'mortal soul!"

"Yer granny!" said Caitlín. "How—"

"She's no teeth, ye know!" said Julia. "But she says that *you* forgot t' pray fer her…and that she's tired out…and that she wants to rest."

Caitlín's mind reeled. "When?" she said. "When did she say this?"

"Last night," said Julia, matter-of-factly. "She was right there, where you are now."

"Last night…" said Caitlín, "…*here?*"

"Yes," said Julia. "She told me that she was my granny. 'I'm yer mammy's mammy,' she said. And she said that it's important: The cat *has* to pray for her mammy's 'mortal soul!'"

Caitlín went to her knees beside the cot and clasped her daughter's hands in her own. "Cat," she whispered. "Dear God."

"Cat" had been a pet name used by no one except Caitlín's mother, Julia's namesake. She had been dead and in the grave for years, the pet name buried with her.

"Are ye alright, Mammy?" said Julia, worried now by her mother's obvious distress.

"Did she say anythin' else to ye, Julia love?"

"No," said Julia. "She just told me to give my mammy a wee message, that's all. Oh, wait—she told me that her and me have the same name."

At this, Caitlín began to cry. "Oh, God forgive me!" she said into the dimly lit, one-room hovel. "How in the name of *God* did I forget m' own mother?" Taking her daughter's hands, she placed them under the child's chin, in prayer fashion, then resting her chin on the tips of her own tented fingers, said, "*We'll* pray for yer granny, won't we love? We'll pray for yer granny's *immortal* soul *every* night from now on! Starting right now!"

Together, mother and daughter prayed fervently to God, and Jesus, and Mary and most of the saints that Caitlín could remember, asking that her mother's soul be received into Heaven. When they were done, and Julia was crawling back under her coarse woolen blanket, she asked:

"Mammy, m' granny said that she lives here…does she?"

Caitlín's flesh tingled slightly. "Well," she said, "no…no, not no more anyway. She…yer granny…she lives in Heaven now."

"But that means she's dead, doesn't it?"

"Yes, it does, love. Yer granny's been dead for seven years. I meant that her *soul* lives in Heaven now."

"Because we prayed for that t' happen?" said Julia.

"That's right."

"Mammy…" Julia fixed her gaze on her mother's eyes, "…will m' granny come t' see me again?"

Another little shiver preceded Caitlín's answer. "No, m' wee darlin'. At least I…I don't think she will."

"But, did her soul live here before?" said Julia. "I mean before we prayed for her."

Caitlín did not want to think about that. "Hush now," she said. "Time for sleep. 'Night, and God bless ye."

In the following days and weeks, Caitlín would often find Julia on her cot, or sitting on the fender, to the side of the fire, talking earnestly with someone invisible. As Julia had not mentioned seeing her granny since that night, her mother decided not to mention the episode to Sean. Secretly she had hoped the incident would turn out to be an anomaly. Now she could see that that was not the case. And although Julia's daily life was otherwise unaffected by these conversations with her invisible visitor, Caitlín found them unsettling.

One evening, she finally broached the subject with her husband, catching him before he made his nightly excursion to the Harbour Inn. "I'm a wee bit worried about our Julia, Sean," she said. "I've seen her sittin' out there, talkin' to herself…well…I mean…talkin' like she was talkin' to somebody…but…but there's nobody there."

Sean was dismissive. "What are ye blatherin' about, wumman," he said. "Sure, she's only a child. She's only playin'."

"No," said Caitlín, "it's not just playin'. I think she really thinks somebody's there; I think *she* sees them." In her mind she saw Julia, earlier that same afternoon, sitting on the old stump that Sean used as a chopping block, talking earnestly with someone Caitlín could not see.

"Well," said Sean, "if the child's talkin' with the *wee folk*, it's because of the *Maher* blood in 'er. Sure, yer ma wasn't right in the head either!" Seeing his wife stiffen, he added, "What's the matter with ye? Sure, ye told me that yerself!"

Sean turned to the child, who was sitting on the hearthstone playing with a ragged piece of cloth. "Julia," he said, raising his voice, "hear me now. Behave yerself, d' ye hear me? Stop worryin' yer mammy with all this nonsense!" Julia, her face a picture of confusion, stared silently at her parents.

"Now," he said, "where did ye put m' cap, wumman?" Caitlín retrieved Sean's cap from the chair upon which he had thrown it earlier and put it into his hand. Sean lowered his voice to a whisper. "I'm tellin' ye, she's alright," he said, donning his cap. "She's a *bairn*, for God's sake. Listen now, I won't be too late." And with that, he was gone.

"Julia," said Caitlín, "C'mon love, it's time fer bed."

Minutes later, as she was about to tuck the child in, the youngster balked. "Wait, mammy!" she said. "Don't ye remember? We haveta say our prayers." So, mother and daughter knelt on the floor beside the little cot, and recited their prayers, after which Julia happily slipped under her blanket. "Night, night, mammy."

Caitlín hesitated by the cot. "Julia," she said, "who was it ye were talkin' to today...earlier on, I mean...down by the stump?"

"Oh, that was Declan," said Julia, without hesitation. "He used t' live here y' know...a long time ago."

"What d' ye mean, here," said Caitlín, "D' ye mean *here*...here in this house?"

"Ach no, Mammy," said Julia, "not in *this* house. Declan told me that he can't find *his* house no more, but *our* house wasn't here before. He said there used to be a big tree in the place where I was sitting, and that he climbed it all the time. Then one day, he fell, and then, he said, he was in the dark."

Caitlín shivered and pulled her shawl tighter around her. "The dark?"

"That's what Declan said. He said there's no colours. He said he could see his mammy and daddy, but nobody could see him, and he couldn't talk to nobody for ages and ages, and then he met *me*! I can see him, and I can talk t' him, and he can talk t' me. But, mammy," Julia looked earnestly into her mother's eyes, "Declan's sad. He told me he doesn't like the dark." Suddenly the child reached out and grabbed her mother's hand. "Mammy!" she said, "I think we should pray for Declan too, mammy…like we do for m' granny…mebbe we can send Declan's 'mortal soul to Heaven too, and then he won't be in the dark no more!"

"Yes," said Caitlín, forcing a smile, "I think we should too." And they did.

Less than a year later Caitlín, hearing a voice, awoke in the middle of the night to find her daughter standing at her bedside.

"In the name of—" she started. "Julia, love, ye scared the life out of yer mammy! What's ailin' ye?"

Julia was sobbing. "It's m' daddy," she said, "he's…he's—"

Caitlín realized then that she was alone in bed. "Yer…yer daddy," she said. "What's wrong with yer daddy, love?"

All at once, Julia was pulling at her mother's wrist. "Come on, mammy. We haveta pray for m' daddy. He's in the dark…and he says he cold…and he's frightened…and he says it hurts." Julia began to cry harder then. "Come on, mammy, ye haveta get up," she cried. "Daddy's hurtin'…we haveta pray fer m' daddy's soul and get him t' the light!"

Later, when Julia succumbed to sleep, Caitlín tucked the child into her blanket, and with her thumb, she made the sign of the cross on Julia's forehead. "'Night, and God bless ye," she whispered and went to sit by the dying embers of the fire.

She was sitting there when, just as the sun rose, they brought Sean McQuillan's body home. Stabbed in a drunken brawl over a game of cards, he had bled to death on the cobblestones, just outside the Harbour Inn. Julia helped her mother wash and prepare her father's body for burial: neither wept.

Caitlín McQuillan, then eight months pregnant with Máiri, and already leery of her daughter, began to consciously avoid unnecessary contact with Julia, drawing away from her, as if she was contaminated. It was ironic, that eight years later, it was she who ultimately contracted typhus and lay dying with her unafflicted daughters at her bedside.

"Julia, see and take care of yer sister, alright?" she whispered. "And listen t' me now Máiri, see and mind Julia…she's yer big sister."

"Yes, Mammy," said Máiri.

"Don't worry, mammy," said Julia, "sure we'll be alright."

Caitlín reached for her elder daughter's hand. "Julia, I—"

"Don't fret yerself now, Mammy," said Julia, "sure, I won't let ye be in the dark fer long…"

<h1 style="text-align:center">2</h1>

It was due to the serious and industrious twelve-year-old, that the sisters managed to survive after the untimely death of their mother. Julia found work as a scullery maid, labouring for the local gentry, and having learned to sew under her mother's tutelage, she took to mending her employers' and neighbours' clothes during what spare time she was afforded. It was through her diligence that the rent for the hovel they inherited was paid, and food graced their table, though at times it was barely enough, and the sisters were no strangers to hunger.

The siblings were as different as night and day—in looks and personalities—with the elder assuming the nocturnal attributes. Julia was dark haired—nearly black—and milky white-skinned, while Máiri was fair of hair and complexion. Julia was taciturn while Máiri was garrulous. Both were attractive, but the younger was more at ease with her allure, so that she was considered the more beautiful by those that concerned themselves with such things.

But Máiri was indolent: When she was deemed old enough, she joined her sister in the sculleries of the many who were better off, but was often dismissed from their employ after only a few days, sometimes hours, of service, although it was never *her* fault.

Because of Julia's meagre income, and Máiri's inability to add to it, the girls depended on the charity of neighbours for the ragged clothes on their backs. It was these same neighbours who came to the realization that Julia had innate, soothsaying abilities, and that her augury was uncannily precise. Thus it was that she became sought after for counsel—even by those in the big houses—and *they* paid cash for her services.

It was after some ugly experiences that Julia learned what and what *not* to divulge in her foretelling. For instance, she discovered early that most women did not really want to know if their husbands were philanderers or not, for what if they were? There was little that they could do about it. And so, the knowledge of the infidelity would fester, until frustration and anger, in need of an outlet, would focus on the *deliverer* of that information.

Julia realized it was better to keep some things to herself.

And she would not foretell of coming death, for the Reaper was a constant companion in her world, in need of no introduction from her.

So, Julia raised Máiri, and watched her sister grow into a lovely young woman who exhibited undesirable character traits. Máiri was not ungrateful, but the teenager did not take advice—nor suffer admonishment—from Julia:

"You're not my mother!" she would exclaim when asked about where she had been, or whom she had been with. "And *I'm* not one of your old crones hanging onto your every word. *I don't believe you can see the future any more than I can.*" But Julia *could* see that it was a black day when Máiri met Donal MacDonnell—and a worse one when he lured her from their hovel...

3

The MacDonnell family no longer held the power it had once wielded with impunity in East Antrim. The clans' resistance to the English crown had crumbled at the beginning of the century and their chieftains' dominance forever diminished. But through the efforts of Connor MacDonnell, a man worthy of the title of chieftain, the name was still held in high esteem in the area. It was unfortunate that Donal, Connor MacDonnell's first-born son and heir, was undeserving of similar esteem among his peers. The younger MacDonnell did not attempt to elicit respect; Donal preferred to use the MacDonnell name, his position, and his size to intimidate and bully others to his will.

In time, a disappointed Connor, rightfully accusing his son of indolence and lacking in moral fibre, disinherited Donal, leaving the young man feeling misused and resentful at the admonition and being left to fend for himself.

Donal was a handsome man. Tall and heavily built, with a mane of ginger curls falling about his broad shoulders. When it suited, he had a disarming, boyish charm about him, but he was first and foremost a bully and a vicious one at that. Donal had a propensity for drinking, brawling, gambling, and whoring—not necessarily in that order. Among the more upstanding inhabitants of the seventeenth-century town of Ballycastle, Donal MacDonnell was known as a *bad egg*, and Julia McQuillan had been correct in her accusatory description of him during their confrontation outside the Harbour Inn...

CHAPTER THREE

1

The gaol in Ballycastle was located under the town hall, amongst its low-ceilinged cellars. Inmates, male and female, child and adult, were held in a large cell, twelve feet wide and twenty-four feet long. Regardless of the season, its stone walls and straw-strewn, flagstone floors were cold and damp. A small, barred window looking out at street-level was its sole source of natural light.

On the narrow stairway, before she reached the subterranean level of the town hall building, Julia's nostrils were assaulted by the acrid stench of human waste. Bending over on the steps, she retched. Briggs, chuckling mirthlessly, nudged her from behind and forced her to keep moving. He selected a key from the assortment attached to a large ring hanging on his arm as they descended.

"Oh, ye'll get used to the stink soon enough," he said.

In the dank atmosphere at the bottom of the stairs, the flame of the torch Briggs carried sputtered, fighting a losing battle with the suffocating darkness.

Briggs did not need a light to find the cell door. "Over there," he said, placing his hand between Julia's shoulder blades and shoving her forward, laughing when she stumbled. "Careful ye don't fall, wumman. We wouldn't want ye to hurt yerself, would we?" He found the keyhole in the heavy wooden door.

"Stand clear!" he cried, while simultaneously kicking the door open and laughing heartily the thud and the loud yelp of pain. "Told ye to stand back." A draught breathed life into the dead flame in his torch, and by its feeble glow, Julia saw the faces of the cell's occupants.

There were many shufflings and scamperings under the straw; apparently the extra light and commotion were not appreciated by some of the cell's smaller inhabitants.

Briggs grabbed Julia by the same bruised bicep he had manhandled earlier and pulled her close. "Stick out yer hands," he said gruffly. Releasing her arm, he deftly removed the shackles at her wrists. As she stood rubbing her chafed skin, Briggs forced her back against the wall and pressed his stinking, sizeable mass against her. "Not so cocky now, are ye?" he said, pushing a hand roughly between her thighs. Julia raked his face with her nails, making him back off, but he slashed at her face with the large key ring. "*Bitch!*" he spat, and grabbing a fistful of hair, he pulled her off the wall, and flung her into the cell with such force that she stumbled and landed on her hands and knees in the damp, rancid straw.

Briggs rubbed the scratches on his cheeks. "There's one for ye, boys," he said, "that's if yer ma will let yiz have at her." He peered into the far corner of the cell, and said, "Alright, Nell? But watch yerselves, m' lads. Yiv seen it for yerselves…that's one nasty bitch!" Turning his attention back to Julia, he jangled the ring of keys at her and smirked. "Now, be a good girl, you, and try and behave yerself, while ye await the judge's convenience." Chortling, he stepped back and pulled the heavy door after him. Julia cringed and shuddered when she heard the key in the lock make a loud *click*.

Julia discovered she was sharing the cell with five others. In one corner, a woman of indeterminate age sat on the floor; Nell, she presumed. The woman's forehead rested on her raised knees, held in place by fingers intertwined at the shins. Nell's hair, long, grey and matted, fell loosely about her face and shoulders. She did not deign to look up.

The rest were males of various age and stature, all of whom looked at their new cell mate with avid interest. Julia scrambled to the nearest wall, and put her back against it.

One of the males, more boy than man, sidled up to her. "Ach, come on now, m' darlin'," he intoned in a voice that did not have the timbre aspired to, "seems like we're goin' to be here together for a wee while, so what d' ye say about ye and me getting' to know each other a wee bit better?" Leering, he advanced, pulling at the drawstring on his britches.

The woman spoke then, and the boy flinched at the sound of her voice. Julia turned to find her staring hard in their direction.

"Ye leave her be, Kieran McGuire!" the woman said. Nodding at Julia, she went on, "Thon's Julia McQuillan, and there's some would say she's not right in the head." The old woman locked eyes with the younger. "And there's some say that she's a whore—just like thon sister of hers." Julia's eyes flashed, but she remained silent.

Nell McGuire continued. "But there are others, mind ye, that say she's a *witch!*" She spat the word onto the straw beside her, and Julia quailed instantly. Being arrested and imprisoned, for disturbing the peace was one thing, being accused of witchcraft was entirely another, and something Julia did not want to contemplate. "But no matter *what* she is," Nell went on, turning her attention back to young Kieran, "You leave her be. Take yerself off into thon far corner and do what ye have to do, if ye must. . ."—the other men laughed at this—". . . but leave *her* be, if ye know what's good for ye!" Nell turned to the still snickering others. "And that goes for the rest of ye, too," she added, scowling. "Mind me now!" The chuckling ceased, and the men, cowed for now, backed off.

Julia knew of the McGuires by reputation only, and had heard rumours that Nell and her four sons were set for transportation to the Americas; apparently. They had stolen one MacDonnell sheep too many. Why Nell felt inclined to offer her a kindness, she did not know. Julia tried to show gratitude in her expression, but the woman just shook her head dismissively and let it fall once more to her knees.

Kieran McGuire scowled at Julia, grabbed obscenely at his crotch, and waggled a finger at her warningly. He slunk away to hunker in the opposite corner, and Julia was left unmolested, at least for the time being.

She spent four days and nights in the cell awaiting the judge's "convenience," sleeping little and eating less. During her confinement, Julia was nipped at and nibbled on by rats the size of kittens, and harassed by Nell's "boys" at every available opportunity. She realized from the start that she would have to go without sustenance, if she could not endure their *accidental*, rough and eager groping while she waited with them at the cell door for their daily rations of stale bread and staler ale. Each day Julia thanked God for Nell's authoritative presence in the cell.

On the morning of the fifth day—which happened to be Julia's thirtieth birthday—she was roughly manacled by a badly hungover Briggs and taken upstairs to stand trial at the Court of Petty Sessions. Customarily, the court was presided over by the local Justice of the Peace, one Thomas Connolly. Connolly had no legal training, was the town's mayor, and was obligated by his position and office to perform the role of Justice of the Peace for no remuneration. He did *not* do so happily. And on top of this, the honourable judge was a drunken misogynist who, by the hour of nine o'clock on the said morning, was already "in his cups."

"Why has this wumman been brought before me?" he asked.

Constable Briggs cleared his throat. "The accused stands before the court accused of bein' a common scold, yer honour," he intoned.

"And how does she plead?"

All eyes were on Julia who was well aware that on that cool September morning her life could be at stake. She surveyed the faces in the crowded room. Many were enjoying her predicament, for whatever the outcome of the trial, there was going to be a spectacle of some kind, and that Julia would be the main attraction. Most of the men wanted to see her punished and humiliated—*cowed*—for her "crime." They were blatantly licentious in their whispered comments. The womenfolk wished Julia chastised because she was the object of their men's lust.

Briggs stepped forward and cuffed her ear, much to the spectators' amusement. "You heard his honour, didn't ye?" he said. "How do ye plead? Guilty or not guilty?"

Julia had heard the word *witch* whispered in the crowd more than once.

"Guilty!" she said at once, before this new and dreadful accusation was considered worthy of further discussion. She flinched as Briggs made to hit her again and added, "Yer lordship."

Briggs hit her anyway. "Yer *Honour,*" he said.

"Yer Honour," Julia meekly repeated, and Briggs cuffed her again—just because he could—and the crowd laughed obligingly and merrily.

Judge Connolly, who paid no attention to the gallery, glared at her with unmasked animosity, exacerbated by the fiery redness in his eyes.

"Julia Caitlín McQuillan," he said, "ye have pled guilty to the charges laid against ye by Donal Connor MacDonnell. Wumman, ye are undoubtedly an abominable scold, and it is the sentence of this court that ye be taken from this place and flogged!" Julia swooned, and many in the audience gasped, surprised at such a harsh judgement. "Silence!" the judge bellowed. "Twenty lashes! Constable, take the prisoner away."

Even Donal MacDonnell was shocked, and it did not take much pleading or cajoling on Máiri's part to make him approach the bench and petition the judge for leniency. After some deliberation (and the promise of a compensatory flagon or two of wine), Justice Connolly reluctantly mitigated the court's original decision; Julia would not be flogged. Instead, she would endure two hours in the town pillory.

2

The pillory stood upon a raised wooden platform in the centre of the square outside the Townhall, and there, while a large crowd gathered jeering and cheering, Julia was roughly stripped to her shift by Briggs (and some willing assistants), and installed in the device.

The pillory had been built to accommodate *male* perpetrators, so Julia was forced to stretch—standing on the tips of her toes—for her head and hands to be secured in the appropriate openings. A box or a log, even a stone, could have eased the prisoner's discomfort, but Joe Briggs thought it unnecessary, and denied the procurement of such an item.

No guard was provided either: MacDonnell told Máiri, in no uncertain terms, that it had cost him enough to have the sentence mitigated, and flatly refused to pay for a guard, even though it was not unusual for prisoners to die in the pillory, killed by an enraged or mob who might throw rocks, instead of the usual offal and rotten vegetables, at the unprotected victim's head and body. Accordingly, if the crime was deemed a minor one, and the culprit's family or friends were willing to pay a nominal fee, a town watchman would be set to curb the crowd's enthusiasm, thereby ensuring the punishment remained strictly one of humiliation and *not* of execution. But Julia had no such benefactor.

It was therefore fortunate, that no one seemed to want the *un*guarded prisoner maimed—or dead, for that matter—but for two, interminably long hours, Julia was denied water, taunted and spat upon, and pelted with rotten fruit and excrement, animal and human. No stones or rocks were aimed at her, but she *was* humiliated further when overly excited children were allowed and encouraged to tear at her shift and thrash her with thin, birch switches readily provided by their elders.

Máiri was horrified at the spectacle and, leaving the leering MacDonnell and his cronies to witness her sister's torment, fled to the harbourside and took refuge in the nearly deserted Harbour Inn. By flirting and cajoling with Dan Flaherty, the portly innkeeper, she persuaded him to supply her with enough wine to dull the sharp edges of guilt that sliced her conscience. In a little over an hour, Máiri succeeded in numbing herself to the extent that when MacDonnell came looking for her in a state of arousal, she did little to thwart his advances.

Pulling her from her seat, he said, "Ye should come and see. The childer have thon crazy sister of yours stripped near-naked out there and they're whippin' her arse with switches, and she just stands there *cursin'* them!" MacDonnell's admiration was apparent. "She won't beg *anyone* fer mercy, that one."

Máiri was drunk, but during the last hour she had transferred the guilt she felt over Julia's situation to the man who now stood before her *smiling*! Blind rage took her then, and throwing herself at MacDonnell, she beat him about the head and face with clenched fists.

"It's all *your* fault," she cried. "*You* could stop them. Julia doesn't deserve *this*!"

MacDonnell pushed her arms aside and slapped her face hard enough to make Máiri fall back against a table.

She winced when touching her fingers to the welt already rising on a reddened cheek. "Julia was right," she said, sneering, "*ye're* not a man at all. Ye're just a bully…a bully, and a *coward*!"

MacDonnell, already excited, was now *incited*. Bearing down on the woman, he slapped her again and began to pull and tear at her clothing.

"Ye'd better close the doors, Dan," he yelled over his shoulder, "and make sure they *stay* closed!" The bartender acknowledged the order with a nod of his head and quickly moved to obey. Máiri, trying gamely to fend off MacDonnell's attack, realized what was happening:

"*No*, Donal!" she cried. "*Please* don't! I *love* you Donal!…sure, ye know I love ye, don't ye?" She looked at the leering corpulent Flaherty with undisguised disgust and snorted. "Why don't ye get out of here, ye fat *pig*?" Then turning back to MacDonnell, she continued in a cajoling tone, "Please, Donal, love, don't." She stroked at his curly mane with the back of her hand. "Not with *him* here, Donal, love. Why don't ye tell him to get out and leave us alone?" She appeared to relax. MacDonnell straightened and, wiping at his mouth with the back of his hand, turned to look at the innkeeper. When he turned back to Máiri, he was grinning. He wrapped Máiri in his arms. "Sure, it's alright by me if big Danny watches," he said. "Don't you pay him no mind, darlin'." Máiri, more frightened than shocked, tried to slither out of MacDonnell's arms and crawl to the door to escape, but the big man lifted her—as easily as he would have lifted a squirming piglet slated for slaughter—and threw her belly down, across the rough-hewn table. Máiri screamed, squirmed, and fought, but MacDonnell held her down with little effort on his part, restraining her with one hand pressed in the small of her back. He hoisted her skirts with the other. "These McQuillan women have *wonderful* arses, don't they, Dan m' lad?" Moving deftly between her flailing legs, he forced them apart with his thighs.

Máiri coiled, stretched, and kicked, but hit air. "Ye *coward*!" she screamed again. "Ye *bastard*!"

A shadow fell across MacDonnell's face and he slapped her naked buttock hard with his open hand. "You shut yer mouth, ye wee *bitch*!" he said. "Or ye'll be sufferin' the same fate as yer sister." He looked over his shoulder at Flaherty and smiled. "Don't be lettin' all this screamin' fool ye, Danny boy," he said, laughing. "Sure, it's all an act with this one. She *loves* this!" He slapped her backside again. "Don't ye, m' girl?" Máiri tried to roll out from beneath him, and push herself off the table, but MacDonnell simply laid his weight across her while he freed himself from his britches, whispering hoarsely, in her ear, "Ye *love* it, Máiri, don't ye?"

3

Máiri made sure that she was in the square when her sister was released from the pillory. She brought Julia a cup of water and some bread, and draped what was left of her strewn clothing over her arm. Julia ignored Máiri's overtures at first, then grabbed the water and gulped it down greedily. Seconds later, she vomited all of it.

Máiri laid her hand gently, on Julia's shoulder. "It's alright, Julia. I'll go and get ye some more."

Julia shrugged Máiri's hand off, grabbed the bundle of rags from her arm, and knocked the bread to the cobbled ground, staring at her younger sister with undisguised loathing. The crowd had thinned upon Julia's release from the pillory, but some tarried with the appearance of Máiri, in expectation of another act in the afternoon's performance. There was an element of anger egging Julia on, goading her to exact vengeance upon her sister, not wanting the "entertainment" to end. When Julia finally spoke, her voice was hoarse and cracking with emotion. Everyone fell silent.

"I curse ye, and wish ye *damned*!" Rubbing at the abrasions on her neck with one hand, she pointed at Máiri. "Ye're nothin' but a *trollop…*" she continued "*…*a slattern…a *whore*!" Máiri shrank before her sister's trembling finger. "Hear me now," Julia went on, "may Hell rip and roast ye, Máiri Brighid McQuillan. May ye suffer eternal torment in the fires of Hell!" In the stunned silence that followed Julia's violent verbal assault and malevolent curses, Máiri fell to her knees before her:

"Julia!" she cried. "No…no…ye can't mean it! Julia! I'm…I'm *sorry…*Julia…*please*!" But Julia had turned her face from Máiri to scowl threateningly into the faces in the crowd. Feeling subdued and chastened themselves, they parted to let her move through unmolested. Because of the stress of the pillory, she could not stand fully erect, and walking was difficult. Julia was bowed, but she would prove to them that she was not broken. Máiri was ignored, bereft and sobbing uncontrollably.

Julia was clear of the crowd when a burly, dark--haired man confronted her, blocking her progress and forcing her to come to a halt. A tense moment passed before she recognized Liam O'Kane; they had been friends since childhood. On this day, Julia was leery of everyone:

"Liam?" she said, warily.

O'Kane carried a stout, blackthorn walking stick across one shoulder, a bundle tied to the end of it.

"I've a mind to walk aways with ye, Julia," he said. He looked around at the faces in the crowd before turning back to her. "That's if it's alright with ye?" Julia hesitated for a second or two before nodding. She was more than aware of the implications involved in walking abroad alone; with evening coming on, she could be followed by these lingering men, some of whom were still excited by the events of the afternoon. O'Kane leaned closer to whisper, "Perhaps ye'd be as well coverin' yerself up a wee bit more, too."

Julia looked down at the filthy, tattered shift that hung from her shoulders and tried to cover herself, pulling the rags that were once her clothes around her frame.

Tears—bred of humiliation, pain, and anger—welled in her eyes, and she turned on the stragglers milling about in the square. "God *damn* ye!" she said. "What are yiz looking at? God damn yer eyes!" Liam quickly grabbed her and, slipping a hand over her mouth, tried to drag her away, despite her struggling.

"Wheesht now, wheesht, Julia," he whispered. "Don't give them cause to put ye back in the stocks."

Then one of the men, stepping forward, managed to tear her shift further. He did not let go. "Ye'd best mind yerself, wumman," he growled. "Mind ye don't have that blasphemous tongue of yours cut right out of yer head."

Liam O'Kane insinuated himself between them and grabbed hold of the man's wrist. "Listen t' me, John," he said quietly, "why don't ye just get yerself home?" He hefted the stick on his shoulder. "I think the wumman's had enough for one day, don't you?"

Reluctantly, John O'Malley, a neighbour of O'Kane's, let go and backed off, watching the younger and bigger man, and eyeing his stick, warily. "I'm just sayin' she should watch 'er mouth, that's all."

Another said, "Aye, but it wasn't her *mouth* we were watchin' today, was it John?" Several of the men laughed and added their comments, and O'Malley grinned:

"Mebbe big Liam here's got some ideas of his own," he said, deeming himself out of O'Kane's reach. He moved further back before eyeing Julia lewdly and adding, "Thon's a fine-lookin' haunch she has on 'er, eh?"

O'Kane smiled sadly and shrugged off his coat. "Ach, away on home, lads," he said, draping the coat about Julia's shoulders. "Sure, yer wives and bairns are waiting on yiz." He took Julia by the arm and led her away from their continuing jibes and ribald remarks. She hesitated and looked at him askance when he directed her towards the Cushendall road. "I'm thinkin'," he said by way of explanation, "that mebbe it wouldn't be safe fer ye to go home tonight, but it's up to you…"

Julia gave it a moment's thought. "Ye're right," she said, hooking her arm in his. "I can't go home…not tonight…or any other night. I won't be goin' home again…ever! I'm done with this town and the people in it." Looking Liam in the eye, she added, "Lead on…"

4

They scarcely made the outskirts of Ballycastle when the air around them thickened and darkened forebodingly.

Peering skywards at the blackening clouds, Liam said, "I don't like the looks of this. There could be a storm brewin'." Right on cue, thunder rumbled, and a huge raindrop hit his forehead with an audible *splot*. Julia laughed at the surprised look on the man's face.

The tumbling walls of *Bun-na-Mairge* lay on their right, with the gateway into the ruin less than a quarter mile further along the dirt road. O'Kane looked at Julia. "D' ye think ye can run?" Larger droplets of rain were beginning to splotch his shirt.

"I'll do m' best," said Julia.

"Well, let's go then!" Although she tried, Julia could not run. At best she managed a hobbling gait. By the time they reached the gateway, both were thoroughly drenched. O'Kane unlatched and pushed the wrought iron gate open, and held it until Julia crossed the threshold. Inside, she stopped and turned to look at O'Kane through thick sodden strands of hair hanging over her face:

"We'll go no further than the gatehouse, Liam." she said. "Agreed?"

O'Kane nodded. "We'll be alright, Julia." He turned to go, but Julia laid a hand on his shoulder.

"Do ye agree, Liam?" she said, holding him with her eyes.

"Aye!"

"Say it. *Say* ye agree."

O'Kane, irritated at the delay, clanged the gate closed; it shook and rattled loudly on its hinges. "Yes, alright…" he said, "…I agree." But when he made to move on, Julia increased her grip on his shoulder and turning, O'Kane saw the dread in her eyes, but also a fire. "Alright, wumman, alright! I *said* I agree. We'll go no farther than the gatehouse, alright? Is that what ye want me to say?"

Julia nodded. "I thank ye." She started to limp along the puddled path.

O'Kane laughed. "Come on," he said. "We'll both *drown* before we get there at this rate!" Over her protestations, he swept her off her feet and, cradling her in his arms, ran into the ruined gatehouse.

Rain fell unchecked through the building's dilapidated roofing. Setting Julia on her feet, O'Kane looked up and snorted. "We're not goin' to be much better off in here, are we?"

Julia laughed too, then began sobbing uncontrollably. O'Kane went to her quickly and wrapped a protective arm around her shoulders. "Sure, that's alright, girl," he cooed. "Ye just let it out. Let it all out."

Julia had never wept like this, and it was several minutes before her sobs subsided. Still, O'Kane held her close and waited. Presently he said, "D' ye feel a wee bit better now, girl?" Getting no response, he tried to lift her chin.

Julia resisted and nuzzled face into the nest of black hair at his chest. "I just need to be held, Liam," she said, hugging him, inhaling him. "Just a wee while longer. Just hold me like this a wee while longer..."

5

Julia awoke naked and alone, and was immediately gripped by a feeling of terror that tightened her throat. When she tried to call Liam, all she emitted was a barely audible squeak. She had no idea what the time of day was, or for that matter, *what* day it was. It was not fully dark outside, and in the dim light she saw a shirt draped—sheetlike—over her nakedness. Knowing that it was O'Kane's shirt, and discovering that his coat was her mattress, assuaged her fear.

The coat was still warm where his body had been, and the scent of him lingered on it. Julia realized they had lain together although she had no recollection of what had led to this event—or what happened during it.

Her tattered clothes hung in a nearby corner. Julia reached for her dress, and took the fabric between thumb and forefinger. It was still damp. Hearing a noise in the doorway, she lay back and covered herself quickly. O'Kane stood there, looking uncomfortable, fumbling with the waistband of his britches. Leather shoes, woolen stockings, and a sleeveless sheepskin jerkin completed his wardrobe. The jerkin was unbuttoned, baring his formidable chest, and Julia wondered if that was deliberate.

Clearing his throat, he said, "So, ye're awake at last." He smiled to show no admonishment. "Well, the storm's passed, but night's comin' on fast." From another corner he produced his stick with the bundle bouncing on the end of it. "Ye must be hungry…"

Julia clutched his shirt to her throat. "How did I…?"

O'Kane busied himself opening the bundle. When he spoke, he kept his eyes on the floor. "Ye were soakin' wet. I didn't want ye catchin' yer death, so…so I…" He looked up, abashed. "I…I took yer clothes off ye and I…I just lay beside ye. Just t' keep you warm, mind, nothin' else. I mean…*nothin'* else happened, like…"

Julia nodded, and smiling modestly, said, "Could ye turn around, please?"

O'Kane cocked his head at her.

"Liam," said Julia, "I have t'…I have t' *go*…ye know…"

Realization hit O'Kane like a smack on the back of his head. Mumbling unintelligibly, he turned his back, and stared at the wall as if it was the most interesting wall, he had ever seen.

"Alright," said Julia, after a moment of rustling, "ye can turn around now." O'Kane's shirt reached down to her calves, and its shoulder seams hung below her elbows. "How d' I look?" she said, smiling.

O'Kane, wide-eyed, could find no words as she walked past him.

"*That* good, eh!" she said, then added, "I'll be back in a minute." She hurried outside. By the time she returned, O'Kane had opened and spread his bundle on top of his coat, and was sitting on the ground with his back against the wall.

"There's bread," he said, "and some cheese…nothin' fancy, mind ye." He produced a swollen, animal skin bag. "And I've got some ale here, too!" Julia grabbed at the proffered bag, but O'Kane cautioned her before he let go. "Just take wee, small sips now, or ye'll throw it all up again."

Sitting down on the other side of the spread cloth, Julia gingerly leaned her back against the cool stone wall. "Thank ye, Liam. I…I don't know what I would've…" Tears welled suddenly, and O'Kane hurriedly pushed a piece of dark bread into her hand.

"Here now, girl," he said, "that's enough of that. Just get that into ye, and ye'll be right as rain 'fore ye know it." The next few minutes were spent in companionable silence—if the munching and gulping could be ignored—until O'Kane spoke again. "Listen, Julia," he said, "ye know I can't stay out here all night with ye, don't ye? I have to go home. I've the chores t' tend to, and…and…well, ye know. I'd bring ye back to our place but…"

Julia could not immediately hide the fact she was crestfallen, but she recovered quickly.

"Sure, don't I know that?" she said. "And don't let it worry ye. I'll be fine here 'til the morn's morn, then I'll be movin' on."

"But ye'll wait for me here, right?" said O'Kane. "I'll be back first thing, and I'll bring ye somethin' to eat, and mebbe I can get ye somethin' to wear…" He let the words hang until Julia caught the inference:

"Oh, Liam!" she said. "I'm so stupid. Of course, ye'll be wantin' yer shirt back, won't ye?"

O'Kane smiled, relieved. "Well," he said, "I can't very well go home to the wife without it. God knows there'll be questions enough. I'm…I'm sure ye understand?" Julia stood and waited while he gathered up his belongings. "I'll wait outside," he said.

Julia changed clothes quickly, but after being wrapped in O'Kane's huge shirt, her damp and tattered clothing seemed inadequate; too much of her scratched and bruised flesh showed through the scant torn material. When O'Kane reappeared in the doorway, his eyes lingered on that exposed flesh. She looked small, and helpless "I'm sorry t' leave ye here like this, Julia," he said, "alone in *this* place."

Julia forced a smile, as she passed him his shirt. "Sure ye've done more than enough, Liam, But ye'd better hurry up now. Like ye said, night's comin' on fast!"

O'Kane threw his coat and shirt, carelessly, over a shoulder. "I'll see ye in the morn's morn," he said, clearing his throat. "Ye'll be alright 'til then."

Julia watched him leave, carefully opening and closing the gate, before finally looking back and waving. Returning the wave, she put a smile on her face, but O'Kane was not fully out of sight before the tears came, and Julia wallowed in feelings of self-pity and despair— and fear—as evening's shadows crept over *Bun-na-Mairge*. She remembered the last time she had been here…

Bun-na-Mairge was built by Julia's McQuillan's ancestors two hundred years ago, and lay deserted since the beginning of the 17th century. It had been twenty years since her last walk among the ruins of the friary. Liam O'Kane was with her that day too.

Julia had reasoned back then that the tightness in her chest, and the feeling of unease she felt when they came through the iron gate was caused by the excitement of being alone with Liam. She knew that he fancied her, and the feelings were returned in kind on her part, so she ignored her trepidation at the ruin's oppressive atmosphere.

Her heart fluttered like a caged bird as they wandered aimlessly along the path through the graveyard. They tried to read the worn inscriptions on the tumbled headstones as each wondered how to proceed. Julia thought that perhaps she should try to affect a fall, when suddenly, tripping on a protruding rock, she *had* stumbled. Liam caught and held her in his arms. But even then, he played the gentleman, and as the moment stretched, Julia wondered if he was going to kiss her or not, despairing that it might be the latter. Then he kissed her—awkwardly and nervously at first—then with a passion that increased when his advances were not repelled. They stood outside an arched opening in the stone wall, and Julia returned the kiss with an ardour that equalled his. It was she who broke the embrace when Liam tried to slip his hand under her bodice. But when he reached for her again, she would have let him put his hand wherever he wanted, had her passion not been quelled upon hearing a low whispered murmuring coming from the shadows that lay beyond the archway.

She pushed Liam away. "Did you hear that?"

Liam tried to renegotiate their embrace. "What? Sure, it's just the wind. There's nobody there...don't worry."

Julia noticed also the atmosphere had thickened and darkened, and when the echoed murmurs rose to become more like chuckling, even Liam could not ignore it.

"W-what..." he stammered. "W-who's there?" Both stood rooted, staring into the opening, watching the blackness beyond it pulse, thicken, and grow. It continued in this fashion until black tendrils crept towards them from the archway. Julia, with breath bated, was horrified to find she could not move.

I'm dreamin'. This is a nightmare.

Then, a thousand voices shrieked as one.

It was the ear-splitting noise that mobilized Julia, and she ran.

Liam was close on her heels. "Run, Julia," he said. "Don't stop…RUN!" The continuous screech rung in their ears, besetting them in their flight through the friary grounds. Colour was drained from the world, so that all loomed either white, grey or black, and Julia's steps faltered when she saw obscure forms, berobed and hooded in black, moving among the shadowed gravestones surrounding the path. Liam saw her waver. "Keep goin', Julia," he shouted. "For the love of Christ, don't stop now. We're nearly there!"

Carried on the wings of fear, driven by that hideous scream, they ran, doggedly keeping their eyes on the path until the gate loomed ahead.

"It's closed," Liam cried, forging ahead of Julia. "Stay close to me now!" Liam reached the gate, unlatched and pulled it open. The scream ceased all at once. Liam, without bothering to turn, grabbed Julia's hand, and together they ran out onto the road beyond the opening.

Liam's clasp on Julia's hand was so tight that it pained her. She struggled to rein him in. "Stop, Liam!" she cried, panting, trying desperately to catch her breath and speak. "The gate, Liam…the gate…we have t' shut the gate!"

"Never mind the gate." Liam was more intent on dragging her away. "Let's go," he urged. "Come on, Julia, let's just get away from here."

But Julia stood firm and pulled her hand from his grip. "I'll do it," she said.

Liam stopped, bewildered. "Alright," he said, "*I'll* close the gate." He started back reluctantly. "But, why, why is it so important to ye?"

"Because…because spirits wander, Liam." There was more, but Julia could not begin to explain it because she understood little of it herself. She knew that gates, when not in use, should remain closed, and latched, especially cemetery gates.

Still, Liam hesitated. "But surely that's just an old wives' tale!" Then, seeing the resolve in Julia's eyes, he puffed his cheeks, and blew his fear into the wind. "Alright, wait here. And don't move!"

Julia heard the gate clang shut and the latch close with an audible *snick*. *Bun-na-Mairge* looked much the same as it had a mere five minutes ago. Liam trotted down the road towards her, smiling.

And why shouldn't he smile? His world has righted itself.

If Liam had seen the black, hooded shapes among the gravestones, he never mentioned it to Julia, and by the time they reached the town square later that same afternoon, Liam was assuring Julia that they simply had over-active imaginations. But Julia harboured no such illusions. She knew that Liam's mind had simply gone into survival mode, softening the edges of memory, and burying that which had disturbed its peace.

And for whatever reason, although Julia and Liam remained cordial enough, their erstwhile romantic relationship withered after that fateful afternoon…

CHAPTER FOUR

1

Having avoided *Bun-na-Mairge* between her first visit and this one, Julia noted that it was Liam O'Kane who had brought her here on both occasions and, although she could find nothing sinister in it, she was disquieted by the coincidence.

Even back then, *Bun-na-Mairge* had frightened her on a visceral level. To her, the *place* seemed malevolently sentient. Julia could not explain those feelings now as she couldn't then, but reasoned it was because she was more in tune with her instincts than most people.

During the years since her last visit, Julia had often warned others—only if asked, and without going into detail—of the danger that lurked in *Bun-na-Mairge*. If pressed, she would try to explain her belief that the ruin was somehow part of the realm of the *Aos Si*— the mythological beings of the *Saoghal Eile*—Otherworld. A place not to be trifled with.

How ironic it was then, to find herself now in the gloom of twilight without a light, or the means with which to produce one, kneeling alone in *Bun-na-Mairge's* gatehouse, praying for protection from whatever the coming darkness might bring.

Julia was raised within the dictates of the Church of Rome, but she had never been overly religious. Her faith in God was profound, and she believed in a Heaven, but not in the ritualistic ceremonies practiced by the Church.

Kneeling in the gatehouse now, Julia found the silence within and without its confines ominous. Her body ached from the cruelty of the pillory and she longed for more comfortable and safer lodgings., But she was loth to stray from the building in search of them. Not for the first time in her life, Julia felt forlorn. With a deep sigh of resignation, she crawled through the deepening dark into a corner and nestled there as best she could. Shivering, she pulled her tattered clothing closer about her and hugged her knees to her chest.

It was going to be a long night—one in which Julia had no intention of sleeping—but intentions are capricious, and eventually, she did sleep. While she slept, she dreamed, and while she dreamt, her soul awakened and wandered. . .

***

The woods were ancient. Julia had never walked among such trees. To her right, dappled sunshine played on the rippled surface of a small river which burbled along happily over its pebbled bed. Muted birdsong tumbled from the canopy and sleepy insects hummed among the wildflowers at her feet. There was no path.

She knew this was a dream, the kind of dream where wakefulness was but a deep breath away, so Julia checked her breathing because she did not want to waken. She meandered along the riverbank, following the river's course. Moments later she heard the sound of another river, this one to her left. Julia walked on, and presently, she stood at a place where the two rivers converged to form a larger third. At this place the ground slowly undulated under her feet—as if breathing—and the air thrummed in her ears.

Through the lower branches of the trees, the third river wound its way to a not-too-distant sea, perhaps an ocean. The landscape, and the shoreline looked vaguely familiar to her.

Then the dreamscape changed. The sunlight disappeared and the air assumed a dark purple tone. The ground still moved beneath her feet, but quicker now, and Julia discovered that she was on a gravel pathway winding its way through skewed headstones. Julia recognized this place. Before her, at the end of the path, set into a stone wall, loomed a familiar archway. A figure, robed and cowled, appeared in the arched opening; it held a rushlight in one hand; the fingers of the other were cupped protectively around the flame. The figure raised its head, and Caitlín McQuillan's smiling face radiated in the lamp's glow.

"Mother?" Julia cried.

Still smiling, Caitlín beckoned her daughter. *"Thig thugainn,"* she said in her native tongue—Come to us.

Julia thought the phrase strange, but walked towards her mother without hesitation and, stepping through the archway, found herself in a stairwell, standing at the foot of a narrow, stone stairway. Her mother smiled down on her from the head of this stairway and repeated her strange command, *"Thig thugainn."*

Julia moved dreamily, climbing the well-worn steps, keeping her hands pressed against the walls, bracing herself because the steps and the surrounding walls had joined in the strange undulations. Upon reaching the landing, the robed figure of her mother stood in the small, dark room beyond it: she held her arms open—welcoming.

Julia crossed the threshold. "I'm comin' mother!" Immediately, her mother disappeared, and a loud susurration of voices filled the darkened room, rebounding her words, mockingly. The whispering grew louder, and Julia shuddered when voices melded to become one.

"Thig thugainn, Julia!" it said.

The movement under her feet made Julia queasy. As she groped in the darkness for some means of support, she heard her name, sounding much like the soughing of the wind, whispered spectrally.

"Julia…"

"Where are ye?" said Julia. "Who are ye?" The voices disintegrated and the murmuring returned to its earlier volume. Some moments passed before Julia heard a distinct, female voice; it hummed a familiar melody—a lullaby. The darkness lifted and Julia saw her mother, smiling and sitting on the edge of a small cot, still bearing a rushlight. "Mammy," said Julia, "is it really you?"

But Caitlin's smile slowly became a leer. Rising from the cot, she spoke with the same fearsome, mingled, whispered voice, *"Thig thugainn!"*

Julia stood transfixed as her mother's visage was swallowed in the folds of her black cowl and her form loomed larger. The horrible voices, once more concentrated as one, now emanated from that cowl.

"A bheil neach-ionaid aice?"—Does she have a surrogate?—the cowl asked.

Julia was confused by the unfamiliar word "surrogate."

The multi-voice speech rose significantly and the question repeated, "DOES SHE HAVE A SURROGATE?"

"No." Julia replied. "I mean…I…I don't think so. I…I don't know what ye're askin'."

The figure moved closer, and assumed a paternal tenor., uttering words Julia could understand. "If ye don't have somebody to take yer place—a *surrogate*—ye can consider yer life forfeit, and yer immortal soul with it. If, however, ye can provide one to stand in yer place, ye may be spared. D' ye understand?" The figure then crouched before her and cocked its cowled head to one side, as if in concern. "So, I repeat the question: D' ye have a surrogate?"

Julia glimpsed a shuffling in the darkness beyond the dim rushlight. She tried to ignore it to concentrate on the question and her situation. Latent memories and fragments of legends and tales told around the hearths of her childhood swirled in Julia's mind. She recalled a tale concerning the bartering of souls—and the creatures involved. *"Sluagh na Marbh,"* she whispered—The Host of the Dead—"God help me!"

Julia's knowledge of *Sluagh na Marbh*—known locally as simply *Sluagh,* or *the Sluagh*—was based entirely on those fireside tales, and ambiguous. Some tales held that *Sluagh* were ghosts of the unforgiven dead; some described them as the tormented souls of people who committed evil during their lifetime and were fated to spend the afterlife roaming the veiled world that exists between life and death; others espoused the view that they were faerie folk gone awry; but all storytellers agreed that *Sluagh na Marbh* are by far the most dreadful of all the beings of the *Aos Si*, for they *prey* on mortals, endlessly seeking souls to add to their "host."

The figure crouching before her straightened. "Aaah," its countless voices sighed, "then ye know of *Sluagh na Marbh*. That's good, perhaps." Soundlessly, it moved away from Julia to hover in the centre of the room. "Provide for us another, and ye'll endure, for that is the contract *Sluagh* made long ago with your forbears. However, if ye can't do this…" With a flourish, the figure discarded its robes. Julia shut her eyes and screamed.

"Look upon me and despair," the thing screeched, "for in me ye see yer future!" But Julia squeezed her eyelids together, closing them as tight as she could. The monster let loose a searing screech. "*LOOK AT ME!*"

And Julia reluctantly opened her eyes:

Faces and bodies appeared and disappeared within an undulating black seething mass of matter in front of her. A host of voices screamed and cried despairingly. Then one shape, a creature, human-like and more distinct than the others, appeared at its centre and spread its arms. Flaccid flesh draped winglike from those limbs, and Julia's nostrils were assailed by a foul stench that brought her to her knees, retching.

Its torso was a mass of grey, wrinkled, sagging skin, dappled with scabbed sores. Julia would look no lower than its paunch.

I know this is a dream. It can't be happening. Please dear God. Please let me awaken!

"Look at me," the monster whispered.

Reluctantly, Julia looked up into its face. Small, deeply set eyes were fixed on her; wattle-like appendages dangling from either side of a beak-like nose swayed to and fro as it spoke. "I am no *dream*," it said, moving towards her with its black, seething mass in tow. "Come, recognize my authenticity…let us embrace."

"*NO!*" Julia screamed. "No! I have another for ye. I have a *surrogate*! Please, *NOOOO!*"

Julia screamed her throat raw., When she was smothered in the creature's fetid folds, and felt its tongue rasp over her flesh, her mind finally abandoned reality and sought sanctuary elsewhere.

2

When Liam O'Kane arrived early the next morning as promised, he was disappointed not to find Julia eagerly awaiting him at the gate. The disappointment turned to concern when he also found the gatehouse empty. Leaving his goatskin bag, stick, and bundle inside the gatehouse door, he followed the path that wound through the ruins, calling out her name.

At one of the lesser dilapidated, stone structures, he stopped, thinking that he may have heard something, and peered into the gloomy reaches beyond its arched opening.

"Julia," he called, "are ye in there?" O'Kane hoped not, for in the long shadows thrown by the morning sun, the archway appeared more like a hungry, yawning maw than a simple doorway. Nevertheless, upon hearing a faint reply come from the gloom beyond, warily he stepped into the *maw* to find himself standing at the bottom of a narrow stone stairwell. "Julia!" O'Kane called into the gloom above, "are ye there?" Among the muffled echoes of his voice, he heard a plaintive voice.

"Liam…?"

The air in the stairwell was oppressive, and his feeling of unease did not lessen when he reached the landing. A slit cut in the stone wall afforded the only light, and directly facing it, O'Kane saw a closed ironclad wooden door. It had a small barred window at eye level. Reaching for the ringed door handle, he peered through this opening.

"Julia?" he whispered, and almost screamed, tightening his grip on the handle to keep from tumbling backwards when her stricken face appeared, pressed against the bars. "Jesus *Christ*, Julia!" he said. "Are ye alright, girl? What's happened to ye?" Steadying himself, he turned the ringed handle and pushed the door.

"No Liam, *don't*!" cried Julia. "Run, Liam, if ye can! *Run*...now! They'll be watchin' ye." There was an unfocused wildness in Julia's eyes that O'Kane found disturbing, but he pushed at the door insistently.

"Who?" he said. "Who's watchin' me, Julia?" Julia just laughed shrilly, but slowly, she backed away, and O'Kane was able to open the door. "My *God*!" he gasped when he saw her. Julia was naked and looked to have suffered a beating. "Jesus, Julia...who *did* this to ye?" Her long, black hair was dishevelled and matted, and raw scratches and abrasions covered her body, not all of which, he was certain, were inflicted during her time in the pillory. When he started towards her, Julia flinched and backed away, trying to cover her nakedness with her arms and hands. But O'Kane calmed her, and removing his coat, draped it over her shoulders. "Ye're alright, girl," he cooed. When Julia winced, he snarled, "The man who did this to ye, deserves to die a slow and painful death."

Julia's shoulders dropped and her hands fell to her sides carelessly. She turned her head towards O'Kane and stared at him as if seeing him for the first time. Her hooded eyes were totally devoid of emotion.

"No *man* did this," she said. Then that awful laugh burst from her again.

O'Kane was horrified. Shushing Julia, he took her in his arms. "Don't ye fret," he said, soothingly. "Nobody's goin' t' hurt ye now." Julia allowed herself to be picked up and cradled like a child. "Now, let's get ye out of this place."

At the foot of the stairs, Julia roused. "Liam, put me down." she said. Snorting, she added, "And where d' ye think ye're takin' me, anyway—to *your* house, mebbe?—oh, I'm sure yer *wife* would just *love* that!" Throwing her head back, she laughed wildly. "Oh yes, she'd welcome *me* with open arms, wouldn't she?" The laughter stopped just as suddenly as it had started, and Julia started to cry softly. "Put me down, Liam," she said wearily. "Please…" O'Kane set her down gently. Julia wiped the back of her wrist under her nostrils and pulled his coat tighter about her. They both stepped out of the archway onto the path. "Ye see it, don't ye, Liam?" said Julia. "*We* can't go *anywhere* together." At the onslaught of further tears, she stamped her bare foot hard on the stony path. "And *I'll* cry no more!" Then, once again, she laughed, shrilly and wildly.

"Just let me think on it for a bit, Julia, alright?" said O'Kane. "Let me think this out…" He sat down on a tilted headstone that jutted from the tall weeds and grasses that grew unchecked among the gravestones and along the sides of the pathway.

Julia went to him, and bringing her face level with his, shook her head resignedly. "But I've had time to think this out Liam, love," she said "I—I think ye should go. I think ye should go…and ye should go now."

O'Kane reached up and gently chucked her under the chin with a curled forefinger. "Now, don't ye worry, Julia, I'm not goin' anywhere without ye. There has t' be somethin' we can do, somewhere we can go." His features hardened. "And, God help me, we'll find who it was that did this to ye, and then…God help him!"

Julia sprang up and put both hands over her ears. *GOD!* she screamed inwardly, and her thoughts swirled and tumbled: *Where was God last night? I called for His help—I screamed for it—where was He then?* She felt giddy, drunk, but she knew it was her madness.

Julia had *felt* her mind snap the night before. Her senses had stretched until they could stretch no farther, and then they tore asunder. "Asunder," she said now, aloud, liking the sound of the word. "Asunder. Asunder…"

O'Kane, watching her, said, "What's that ye say?"

Julia looked at and beyond him. She wasn't surprised to see her mother standing there.

Caitlín McQuillan spoke. "He's just another man, Julia, love. Sure, he's nothin' to ye."

Julia looked at O'Kane who apparently had heard nothing. "He's a good man!" she said. O'Kane smiled at this, and Julia returned the smile, awkwardly.

"Ye know what this lad wants, don't ye?" her mother continued. "Sure, he's just like all the rest of them, lass, make no mistake. Why would ye concern yerself about Liam O'Kane?" Caitlín snorted a laugh, but then her mien darkened. "Don't tell me ye'd rather *he* takes *your* soul instead of this one's! Ye saw them others, didn't ye? Ye heard them screamin'. And ye saw *his* slaves. D' ye want t' become one them?"

"They *ravaged* me!" cried Julia.

At this, Liam was on his feet. Caitlín vanished.

"*They!*" he cried. "So, there was more than one. Well, no matter; we'll find them…and they'll still pay!"

But by then, Julia had decided that her mother was right after all— she had no choice.

3

Julia wiped her face and eyes and, pushing her fingers through matted strands of hair, lifted it off and away from her face.

"Lord love us," she said, chuckling and smiling coyly. "Just look at the state of me, would ye. I must look a right sight."

O'Kane was nonplussed by this change of demeanour, but he too, had made a decision:

"Julia," he said firmly, getting to his feet, "I want ye t' come away with me. Will ye come with me, now? We'll go to Armoy. We'll get ye cleaned up there, and get ye something to wear, and then we'll decide what we're goin' t' do, and where we're goin' t' go."

Julia went to him, and eased him back down onto the headstone. She quickly straddled him, draping her arms around his neck.

"But sure, there's nothin' we can do in Armoy that we can't do here, Liam, love..." She cocked her head coquettishly, and pressed her lips on his. At first, O'Kane was shocked and did not respond, but Julia's mouth was insistent, and soon he was returning the kiss fervently. He was disappointed and confused when she broke the kiss and dismounted, saying, "I'm sorry, Liam. Please forgive me."

"Forgive ye?" said O'Kane. "Forgive ye for—" He stopped mid-sentence and his chin dropped when Julia shrugged his coat off her shoulders and stood naked before him.

"I know," she said, seeing his reaction "I know, I'm befouled. And ye must find me ugly."

"No, no, Julia. It's...it's just that we—"

Julia fell to her knees in front of him and laid her head on his lap. "Are ye wantin' me to beg?" she said, smiling lopsidedly up at him. "What would ye have me do?" When she suddenly nuzzled her cheek into his groin. A surprised O'Kane fell off the headstone, landing on his back among the tall grass. Julia, laughing that unnaturally shrill laugh, crawled to him and made to straddle his hips again. At first, O'Kane resisted, but when she lowered her breasts onto his face tantalizingly, he groaned and reached for her.

Julia pulled back teasingly, then lowered her mouth on his while grinding herself against his hardness. O'Kane responded impulsively, thrusting at her heat. Julia pulled at his britches which O'Kane, slid to his knees. Feverishly he sought entry while Julia, eased herself along the length of his erection until access was almost achieved. Then suddenly, she stopped his progress by pushing herself up to straddle him once more. "Wait Liam!" she said, looking about anxiously, "Not here." Clambering off him before he had a chance to argue, she picked up the discarded coat and draped it around her shoulders. Grabbing his hand, she gestured towards the archway. "Come," she said. "Quickly. It'll be safer there."

"Safer?" said O'Kane, trying to hitch up his britches. "Safer from what?" He looked bewildered, holding his britches at mid-thigh, with his rigid penis peeking from beneath his half-rucked shirt bouncing and swaying in a way that, under different circumstances, would be comical. Catching her look, O'Kane self-consciously pulled his britches back up his thighs in an attempt to cover himself. "Julia, I—"

"Ye don't want me!" said Julia, her face crumpling.

At this, Liam O'Kane swallowed hard. "*Want* ye?" he said. "Julia…I…I think I *love* ye!"

Julia felt her resolve faltering then. "Liam—"

"I…I think that…that perhaps, I always have." Going to her, he cinched his arms about her waist. "Julia—"

Julia fell into him, put her arms around his neck and raised her face to his. "Ye must think me a *whore*," she said, to give reason for the tears that streaked her cheeks. Then she kissed him and felt his manhood, hot and hard, against her lower belly.

"Julia," O'Kane whispered huskily and tried to hoist her once more onto his hips.

Juia heard her mother's voice in her head: *He's just a man…just like all the rest of them…*

"I said, not here," she said. "Quickly, follow me."

O'Kane followed her back to the small cell at the top of the stairs. There, they embraced and kissed again. He made to close the door, but Julia, hearing her mother's voice once more, stopped him and took his hand. "Leave it open," she whispered, "that way we can hear anyone coming."

O'Kane started, "But who—" He quieted when Julia once again discarded his coat, and taking both his hands in hers, walking backwards, she led him to the cot. She lay down and pulled him on top of her. When she winced at the pain this caused in her misused limbs and damaged flesh, O'Kane raised himself onto his hands and looked down at her, concerned. Julia, dismissed his anxiety with a shake of her head, grabbed his buttocks, raised her hips off the mattress provocatively, and pulled him into her.

Moaning her name, O'Kane lowered his face to hers. Julia offered him her throat instead, and he kissed her there, tentatively and tenderly. Julia, writhing under him, invited and incited him to be more assertive.

"I need ye, Liam," she breathed huskily, pushing herself at him and pulling at his shirt. "God, how I need you." She caressed his chest as she worked his shirt up and over his head, until it covered his eyes. "Oh, yes," she said, sensing his hesitation, "oh, that's it, Liam…oh, yes!" Although confused, O'Kane could not help but be aroused by Julia's wantonness, and soon his movements matched hers, and pure, unadulterated lust replaced propriety.

Julia's fear-driven gasp, when she saw the ruined, cowled creatures creeping silently from the shadows beyond the doorway, went unnoticed. "Oh, don't stop, Liam," she panted. "Please…don't stop!" They crept closer, seemingly emboldened by her obvious revulsion of them—bloated by it. Julia held her breath when she felt O'Kane's body stiffen. He grunted, once…twice…and then…then, they were on him! Pulling at his arms and legs, they dragged him off her, and Julia screamed, "*No! Stop*! Dear God, *Liam*! I'm…I'm sorry!" In his struggle to escape their grasp, his shirt fell clear of his head. The naked terror in his eyes when he saw what held him, made her sick with shame. Julia buried her head in her hands, so that she might no longer see his face, as they dragged him away.

"*Julia!*" he screamed, and she was left to wonder whether he screamed her name as a question or an accusation. But Julia knew that

Liam O'Kane was dead, even as his emission, still warm, seeped onto the tick mattress beneath her…

4

A thin shaft of sunlight warmed her face, blushing the insides of her eyelids, and Julia awoke. She was back in the gatehouse, wrapped in O'Kane's coat, and for a fleeting moment she hoped that it had all been a horrible dream. From the direction of the sunbeam, Julia knew it was morning…but which morning? Had she slept for one night, or more? Her throat was parched, and pangs of hunger gnawed at her stomach. Moving slowly, for her body ached, she rose and shivered. The gatehouse was cool and damp. Wrapping O'Kane's coat tighter about her, she was about to step out into the morning sun when she spotted his bundle and goatskin bag lying on the floor, inside the doorway. Waves of memory crashed over her and drove her to her knees.

"Oh, Christ, Liam!" she cried aloud. "I'm sorry…I'm so sorry!"

Rising, Julia stepped out into the morning sun. Spreading and lifting her arms, she let the coat fall to the ground at her feet. Julia McQuillan, in her thirty years of existence, had never stood naked in the sun, never felt its nurturing warmth on her body—all over her body—and she luxuriated in it.

Julia had never felt so free, and was moved to laughter. Lightheaded, naked, and emboldened, she started down the path, towards the gate; she would leave *Bun-na-Mairge* and never return. She had not gone more that a few yards when, realizing that her nudity would not go unnoticed beyond the confines of the ruins, she turned to retrieve Liam's coat. As she approached the gatehouse, the morning light dimmed and darkened, and two figures, robed and cowled in black, appeared in the shadowed doorway.

One of them spoke in a rasping, high voice—*A woman?*

"Ni féider leat imeacht," it said—Ye can't leave—and Julia trembled.

Addressing the creatures in her native tongue, she said, "I don't understand. Why can't I leave? We…we…we had an agreement. He said—"

The other figure spoke in Gaelic, "Ye can't leave." The voice was deeper—male—seeming the more malicious for it. "Yer *lover* is kept."

"What?" said Julia. "My *lover*! My lover is…is *kept*. What does—"

"Gleidhidh borgaire anama a chuid," said the first—The Burglar of Souls is keeping him—"His soul's captive," she continued. "It belongs t' the Burglar, but he didn't take it unto himself, nor is it destroyed."

The "male" spoke again. "Aye," he said, "the Burglar keeps it…safe and apart…but, if ye try t' leave…he'll consume it."

The "female" said, "So, if ye value yer lover's soul, ye can *never* leave this place, even when yer own mortality ends, ye can't leave. Here ye are, and here ye'll stay. The Burglar will honour yer pact. Ye provided a surrogate, so he'll not take *your* soul, but he *owns* yer lover's, and if ye don't want it destroyed, ye'll bide here…*forever!*" Both of them laughing, backed into the gatehouse and were swallowed by the shadows within.

Julia, turning from her path to the gate, covered her ears in an ineffectual effort to block the mocking laughter. She circumvented the gatehouse and ran back along the path, helplessly hoping against all reason that she might find some kind of sanctuary back in the small space of the cell at the top of the stairway: she could think of nowhere else to go.

CHAPTER FIVE

1

A posse, led by Constable Joe Briggs, arrived at *Bun-na-Mairge* a few days later. Julia, hearing their approach, ran to the stairwell and, from the window slit on the landing, watched them wend their way slowly along the path. There were seven of them, including the constable, all men, all on foot. Some shouted out Liam O'Kane's name as they advanced, raking the long grass between the gravestones with their walking sticks as if searching for his body.

They were visibly startled when Julia appeared in an archway. She did not speak, but stood there, leaning a shoulder against the wall, smiling inanely. Briggs, and the rest, gaped stupidly.

It was her fixed look and malevolent expression that disturbed the men and kept them at bay. Briggs was more concerned than his cohorts, for it was on him whom Julia fixed her gaze.

Even so, he strode forth, coughing importantly, and stood with feet apart and hands on hips, twenty paces from the archway.

"Wumman," he announced, "we're looking for Liam O'Kane. Is he here?" He was trying gamely to sound brusque. Julia gave no answer, nor any indication that she had heard the question. "Did ye hear me, wumman? I asked ye if Liam O'Kane is here."

The men jumped when Julia pushed off the wall and let out a piercing shriek. Mimicking Briggs's stance, she stood as tall as she could, kept her eyes on the constable, and spoke. "And is there none lookin' for me?" Briggs did not respond, so Julia shrugged and went on, "Liam left me here to go home to his wife and bairns." She ran her eyes over the line of men. "Where all of *youse* should be!"

The men muttered and grumbled, and some made to advance, but Briggs, holding out his walking stick, stayed them without a sideways glance. "And, when was that?" he asked.

"The same day ye had me pilloried," Julia spat.

Neither Briggs, nor his posse, seemed at all perturbed by these words, and Julia knew she would find no sympathy here.

"And ye haven't seen him since," said Briggs, "ye're sure of that?"

Julia threw her head back and laughed, and once again, Briggs and company were shaken by her outburst.

The constable regained his composure quickly. "What is it that ye find so funny?"

Julia stopped laughing. "I've seen neither hide nor hair of him since," she said. "Why d' ye ask?" One of the others spoke up. "That's *none* of yer business, wumman!"

Before Julia could respond, Briggs broke in using a more conciliatory tone. "Listen, Julia, are ye…are ye alright, wumman?" And as he withered under her malignant scrutiny, he tried once more for the upper hand. "Ye know now, that ye can't be stayin' here."

Julia laughed again. It was an equally disturbing sound to the posse, but this time with more disdain than hysteria. "And why not?" she asked. "This is McQuillan land, and I'm a McQuillan!"

The other, who had spoken before, spoke again. "Aye, but it was a long time ago that it was McQuillan land. It's *MacDonnell* land now…has been for a hunderd years, or more. Ye should know that."

Julia turned her icy gaze on the speaker. "Well, seems to me that there's none too many MacDonnells about the place now." Her eyes blazed as she added, "And it'll be a cold day in hell when I need a history lesson from the likes of you, Dessie O'Connor!" Turning her glare into a leering grin, she chuckled. "And how is it ye're here anyway? Shouldn't ye be back in the Harbour Inn, kissin' big Donal's arse, as usual?" Some of the others guffawed at this, and O'Connor, abashed, had no other retort but glared hatefully at Julia McQuillan.

Briggs coughed once more for attention. "Hear me now. If ye *do* see Liam O'Kane, tell him to report to me, immediately!" Julia let that mind-rattling smile return to her otherwise slack features, and after an uncomfortable thirty seconds, Briggs said, "Let's go, men."

Some of the men balked, but the police constable quieted them. "We're here on *official* business today, lads, but sure there's time enough for this one to get what's comin' to her, eh?" Some of the men nodding, chuckled and nudged one another. Turning to Julia again, Briggs attempted a bolder demeanour. "Now, we'll go, and we'll check O'Kane's house again, but if we can't find 'im there," here he beetled his brow threateningly, "we'll be back." He leered openly at her and her lack of adequate clothing. "Mebbe we'll come back even if he *is* at home, eh lads?"

The *lads* laughed dutifully at this, but their laughter was short-lived, and Briggs's smile faded when homing in on the big man, Julia fixed him with a stare steeped in malice. When she made to move towards the group, Briggs quailed visibly.

Then Julia spoke, "Well, Joe," she rasped, her eyes glistening, "I'll be here, waitin' for ye. Ye can be sure of that."

Briggs abandoned all further attempts at bravado. "C' mon lads," he said, sullenly, "let's go." Turning, he led them back down the path towards the gate. Julia followed at a distance.

At the gate, Dessie O'Connor stopped to confront her. "Donal will hear of this. And he won't be too happy about it, mind ye!"

Julia moved menacingly towards him, and O'Connor quickly pulled the gate closed—too quickly—and he was embarrassed when it clanged, and jangled loudly on its hinges. Julia heard some of the others laughing—openly contemptuous of the little man. Knowing that only O'Connor could see her because of the obstructing wall, she turned her back, bent over, hoisted her ragged skirt and, making loud kissing sounds, waggled her naked buttocks at him. "Bitch!" he shouted, but Julia was laughing, and already disappearing down the path.

2

And so it was that Julia McQuillan, coddled in her madness, settled in *Bun-na-Mairge*.

The cell at the top of the stairwell offered a cot and a small fireplace, beside which she found a tinderbox and some rushlights. Inside a wooden box under the cot, reposed a large, iron key which fit the lock in the door to her cell, a well-worn book, with a cross embossed on its cover and, a small, wicked-looking lash made of leather and rope. Grimacing, Julia picked up the lash. Like the Bible, it appeared to have been well used; it had seven, knotted cords, each of which was darkly stained. It was a scourge—a *discipline*—a small, cruel device used for self-flagellation by a penitent seeking atonement for their sins; she shuddered, wondering how many had suffered its usage.

Julia never attempted an escape. She believed her erstwhile presumption that *Bun-na-Mairge* was part of the Otherworld, and that the creature with which she had made her bargain, that which called itself *Borgaire anama*—the "Burglar of Souls"—was some kind of spirit or demon, and was master here in *Bun-na-Mairge*. And Julia believed what she had been told by the two hooded ghouls at the gatehouse: Liam's soul was somehow held captive, somewhere. She believed too, that because of this covenant, her own, immortal soul was ultimately damned.

Julia decided then that her discovery of the box and its contents was fortuitous and, although she was illiterate, in a daily act of penance, Julia stood before the old wooden altar in the chapel, holding the Bible in one hand while she scourged herself with the other, praying desperately for absolution and salvation.

She soon discovered that those black-robed and cowled ghouls were not the legendary *Sluagh na Marbh* as feared, but were in fact revenants—cadavers in various stages of putrefaction. They were the Burglar's minions, controlled and accountable to him—*whatever* he might be.

Because these minions shunned the light of day, Julia found that interaction with them could be avoided simply by spending daylight hours outside, keeping away from dark corners and shadows. If there was a chance encounter with them, her scourge was a viable deterrent to their unwelcome advances when wielded with courage and vehemence. Thus, it became her constant companion. Julia found too, that her cell door, closed and locked, was a sufficient barrier against the servants of the Burglar.

But she had to sleep; and it was while her body rested that her soul wandered in the twilit Dreamworld of the Burglar, and the ethereal Julia was immersed in terrifying scenarios, which left her body unscathed, but continued to gnaw at her sanity long after she wakened.

And yet, she endured.

Julia had water from the river. When word spread that she was living alone, some of those who believed she had been unfairly treated left gifts of food and clothing at the gate so that death by starvation or exposure was thwarted.

Julia McQuillan already owned a reputation of dabbling in the Black Arts, and because of this, she was feared by those who wished her harm. And so it was that Julia was left alone and, for the most part, unmolested in *Bun-na-Mairge*.

It became her refuge…and her prison.

CHAPTER SIX

Ballycastle
Friday, 14 August, 1665

Dessie O'Connor found his employer sitting at his usual table in the Harbour Inn.

"She's back," he said, without preamble.

Donal MacDonnell did not look up. "Where?"

"She's at the wee cottage, on the Rathin Road," said O'Connor. Glancing at the cup in front of MacDonnell, he licked at his lips, and doffing his cap, said, "Any chance of a wee drink, big man?"

MacDonnell ignored the question. "When?" he said.

O'Connor wrung his cap in his hands. "She got there early this afternoon," he said, then tried again. "I wouldn't say *no* to a wee drop…"

MacDonnell removed a coin from a leather pouch that hung from his belt, and threw it carelessly onto the table. O'Connor snatched it up.

MacDonnell nodded at his empty cup. "Take that with ye and bring me another." As O'Connor hurried off to the counter, coin in one hand, cup in the other, he added, "and bring me my change."

Some twenty minutes later, they were standing on the doorstep of the small cottage that MacDonnell owned, and Máiri McQuillan shared with three other women. The big man signalled to his toady who immediately threw the door open and stepped inside. Two women jumped up from the table they had been sitting at. MacDonnell fixed his gaze on Máiri McQuillan, ignoring Maura Leahy for the moment.

"So-o-o," he said, "where were *you* last night?" His bulk filled the doorway, all but blocking the light of day, and leaving his features silhouetted. Máiri, unable to discern his mien remained silent. A smaller chair, missing its back, stood in front of the small fireplace in which a turf fire sputtered gamely. MacDonnell moved there and sat himself down. Máiri could see now that he was wearing a smile that did not quite reach his eyes. When he patted his thighs playfully and held out his arms, she quickly went to him and lowered herself onto the proffered lap. "Well, darlin'," he said, "are ye goin' to tell me where ye were?"

Máiri turned her face to him and smiled coyly. "Sure, don't ye remember, Donal?" she said. "I told ye yestermorn that I had to go to Armoy t' see m' Aunt Lily? I told ye she was sickly, Donal. D' ye not mind me tellin' ye?" Warming her smile, she stroked the rough, ginger bristles on MacDonnell's cheek with the back of her hand.

"Did ye, now?" said MacDonnell, fondling her rear end. "It's strange isn't it, that I *don't* mind ye tellin' me that all?" His expression did not change and he kept his eyes on Máiri when he spoke next, "What about *you*, Dessie, boy? Do *you* remember Máiri here, saying anythin' about her Auntie Lily bein' sick. and about her goin' t' see her in Armoy last night?"

O'Connor, assuming a bemused expression, said, "No, I don't, big man. I don't mind her sayin' *anythin'* about her Auntie Lily."

MacDonnell ran his other hand up and down Máiri's thigh slowly. "Did ye hear that, love?" he said, quietly. "Dessie there, doesn't mind ye sayin' anythin' about goin' t' Armoy either."

Maura Leaghy spoke up then. "She told me she was—"

The big man's head swung in her direction. "*You!*" he shouted. "*You* shut yer mouth!"

"But I—"

"What are ye doin' standin' there anyway? Have ye nothin' better to do?" Maura Leahy looked at the floor while she fumbled for her shawl. Although she wore nothing but her shift, she was out of the door before Donal MacDonnell could say, or do, more.

Beyond the door, she stopped momentarily, to catch her breath. Maura had agreed to substantiate Máiri's story when asked, but that was before she saw Donal MacDonnell in no mood to be cajoled. So, Maura Leahy took herself off, as ordered, considering herself lucky to be given the opportunity.

Inside, MacDonnell had Máiri's full attention. "Now," he said, still smiling that dead smile, "are ye goin' to tell me where ye were last night?" The hand on her thigh stopped moving, and he gripped her leg hard, above the knee, and dug into her flesh, so that she cried out in pain. "Where were ye?"

Máiri mewled, "Please Donal, don't. Please…ye're *hurtin'* me, Donal! I was in Armoy, I tell ye. I went to see my Auntie Lily. They think she's got the consumption!"

Donal tightened his grip. "Ye never told *me* that!" he said, squeezing harder.

Máiri screamed and pushed insistently on his chest, until MacDonnell released his grip and allowed her to escape his lap. Standing before him, she rubbed at her knee. "That hurt!" she said. "Ye bastar—" MacDonnell was suddenly on his feet and had a hand at her throat.

He spoke into her ear, "Listen t' me, girl," he said. "If I find out ye've been puttin' it out behind my back, I'll *flay* ye alive! D' ye hear me?" Máiri hung on to Donal's wrist with both hands, her feet off the ground. struggling for breath. Several more seconds passed before he released her, and let her slide down to the rushes that covered the earthen floor.

"Now," said MacDonnell, unbuckling his belt, "I know ye weren't doin' *me* any good last night—*wherever* ye were—and I *know* that ye told me *nothin'* about goin' to Armoy!" Máiri, still recovering from the chokehold, scurried away from him on her hands and knees. Angrily,

Donal kicked the backless chair into the air; it landed, broken and askew, on its side, in the centre of the room. He held the belt by its buckle in his right fist. "And here's somethin' else for ye t' think about," he said. "Ye haven't given me—or wee Dessie here—any coin this mornin', or, for the last *few* mornin's, for that matter!"

Methodically, he wrapped the belt around his fist, leaving a foot of well-worn leather dangling. An authentic grin split the lower part of his face, but it was the cold glitter in his eyes that was frightening—there was no spark of kindness in them. "I *hate* t' do this to ye, Máiri, love," he said, stepping towards her, "but it seems t' me that ye need to be taught a wee lesson." Máiri scrambled to her feet and struck for the door, but O'Connor easily blocked her escape, and wrapping her in his arms, he half dragged, half carried, the struggling woman back into the room towards his boss.

MacDonnell reached for her and snatched at the front of her shift; the threadbare fabric ripped as if it was paper.

"No, Donal, wait…listen…*please!*" she cried. "I *was* in Armoy. Ask Maura, she'll tell ye." MacDonnell snorted dismissively, and between them, he and Dessie O'Connor threw Máiri across the wooden table as though she was no more than a ragdoll. Máiri fought back viciously, for she remembered vividly the last time this man had stretched her over a table. "No, Donal!" she screamed. She lashed at him with her feet and bit O'Connor's hands and fingers where he held her wrists. "Let go of me, yiz *bastards!*"

But MacDonnell easily parried the blows of her flailing feet with his forearms. He ripped and pushed the remnants of her tattered shift aside, and roughly thrusting his leather-bound hand between her thighs, groped at her sex.

"Well now, ye wee *bitch*," he said. "Seems to me, that ye need to be taught that ye can't go puttin' *this* out for nothin'!" Withdrawing his hand, he slashed the dangling end of the belt across her hindquarters. "Where were ye?" he demanded. Máiri, screaming in pain and frustration, cursed him. "That's nothin' to what's comin'. Where were ye last night?" He lashed her buttocks with the belt, and she yelped again. He lashed her once more. "Tell me where ye were last night, ye wee *slattern*! Who were ye with?" In a frenzy now, MacDonnell lashed at the distraught woman repeatedly, oblivious to her screams. ignoring her pleas for mercy.

Dessie O'Connor, a happy accomplice at first, quickly became concerned. He did not want to be involved in a murder—even if the victim was a trollop. "Donal…" he said, "…big man…don't ye think that mebbe that's enough?"

When Donal ignored his accomplice's pleas for leniency, Máiri realized with horror, that MacDonnell might well continue to beat her until…

"*Donal!*" she screamed. "Donal, wait! Please, Donal! I'll tell you! Stop, sweet *Jesus*, stop! Wait, I said. I'll tell ye where I was last night…I'll tell ye everything!"

MacDonnell stayed his hand, and standing beside the table, panting, he laid the belt gently across Máiri's injured flesh. "Well…?"

Máiri stifled her sobs. "Will ye let me rise and fix meself first, Donal?" She contorted herself on the tabletop, trying see the big man's face, attempting to find his eyes with hers, hoping she still might find a hint of mercy in them, that maybe—just maybe—MacDonnell had some feelings for her. O'Connor cast an enquiring glance at his boss.

"Just ye hold on to her, wee man," said MacDonnell, "'til I tell ye elsewise." Keeping himself out of the woman's line of vision, he stroked the belt over Máiri's injuries. "Alright then, Máiri, love," he said, softly. "Now, tell me…where were ye?"

"Well, after Armoy, I went to see my sister," she said. "I haven't seen her in a while, and I was worried about her, and—"

The lash was sudden and vicious. "*Bollocks!*" said MacDonnell. "Bollocks, I say! Ye're tellin' me ye went t' see yer sister? Thon crazy bitch *hates* ye! She cursed ye into hell, and out of it!" Turning to his sidekick, he added, "Do ye know what they're callin' her now, Dessie, boy?" He did not wait for an answer. "'The Black Nun *o' Bun-na-Mairge*'! What d' ye think of that? And there's talk that she's conjured up *all* sorts of demons out there. Who can say she's not humpin' the *Wee Man* himself, eh?" Leaning over Máiri, he pushed his elbow into the small of her back, smiling when she winced, and put his lips close to her ear. "And here ye are, tellin' me that ye went out there all by yerself, mind ye, in the middle of the night, because, all of a sudden, ye're worried about yer *mad* sister."

Máiri started to blubber. "I did go there, Donal. honest to God, that's where I went."

MacDonnell grabbed a fistful of her hair and pulled her head back and off the table. Producing a small dirk from his stocking top, he waved it menacingly in front of her eyes and traced the contours of her body with the pointed end of its blade. When he stopped and laid the cold steel blade against the tender skin of her rear, Máiri craned her neck to see what he was doing.

"Now, listen to me, Máiri, love," he whispered, "I'm just about done with all yer lies." As he spoke, he ran the dagger's point across her buttocks, momentarily mesmerized by the thin white line it created and left in its wake. Seconds passed until MacDonnell, blinking twice, swallowed audibly and increased the pressure on the knifepoint. "Now," he said, huskily, "either ye start tellin' me the truth, or I'm goin' to carve my name right here on yer *arse*!"

Máiri wiggled and squirmed on the table between the two men. "No Donal, no more, *please*! I'll—" But there was no immediate attack. She heard MacDonnell's heavy breathing. heard him swallow loudly again. On the periphery, she saw O'Connor lick his lips while he ogled her, feeling his sweaty palms on her wrists.

Máiri writhed, accentuating the movement of her body on the tabletop. "Please," she whimpered, "don't cut me; and don't beat me anymore, I beg ye, please, Donal. I'll tell ye *everythin'*! I know ye don't believe me, but I saw Julia last night; I *was* in *Bun-na-Mairge*, I *swear* it!" Twisting, she tried to see MacDonnell's face, to gauge his reaction. "Donal, love, listen to me; there's *treasure*, Donal! Julia's found the monks' *hoard* of treasure!"

The men looked at each other across the woman's prostrate body. For moments no one spoke, but Máiri, pulling, and continuing to move her lower body provocatively, drew the men's eyes back to her.

MacDonnell stepped closer. "It's the truth, Donal," she said. "Julia showed me this old…this old, wooden chest. It…it was full of gold coins, Donal! And…and…and all *sorts* of precious stones! I was goin' to tell ye about it, Donal. I swear to *God* I was!"

The pregnant pause that followed was broken when O'Connor snorted, "She's *lying*, big man. I'd wager she was nowhere near *Bun-na-Mairge*, last night; she probably *was* in Armoy, but it was no sick aunt *this* one was visitin', *that's* for sure! The bitch is lying, Donal. Sure, ye can see it in her eyes."

Máiri struggled and raised herself on her elbows, offering O'Connor an unobstructed view into her cleavage.

"Ye can see it in my *eyes*, can ye?" she spat. "Ye've never, ever *seen* my eyes, ye little *runt*! Ye can't raise yer eyes any higher than my *tits* whenever ye're around me!" Distracted, and angered, O'Connor let go of one wrist to backhand her. Máiri twisted out of his slippery grasp, turned snake-like and raked the surprised MacDonnell's eyes with her fingernails.

MacDonnell, lost his grip on the dirk and, before he could react, Máiri slid from the table and went to her knees in the straw. She rose, brandishing the small dagger before her. The men hesitated momentarily, and in that instant, Máiri spun on her toes and ran for the door. She had forgotten—and failed to notice—the broken chair in her way, and tripped and tumbled headlong over it.

The fall knocked the wind out of her, but Máiri was back on her feet instantly, determined to make her escape. She was confused to see the hilt of the knife protruding rudely from her abdomen. She wondered what it was. There was no pain—only the dark red, swiftly-spreading stain on her shift. Blood—her blood—pulsed from the wound, soaking her shift; it ran onto her thighs, where she felt the warm stickiness of it. And then—then, the pain.

Turning to face the men, she blurted, "Lord, save me!"

Donal MacDonnell, shocked by the sight of blood, quickly surmised what had happened, and moved towards her. "Máiri..."

"No! Let me be! Don't *touch* me!"

Ignoring her warning, MacDonnell closed on her, concern etched on his face. But Máiri snarled and, with unexpected speed and viciousness, pulled the blade from her abdomen and swiped it at MacDonnell's crotch, catching him high on the inside of his upper thigh. Then, stepping back, she hurled the weapon at his head. MacDonnell instinctively threw his arms up to protect his face. When he dropped them a second later, Máiri was gone.

CHAPTER SEVEN

Bun-na-Mairge
Friday, 14 August, 1665

1

Máiri McQuillan was dying. Death hung like a sodden shawl on her shoulders, and she knew that should she stumble and fall, she would die out there among the dunes, alone and unshriven.

Blood seeped steadily from the wound in her belly and coursed freely over her upper thighs; the hand she held tightly pressed there did little to stanch the flow.

The torn remnants of her shift were pasted to her body by the driving rain so that even as the light of day receded, the wounds inflicted on her were starkly visible. Máiri rested momentarily in the overhang of a larger sand dune. Her eyes closed as she slid to the ground.

Through a smoky yellow haze, she saw her mother sitting before the embers of a turf fire, in the hovel Máiri had once called home. She was crying.

"*Carson a tha thu a' caoineadh, a máthair?*"—Why are you crying, Mother?

Without turning or looking up, her mother replied, "*Air son anam mo nighinn.*"—For my daughter's soul.

Which daughter?

Her mother barked a laugh. Startled, Máiri opened her eyes and was surprised to find herself standing before the gate of *Bun-na-Mairge.*

The gate was closed and latched but there was no lock upon it. Lifting the heavy latch in her current state proved no easy task, and the pain bit when she put her shoulder to the gate's iron bars to force it open. The hinges screeched in protest, and she cringed at the sound, but still, she pushed until the opening was wide enough to afford her entry.

Inside the gates, Máiri faltered. It was as if she had just pushed her way through a huge cobweb and parts of it still clung to her. Máiri rubbed her arms and brushed her face and legs. She felt insubstantial, so light that she could not feel the ground beneath her feet. The world rippled and weaved around her. It was still raining, but the drops fell in slow motion, floating to the ground. The wind caressed her enquiringly and traced the contours of her body, much as a blind man uses touch to see.

Someone spoke, a female, and Máiri, looking for the source, saw a strangely dressed fair-haired woman standing a short distance away. She was staring, wide-eyed at Máiri. Then…she was gone.

As the next moments passed, Máiri looked back towards the gate, then scanned the path ahead, weighing her options. With a great sense of unease, she chose to continue along the path.

A faint buzzing came to her ears—like many voices whispering—and, as her anxiety increased, so too, did the volume of the buzzing. A few yards ahead, a gatehouse straddled the path. Máiri halted when she saw movement in its doorway. Standing motionless in the strange rain and caressing wind, she peered intently. It was difficult to keep the building in focus, for the walls seemed to be in motion, but again, she saw someone, or something, moving within.

Máiri whispered loudly…hopefully, "Julia! Julia, is that you?" There was no reply. All was still. The sudden sound of the gate *clanging* shut behind her roused Máiri and—her pain momentarily forgotten—she ran without looking back. She would not enter the gatehouse, choosing instead to leave the path, stumbling through the undergrowth until she found it again on the other side. There, the momentarily forgotten pain flooded back and she stopped for a moment, to catch her breath before walking on.

***

Julia McQuillan sat motionless on her cot, controlling her breathing. She listened harder, sure she had heard the sound of the gate. Rising, she stole to the slit window on the landing beyond the door and, although rainfall was a curtain and nightfall crept inexorably across the grounds of the friary, she detected movement on the path. Someone was headed in the direction of her quarters, and whether they knew it or not, they were being stalked. Dark forms coursed through the headstones, keeping pace with the visitor. Juli went back into the room, closed the door and waited.

***

Máiri, stumbling through an arched opening in a wall, found herself in a stairwell. Thinking she might rest for a moment, she sat on the steps and leaned her forehead against its cool stones. A sudden noise, possibly a voice, coming from the dimness above, startled her.

"Julia?" she cried. At first, only the sound of her own voice echoed in the stairwell, then other voices—male and female, whispering and laughing—mingled with the ebbing reverberation of hers. "*JULIA!*" Máiri screamed the name this time, and around and above her, the whispering increased and grew louder. "Julia! It's yer sister! Why don't ye answer me?" Holding her body taut as a bowstring, she listened until the echoes faded and all was ominously silent. Outside, the wind had dropped and the sounds of the strange rainfall had diminished. Máiri smothered in the suffocating silence, until the whispers began again and she saw creatures crawling down the walls…like spiders…towards her.

***

Julia found the woman in the stairwell, half naked and sprawled across its lower steps. Her torn shift was blood-stained and a small pool of blood was forming on the stone beneath her, but she was breathing. Julia leaned over and laid a hand on her shoulder, but recoiled when the woman stirred.

"Julia?" the woman said, "I pray t' God it's you."

Julia MacQuillan crossed herself instinctively. "Máiri!" she cried. "In the name of God, what's happened to ye?"

A few revenants appeared in the stairwell then, whispering and chuckling. Julia brandished her lash threateningly at them. "Let us pass," she said, then stooping, she pulled her sister onto her feet, wrapped an arm around her, and began their ascent. "Leave her be!" she snarled, as she fought her way to the door of her cell and safety. "Do not *touch* her!"

2

The voice sounded faint as if it was coming from another room…from the other side of a thick wall. Máiri had never felt so tired; she did not want to waken, but when she heard her name spoken again, louder and more clearly, she forced her eyes to open.

"Julia? I can't believe it. Is it—"

Julia touched a cool, damp cloth to Máiri's fevered brow. "Quiet now, m' wee love," she said. "It's alright, ye're safe now, but I see ye're tired. Try to get some rest now, and we'll talk later."

"No!" said Máiri. She saw the tendrils of an approaching grey fog reaching for her and began to panic. "No, Julia! We…we have t' talk now…there won't *be* any later." She tried to rise using elbows but the pain in her belly prevented movement. "Please, Julia, I'm sorry; will ye please forgive me? Please don't let me die unshriven. Will ye forgive me my sins, and pray for my soul?"

"Hush now, love. Sure, who am *I* to forgive anybody?"

Máiri grabbed her sister's arm. "Julia, listen," she said, urgently, "he's goin' t' come lookin' for me. Lookin' for *us,* unless…unless he's dead. Aye, mebbe he's dead, Julia. I cut him, ye know." She squeezed Julia's arm tighter. "I'm sorry! He was goin' to *kill* me! He wasn't goin' to stop, d' ye see? so I *had* to tell him somethin'—*anythin'*—to make him stop."

Julia took both of her sister's hands in hers and held them tightly. "Now, stop your blathering, Máiri." She had cleaned and tended to Máiri's lesions, and stitched and dressed the awful wound in her abdomen as best she could, but fresh blood was already staining the bandages. "Ye'll have to lie still, Máiri. Just rest yerself, now. Ye'll be alright. I'll take care of ye now, love."

But Máiri wouldn't be calmed. Stiffening, she raised her shoulders from the cot. "But he'll come here lookin' for it, Julia!" Her eyes were wild. "I cut him, I *know* I did, but mebbe I didn't cut him bad enough. And if he's able, he'll come here lookin' for me…lookin' for *it.*"

"Who'll be comin' here?" said Julia. "What's he lookin' for?"

"Donal," said Máiri. "He wants the treasure!"

"Treasure!" said Julia. "What treasure?"

3

Máiri slept, and Julia left her to go outside. The rain had stopped and the sky was clear and star-laden. A waxing moon peeked over the walls of the courtyard where Julia walked. She kept to the centre, staying in the moonlight, away from the shadows along the walls.

Craning her neck to look skyward, she studied the moon, as she had done countless times, wondering what it was and why it shone and why it changed shape. The stars dotting the sky were another mystery to her. Realizing her mind was wandering, Julia slapped her face with both hands in frustration, laughing and crying simultaneously:

"Please God," she cried, "forgive my sister Máiri her sins. In the name of Jesus Christ, your son, forgive her!"

Forgive her! But what is forgiveness? Can I forgive?

The word sounded foreign in her mind, so she said it aloud "Forgive, forgive, forgive…'Forgive us our trespasses'…what does that mean? Trespasses, trespasses, trespasses." In concert with the hiss of the last syllable of the last word, the whispers started, and Julia shivered and hugged herself. Dark shapes were milling in the shadows. She had forgotten her scourge. As if realizing this, some forms left the shadows to close on her. "*No!*" she cried. "Not now…not tonight. In the name of Christ and all that's holy…LET ME BE!"

Immediately, the atmosphere in the courtyard began to crackle and thrum; it grew louder by the second. Julia looked towards the stairwell, for the humming sound seemed to be coming from there. A bolt of brilliant light flashed from the window slit at the landing, cleaving the darkness and leaving her momentarily blinded. The humming grew exponentially, and the air exploded with an ear-piercing crack. Julia screamed and threw herself on the ground. The light was gone in a second and all was still.

Julia's ears rang, and the air vibrated and tingled on her skin, but her sight began slowly returning. "Máiri!" she whispered and crawled towards the stairwell. She hesitated on the threshold: it was empty. On the landing, her eyes were drawn to the door and the soft blue light that flickered on the bars of its window and seeped onto the floor from the crack at its bottom.

Cracking the door open, she whispered, "Máiri?" Getting no response, she pushed further into the room. "Máiri…it's me…it's Julia." The room thrummed quietly, and all was bathed in a pale blue glow. The light came from an object, shaped like a large trencher, which hovered over Máiri's inert body. Julia approached the bed slowly, mesmerized by the pulsing, translucent blue platter.

Drawing closer, she heard her sister sigh her final exhalation and watched a small bead of light, similar in colour to that of the trencher, escape Máiri's lips to immerse itself in the greater light which flared brilliantly and expired.

A rushlight, burning bravely beside the cot, saved the room from total darkness. Julia approached the side of the bed to lean over her sister's body. A beautiful, peaceful smile adorned Máiri's features. Julia, feeling her madness abate, kissed her sister's still-warm brow. A noise on the landing attracted her. Straightening, she turned, placing her body between the bed, and the doorway. A fierceness overcame her, a potency that not even the sight of the vile creatures milling upon the threshold could quench. Throwing her head back, she laughed. "My sister's soul is safe with God," she said. "Yer master's denied it!"

The creatures advanced, and, reaching for the lash on the bedside table, she wished with all her heart that she had remembered to close the door.

CHAPTER EIGHT

Bun-na-Mairge
Saturday, 31 October, 1665

1

Days passed, summer turned to autumn, and when there was no sign of anyone looking for Máiri or her, or the 'treasure,' Julia started to forget. During the three years she had lived in *Bun-na-Mairge*, moments of lucidity had become fewer and farther between and, for the most part, unwelcome.

Beneath her madness, Julia's faith in a merciful God was restored, for she had seen his mercy. With her own eyes and ears had she not seen and heard Him, or some emissary of His, take Máiri's soul to Heaven?

Julia believed fervently that her subsistence, and the abuse she suffered, was God's judgement on her—and that it was just. But she could not die unshriven: Julia knew that she needed to make herself worthy of God's mercy for her sins to be forgiven, for the sake of her immortal soul.

And so it was, that on the last day of October, Julia stood solemnly before the altar in the old chapel. It had rained all day, but the clouds had broken, and slanting rays of the setting sun laid her shadow across the chapel floor. It was late in the afternoon, but Julia deemed there was enough daylight left.

The scourge lay coiled upon the altar, like a snake about to strike. Julia slipped out of her homespun habit and laid it on a small stool nearby. Removing her cap, she shook her hair loose and let it fall about her shoulders and back. Goose pimples covered her flesh, and her nipples hardened in the cold air, and in anticipation of what was to come.

Laying her cap carefully atop her discarded habit, she picked up the lash, took one step backwards, and knelt on the packed dirt floor. Lifting her long tresses from her back, Julia gathered them and draped them over her left shoulder. The scourge felt heavy, and eager, in her hand; she brought it slowly to her lips and softly kissed it. She wondered at the sounds of rustling and scrabbling along the walls and was surprised to see that they were already deeply shadowed. Had she miscalculated? Surely, nightfall and darkness were still hours away. The Burglar's minions rarely entered the confines of the chapel. A lingering atmosphere of consecration kept them at bay, she presumed. Nevertheless, she sensed them gathering and was disconcerted. But she had her lash and felt she would be safe and unmolested here within the chapel walls.

She hefted the scourge and hesitated before closing her eyes. The first lash was the hardest to administer—and to bear—and when Julia whipped the cords across her shoulders, she bit on her bottom lip to curb a cry of pain. Whispering, cackling laughter issued from the shadows. Again, she was perturbed and hesitated. Trying to clear her mind, she lifted her face to the ceiling.

"Father in Heaven, please shrive me of my sins and deliver me from evil," she prayed, then forced herself to inflict a second lash. Inhaling deeply and holding her breath, she lashed a third time. "*Mea culpa*," she cried. "Forgive me, dear Lord! Please, absolve me of my sins!" Another lash. "*Mea culpa!*" Julia struck again, more forcefully this time, and cried out, "*Sweet Jesus!*"

A man's voice reverberated in the chapel.

"'Sweet Jesus', she says!" Donal MacDonnell and Dessie O'Connor stood in the arched opening at the end of the aisle, behind

Julia. "Did y' hear that? 'Sweet Jesus'. Who does she think she is, talking about our Lord and saviour like that?" He laughed and O'Connor joined in, his eyes shining as they roamed greedily over Julia's naked body. Both men were drunk: had they not been, the more likely it was that they would not have been there.

***

They had spent the afternoon in the Harbour Inn where MacDonnell had talked himself into a foul, vengeful mood, saying that he wanted to go to *Bun-na-Mairge*, to find "that bitch" Máiri.

"Mother of God, big man!" O'Connor had said then. "Tonight's *Hallow-e'en*, for Christ's sake! Now, ye don't want to go to thon place *any* night, but 'specially not this one."

"That bitch cut me!" said MacDonnell. "And she's made me a laughing stock, and she'll pay for it!" Gulping his whiskey, he poured himself and his sycophant another. "And don't be forgettin' that treasure. I want it. It's mine by right!"

Dessie O'Connor was all but certain that there was no "monk's treasure" in *Bun-na-Mairge;* he was sure that Máiri McQuillan had concocted the story just to stop a raging MacDonnell from beating her to death for whoring on the side.

"So, Dessie boy," said MacDonnell, staring darkly at the little man, "I'm for *Bun-na-Mairge*. Are ye with me, or aren't ye?"

O'Connor had known then that there was no choice, and so, here they were...

***

Julia stayed kneeling on the floor and did not turn around.
"Who are ye?" she demanded. "And what d' ye want here, in the house of the Lord?"

Low whispering, like the buzzing of bees, began once more in the shadows, but as MacDonnell was still chuckling at his sense of humour, he either didn't hear or chose to ignore it.

73

"Have ye ever seen the like of it?" he said. "Here, in the *house of the Lord*, on Hallow-e'en, mind ye. Some *wanton,* naked as the day she was born, whipping her own arse with a knotted rope."

He waited for a response, but Julia was momentarily stunned.

How in God's name did I forget that it's Haleve Nicht?

A week previous, the night of the full moon, she had remained in her cell, knowing that the strength of the *Aos Si* waxed with the event, but tonight was a more perilous one: *all* creatures of the *Aos Si* were at their strongest on Hallow-e'en. It was inconceivable to Julia that she could have forgotten. Beyond the chapel walls, it had become darker in only the last few minutes. Julia, recognizing this to be a contrived phenomenon, knew that it was imperative that she get to the safety of her cell as quickly as possible. She reached for her clothes.

"Stay!" cried MacDonnell. "Stand up, *witch!*" He smiled when Julia flinched at the word and complied with his command. Winking at his cohort, he continued, "Oh, we know *all* about the Black Nun of *Bun-na-Mairge.* Is that what's goin' on here? Are ye practisin' yer dark arts, *witch?*" He stepped closer. "Do ye know what they do with witches in this part of the country?" Snorting, he added, "It'll cost ye more than a couple of hours in the pillory, I'll tell ye that!"

Julia recognized the voice and its mocking tone; she knew who taunted her. Looking straight ahead, she raised her voice, "I ask ye again, Donal MacDonnell…what do ye want?" The thrumming around the walls increased in volume. This time MacDonnell heard it too and looked unsettled by it. He tried a laugh but it caught in his throat, making him cough loudly instead.

"I want thon *bitch* of a sister of yours?" he said. "Where is she?" He scanned the chapel for the source of the strange sounds which seemed to be increasing in volume by the second. The walls appeared to be seething. Peering into their shadows, he could see nothing. MacDonnell brought his attention back to the woman. "Did ye not hear me, wumman? Where's Máiri?"

Julia slowly turned to face the men and lifted her arms out to the side. She smiled, then laughed crazily at the expressions on their faces: one angry, the other shocked.

Then she said, "Search me."

She anticipated MacDonnell's lunge and, moving quickly, snatched her habit and threw it at his face. The big man stumbled and stopped, momentarily blinded. Julia flew past him, evading his flailing arms.

O'Connor came at her, but she caught him full in the face with the lash. He yelped, cowered, and covered his head with his arms. Julia darted past him too. She ran through the chapel's arched doorway, hoping that she could safely reach her cell.

But the shock of what she saw outside, brought her up short. The ground seethed with black beetle-like shapes, while other winged forms swooped, or hovered, bee-like, in the air. Julia stood aghast at the sight.

"*Sealg Fiadhaich!*" she said, awestruck—The Wild Hunt: Julia had never seen anything like the scene evolving before her, but she was well-versed in the folklore of her native land: It was *Haleve Nicht*— Hallow-e'en—and the *Sluagh na Marbh* had been incited to muster. Julia knew that these beings were not the familiar revenants of *Bun-na-Mairge*…and knew also that she had no pact with them.

Their terrifying ear-piercing shrieks when they saw Julia emerging from the chapel, rooted her momentarily. She knew, for the sake of her soul, she had to reach her cell and find sanctuary there.

Julia aroused and surrendered herself to her madness. Screaming a blood-curdling shriek, she attacked. Brandishing her lash with wild abandon, and mingling her screams with theirs, she launched herself at those beings who wished her nothing but harm.

2

No one had ever accused Desmond O'Connor of being a brave man, and the screaming and wailing that came from the sudden unreal darkness outside the chapel walls filled him with more dread than he had known. He grabbed at MacDonnell's cloak as he tried to pass.

"Don't go out there, Donal," he begged. "Can ye not hear that? It's like the gates of Hell have opened!" MacDonnell yanked his cloak from the smaller man's grasp and grabbed him by the shirtfront. O'Connor saw madness in MacDonnell's eyes.

"Ye're craven, Dessie," said Donal. "Sure, that's just the wind screamin' around the walls of this old place, and playin' tricks on yer ears." Hawking, he spat and threw O'Connor to the ground. "Now, if ye're ascared, get yerself back to the gate, and make sure they don't try to get out that way, but I'm goin' after thon bitch, alone, if I have to!"

MacDonnell, turning to leave, hesitated when he heard another unearthly scream from the darkness beyond the chapel door.

O'Connor sat on the ground, a picture of misery and fear. "Donal," he said, "listen t' me, big man. It's *Hallow-e'en*, Donal. I...I think that mebbe that's *Sluagh na Marbh* doin' all that screeching out there. So, for the love of Christ, let's you and me find another way out...let's get out of here, big man...let's go home!"

MacDonnell looked down at his sycophant. "*Sluagh na Marbh*," he sneered. "What are ye bletherin' about? Nothin' but tales and legends! Get a hold of yerself, fla ye! Stand up and be a man, for once in yer life!" But Donal himself quailed when a singularly blood-curdling screech rose above the cacophony outside.

O'Connor got to his knees, his features contorted and squeaking with fear. He saw the big man falter.

Swallowing, he said, "Donal...big man...let the bitch go. Let *them* have her, and mebbe they'll let *us* go!"

For a moment MacDonnell considered doing that. The nerves on his body tingled, and flight appeared the better option. But he was Donal MacDonnell who had never run away from a fight in his entire life! He straightened his shoulders and summoned enough saliva to spit again.

"I want that treasure," he said. "It's mine by right." He pulled his dirk—the same weapon that had done for Máiri McQuillan—from his stocking. "Máiri said she seen it, and thon crazy bitch of a sister of hers knows where it is!" Before he had time to reconsider and change his mind, he hurried through the archway, into the blackness beyond.

O'Connor meanwhile, swept the walls of the chapel with his eyes, searching for another way out. Noticing a small glimmer of light in the far corner, he began to crawl slowly, towards it.

The sound of the voice was sudden and close. *"Cá bhfuil sé ag dul?"*—Where is he going?

Startled, O'Connor rolled over and sat on his backside, trembling: "Who's there?" he said. "Who is it?"

The blow to his ribcage was unexpected and vicious.

He struggled to catch his breath and tried to get to his feet, but many hands were on him, and he could do nothing to stop from being dragged across the chapel floor.

Moments later, O'Connor was sitting on the floor of a small room where several monks milled about. They laughed softly and whispered.

"Who are ye?" wailed O'Connor. "What d' ye want with me?"

The monks quietened and parted to let another robed and cowled figure approach him. Slowly this figure pulled back its hood, and O'Connor's eyes bulged with wonder.

"Máiri?" he whispered, and watched, spellbound as she tugged at the front of her robe until it parted. The woman was naked beneath its folds, and O'Connor's astonishment was such that he struggled a little as the other monks tore his clothes from his body, and placed him, face up, on a roughly-hewn tabletop. Máiri smiled and whispered something—something unintelligible for the most part, and O'Connor thought her voice sounded different—it was more cackle than voice. It was this cackle, and the glazed hungry look in her eyes that caused the increase in his dread, so that he started to resist in earnest, but to no avail. He was held, spreadeagled on the tabletop by his captors.

Máiri approached, and O'Connor flinched when she ran the fingers of one hand down his cheek, across his chest and over his abdomen. He gasped when her icy cold fingertips caressed his shrunken penis.

Moving her free hand between his legs, she cupped his balls in its frosty palm, and widened her smile for him. O'Connor, tried gamely to smile back. Máiri spoke again in that cackling voice. "What's the matter, Dessie?" she said, turning her head to look sadly at his unresponsive genitalia, "Is m' touch not pleasant enough for ye?" She brought her lips to his ear then. "Well," she whispered, throatily, "Let me try somethin' else…"

O'Connor's smile became a grimace when Máiri's long tresses trailed over his body as she lowered her head to his crotch. He shuddered involuntarily at the feel of her cold breath there.

The sudden pain in his groin made O'Connor scream. Writhing, he increased his struggling and screamed louder when he saw the ghoulish creature leering at him now from between his splayed thighs. Its features were in an advanced stage of putrefaction, and it held the bitten-off part of his penis between its rotting teeth.

Slowly, the thing climbed onto the table, and O'Connor shrieked continuously as it crawled up his body towards his face. It stared at him with cold, lifeless eyes and grinned obscenely while O'Connor's blood dripped from its chin onto his face. Then slowly, it lowered its face, its mouth, to his.

O'Connor vomited, and was held amid whispering laughter while he died, choking on the mixture of ruined flesh and the matter which had spewed from his stomach. As O'Connor expired, the translucent blue marble of his soul escaped his ruined body, but was immediately captured and ingested by his attacker: The Burglar was desirous of its sustenance.

And it was then when O'Connor learned that death does not necessarily end one's existence, and what arose from that torture table was *not* Desmond O'Connor, for *he* was no more.

3

Just beyond the archway, Donal MacDonnell stopped dead in his tracks. Though it was very dark, he could see a mass of darker shapes, on the ground, and in the air, fighting or dancing with each other. It occurred to him that it was from these creatures that the blackness emanated and contaminated the air.

He was espied and had to cover his ears to deaden the screeching din that accompanied his discovery. He discerned he was under imminent attack from these fiends.

MacDonnell was about to turn tail and run when, through the advancing mass, he caught a glimpse of Julia McQuillan. Naked as a newborn, her skin emitting a pale blue light, she wielded her lash ferociously, slashing and fighting her way through the creatures that sought to destroy her. The sight of her reminded MacDonnell of some mythical female warrior of legend, and he was suddenly ashamed of his cowardice.

Summoning a war cry, he threw himself into the fray, slashing with his dirk at anything and everything that came near. The gap between man and woman was closing when all at once, MacDonnell saw Julia taken into the air by two of the bat-like monsters. With a yell and renewed vigour, he leapt at her attackers, and slashed at them with his knife. Grabbing one of Julia's arms, he pulled her from their clutches.

To MacDonnell's astonishment, Julia hit the ground running. "Quickly now," she called over her shoulder, "follow me!" MacDonnell made to comply, but something wrapped itself around his legs, and before he knew it, he was on his way down.

"Julia!" he screamed, seeing what held him. "Julia, wait, *help* me!" And in a moment, she was there, screaming and lashing at his attackers viciously with her scourge. MacDonnell, slashing blindly with his dirk at the creature pinning his legs, finally broke free of its grasp.

"Stay close t' me, now!" said Julia and together, back-to-back— him bathed in the issuance of her strange, blue light—they fought their way to the archway before the stairwell.

Once inside, they could not be surrounded, and it seemed the creatures were loth to engage them face to face. MacDonnell, breathing heavily, silently congratulated himself on his bravery.

"It's alright," he said, turning to Julia, a few steps above him, "ye're safe now. I think I can—" His bragging was cut short, and he screamed, when several pairs of hands reached through the archway to grab and pull at him. They would have succeeded had not Julia come to his rescue, yet again, repelling his attackers with her lash.

Grabbing his arm, she pulled him up the stairs. "Come on. Quickly now!"

Once in her cell, Julia closed the door and leaned against it, breathing heavily. A rushlight sputtered at her bedside. She found a replacement, lighting it from the former's dying flame, so that its feeble light battled the pervading darkness in the little room. The silence beyond the door had become palpable, and Julia peered at the landing beyond through its barred window.

"Can ye see any of them?" asked MacDonnell. "D' ye think they've gone?"

Julia shrugged.

MacDonnell stared at her body. "What's that light around ye?" he said.

"Angel light," Julia said.

MacDonnell chuckled. "Alright, have it your way, but tell me this, d' ye know what in the name of *Christ* those…those…*things* are?"

Julia still did not turn around. "*Sluagh-na-Marbh*," she said.

"*Sluagh-na*——" said MacDonnell. "I don't believe——"

Julia turned to face him. "Ye're a fool!" she said. "Why else would ye come to this place, of *all* places—here—to *Bun-na-Mairge*, on *Haleve Nicht*? Have ye never heard of the *Sealg Fiadhaich*, Donal MacDonnell?" Throwing her head back, Julia laughed uncontrollably, turning hysterical. "How could *I* have forgotten what day it is?" she said. "How could I have forgotten what *night* it is! It's *Sealg Fiadhaich*, Donal…the Wild Hunt! All of *Hell* is let loose!"

Donal became angry. No one had called him a fool in a while, and he did not like it, especially coming from this woman.

"Where's Máiri?" he snapped. Julia stopped laughing and looked at him with exaggerated surprise. "Ye crazy bitch! Where's yer sister?" With effort, he calmed himself and spoke more softly, "Listen, Julia I only want to *talk* to her…that's all."

Julia guffawed, turning coy. "Is it about the treasure, Donal?" she said. "Is that what ye want to talk to Máiri about?" She caught the look in his eyes as they roamed over her nakedness. "Look, Donal, *I'm* right here. Why would ye want t' talk to my sister about some silly treasure?"

A low whispering began outside on the landing, and MacDonnell jumped when something banged loudly at the door. Ignoring it, Julia slowly ran her hands over her breasts and along her body to rest on the flare of her hips. "D' ye think me pretty, Donal?" she said. The whispering on the landing grew louder, and something hit the door, so hard this time that it shook on its hinges. Julia still did not react.

"Julia," said MacDonnell, "listen to me. It doesn't matter right now. Is there another way out of here, wumman?"

Julia brought her hands to her breasts once more, hefting and kneading them. "Liam thought I was pretty," she said, "and I liked *him* too, but…" Without warning, she began to cry. "But I had no *choice*, don't ye see? He would have burgled *my* soul!" As suddenly as she began, Julia stopped crying and smiled at MacDonnell mischievously. "They wanted Máiri's soul as well, but they didn't get hers! *I* saved her!" Crossing the floor to where MacDonnell stood, she raised herself on tiptoe and draped her arms loosely about his neck. "Mebbe I can save your soul too."

MacDonnell stared into her eyes and realized that Julia was a stranger to sanity—or worse! Grabbing her wrists, he pushed her away, then he crossed himself. He was not a religious man and until this night had never known real fear. But now, in this tiny room, alone with this woman, with those creatures outside trying to get in, an unbridled terror coursed through his veins.

"I have to get *out* of here!" he said. Going to the door, he did not dare to put his eye to its window but laid an ear alongside its timbers. The whispering had increased in volume so it was hard to hear Julia when she spoke.

"But what about Máiri and the treasure, Donal?" she said. "I thought that that's what ye came here for." MacDonnell turned to find Julia on her back, writhing on the cot. The light from the rushlight by her bed crowned her glowing breasts with flickering tiaras of gold, and shadowed the recessed areas of her form. MacDonnell's eyes were drawn to the deeper darkness below her belly.

"My God!" he grunted. But the door rattled suddenly, and his growing lust abated quickly when reminded of the peril he was in. Turning his attention once more to the door, he reached for his dagger…

"Is *this* what ye're lookin' for, Donal?" said Julia. The blade glinted in her hand.

Two blows, in quick succession, pummelled the door, and MacDonnell noticed the frame shifting after the second.

He turned back to the bed. "Give me that!" he snarled, striding towards the cot. But Julia, scurrying across the mattress, put the bed between them. Laughing, she brandished the dirk.

"Is this the knife ye used to *murder* my sister?" There was naked hatred in her glare, and MacDonnell, sensing its encircling tendrils, felt his skin shrink.

"Listen," he cried. "It was an *accident*, Julia! I swear to Almighty God, I meant Máiri no harm!"

"Harm!" Julia screamed. "Ye almost beat her to death first, y' bastard!"

"Julia…listen to me. Sure, I gave the girl a bit of a latherin'. Lord knows she had it comin', but I never cut her. I swear it!" He stretched out his hand. "Now, Julia, just give the knife to me, and I'll get us out of here."

Julia struck at his outstretched arm with the blade. Blood spurted from the wound, and with such force that it spattered her face and breasts. Arteries in MacDonnell's arm had been severed, close to his wrist. Clasping his free hand around the wound, he stood watching wide-eyed as his blood spurted through his fingers to soak the cot.

"Christ, wumman!" he gasped. "What have ye done?" His strength drained from him as he fell to his knees. Julia scampered past him, and threw open the door. She hid behind it while many creatures spewed over the threshold and fell on the already unconscious man. Seizing the opportunity, Julia escaped the room. Wielding the knife, she slashed at the creatures still on the landing, fighting her way through them, screaming and cursing. She faltered when the hood of one of her attackers fell back and the putrefied ruin of Liam O'Kane's face hovered before her. Julia stumbled and tumbled head-over-heels, down the stone stairway screaming his name.

Moments later her lifeless body lay crumpled in the stairwell entrance at the bottom of the stone steps with the slim blade of Donal MacDonnell's dirk buried in her heart.

The light was bright and welcoming, and Máiri stood at its centre, arms wide open. She smiled as she beckoned her sister thither, but Julia balked.

"No, I can't Máiri," she said. "Sure, Liam's long gone, but I know his soul yet exists. The Burglar keeps it, and will destroy it if I travel on with ye. I can't—I won't—forsake Liam again."

The light dimmed and Máiri lowered her arms:

"Then," she said, "we must rescue him."

PART TWO

August, 1971

CHAPTER NINE

Ballycastle, County Antrim, N.I.
Friday, August 6, 1971

1

After they left the Harbour Bar, Bill and Carol, strolled hand in hand, following the contour of the seawall. Carol, laughing self-consciously and drawing the attention of her fellow tourists, fought the strong sea breeze for control of her hair and flared skirt. Bill laughed too. He enjoyed watching her and knew by now that Carol loved being watched.

Carol had elfin features, and long, straight, blonde hair, which cascaded over slender shoulders to the middle of her back. She had a tall, lean athletic build, and complained that her body looked more like a young boy's. Bill did not agree with that self-appraisal, nor did Carol, he suspected.

Walking further east along the seafront they came to the outdoor courts of the town's tennis club where several games were in progress.

"I wish I'd brought my runners," said Carol. Turning to Bill, she struck a pose and, in a distinctly Southern United States drawl, added, "I bet I'd wup yo'r ass on the tennis court."

Bill laughed dutifully. "Well," he said, "at least you're wearing the right type of dress."

Carol plucked at the hem of her dress, lifting it and inspecting it closely. "What, this durn thang? Why, it's so long it would cramp my style!"

A few players stared at Carol holding up the skirt of her dress.

"Carol!" Bill whispered, nodding in their direction.

She turned and looked. "Well, *land sakes!*" She let her skirt fall into place, and giggling into a cupped hand, took off hurriedly down the sloping sandy path with Bill in hot pursuit. At the bottom, to the right, there was a building marked "Public Toilets." They stopped under its overhang, laughing and trying to catch their breath. The doors of the building, marked "Gents" and "Ladies," were closed, and no one was in sight.

"Were you trying to get us arrested?" said Bill, panting. "I don't—"

Carol, interrupting him, threw both arms around his neck and kissed him on the mouth. Breaking the kiss, she said, "Did you see the looks on their faces?" She was flushed and breathless. "I got the impression they liked what they saw." Stepping away from him, towards the wall of the building, she lifted her skirt again, this time slowly and sexily. "Do you like what you see?"

Bill looked around furtively, and seeing no one, went to her, took her face in his hands, and kissed her, this time with more fervour. Carol, returning the kiss with equal passion, held and squeezed Bill's buttocks as she ground herself against the front of his jeans. Bill mirrored her actions, then reaching around and under her dress, slipped his hand between her legs. Carol moaned and parted her thighs, allowing him access, coaxing his erection with one hand and reaching for his belt buckle with the other.

"I got it," Bill whispered. He undid his buckle and jeans, and pushed them down his thighs. He swallowed drily, watching Carol as she reached under her dress and tugged her panties down to her knees, working them from there to the ground and kicking them off her feet. A moment passed—a pause—where they gazed at one another, and then the two were desirously entwined.

The sound of a toilet flushing within the building broke their embrace abruptly, and they hightailed it back up the path, Bill struggling to fix himself as he ran. Both were laughing uncontrollably by the time they were back beside the tennis courts.

"Jesus Christ!" said Bill. "You *are* trying to get us arrested!"

Carol slapped at his shoulder. "Me?" she said, looking down. "You're the one running around with his jeans undone!"

Bill zipped himself quickly. "Jesus!" he gasped. "I need a drink. Come on." Taking Carol's hand, he started back towards the seafront.

But Carol balked. "What about Bonawhatsit?" she said, looking at her wristwatch. "You said we'd go there, and it's almost five o'clock."

"Listen, we'll go there," said Bill. "We've got loads of time, but how about a wee drink first to give us courage. The place *is* haunted, y' know!"

2

Back at the Harbour Bar, they opted for the door marked BAR this time, and made their way to a table in front of a window. The long, knee-high trestle table sat in the mouth of the red vinyl-covered bench seat that curved around it in a semicircle. Carol slid into this cozy alcove.

"What would ye like to drink?" Bill asked.

"Isn't there a waitress?"

"This is the bar," he said, "the *pub*." Then in a posh English accent, he added, "In a pub, madam, one is expected to serve oneself." Back in his natural brogue, he said, "Now, what can I get ye?"

"I think I'd like a vodka and coke."

Carol surveyed her surroundings: The bar was low-ceilinged, with old wooden beams, thick and wide. The furniture was sparse, wooden and heavy, mostly benches and low trestle tables like theirs; the flagstone floor was unadorned by rug or carpet.

The bar was huge, ornately carved and visually impressive, and through a pall of smoke, Carol could see nothing but men standing at it—not a single woman. It seemed that every one of the men smoked, mainly cigarettes, but she noticed a few pipes too. It seemed also, that everyone was staring in Carol's direction, some surreptitiously, some not so much, and some ogled her blatantly. She was the only female in the place. She tugged at the hem of her short skirt and was glad when Bill returned with their drinks. "What's with these guys?" she said. "Haven't they ever seen a woman before?"

Bill chuckled. "Not a woman who looks like you, honey," he said. "Most of the fellas in here are retired, or they've just got off work, and I'd bet none of them is going home to someone who looks as good as you."

Carol tossed her head, flicking her hair off her face. "Am I supposed to be flattered by that?"

Bill laughed. "No. But ye don't have to be stuck up about it either. Listen, don't ye worry about them lookin' at ye. I'm not." *And I have the feelin' ye'd be more upset if they didn't look.*

Carol grabbed her cigarettes from her purse. In Canadian fashion, she did not offer one to Bill but left the opened pack on the table in front of her. "So," she said, drawing the smoke into her lungs and relaxing, "tell me more about how you misspent your youth in Ulster." She exhaled and smiled, showing her white, straight teeth.

He spent the next twenty minutes regaling her with tales of his past exploits, with much embellishment. Draining his pint, he said, "Right, one more for the road, okay?"

Carol bristled, uncrossed her legs, and sat up straight, glowering at Bill. Regaining her composure quickly, she smoothed the fabric across her lap. "Okay," she said, "but that's it, Bill! I mean it. One more and then we go to that old friary place, right?"

Bill slipped out of his seat, stood at attention, and saluted. "Right you are, ma'am."

Carol giggled, then beckoned him closer. "Is this place…this…this Bonamargy…is it secluded," she enquired. "You know, not too many people around?"

Bill shrugged and started to say something when she quickly flicked the front of her skirt up and down.

Bill actually gasped. "What the—"

Carol laughed at his astonished expression, then shushed him, putting her finger to her pursed lips and crossing her legs demurely. "Go get the drinks," she said. "Hurry up! The sooner we finish them, the sooner…"—here she nodded towards her lap—"…you know…" Bill made his way to the bar, shaking his head, but he was smiling.

3

Bill had been gone less than thirty seconds, when one of the men approached their table. He was shorter than Carol and slight of build with pleasant features. He looked to be in his twenties, and wore his fair hair fashionably long, but not styled or cut distinctively. The name "Marty" was emblazoned in yellow across the left pocket of his light brown work shirt which matched his trousers. He held a half-full pint glass in his right hand and spoke before Carol realized it. Giving her head a little shake, she tried to concentrate:

"I'm sorry…?" she said.

"Oh, no problem," said the little man. "I just asked if ye'd mind if I asked ye a wee question."

Everything's wee this and wee that. "No," she said. "I mean, no…I don't mind. Go ahead."

"Are you and yer man Americans?" he said.

Marty Doyle knew that her man was not an American—he had heard him speak—and he did not care if this woman was American or not. He saw Carol come into the bar, slink over to the table by the window, and hadn't taken his eyes off her since. Doyle thought her the most beautiful woman he had seen. And then, just minutes ago, when she lifted the front of her skirt…just for that wee second…up and down again…well, Doyle was astonished by what he saw, and since that moment, meeting her—and talking to her—became an obsession. He felt inexplicably drawn to her, and as soon as her companion left the table, Doyle acted in an uncharacteristic way by making his move quickly and decisively.

"No," she said, "we're not." Carol was undecided whether or not she should elaborate when Bill returned with their drinks. Bill nodded at the little man who stood, innocuously enough, before their table.

"What's going on?" said Bill. "Is everything alright?" Before Carol had a chance to answer, he set their drinks down and turned to Doyle, giving him all his attention. "What about ye, mate?" he said, his face a mask. "What can we do for ye?"

Doyle started. "I was just—"

Carol, reading more into her boyfriend's stance, interrupted, "It's okay, Bill, he only wanted to know if we were Americans." She gave a little laugh.

"*Americans!*" Bill said incredulously, sliding back into his seat beside Carol. "Do I sound like an American to you, mate?"

Doyle smiled self-deprecatingly. "No. no, ye don't, now that I hear ye speakin' more than a few words at a time, but I was wondering if yer wife—"

Carol interrupted, "Oh, I'm not his wife." She was a little annoyed. Did this little man think she couldn't speak for herself? "We're not married. And I'm not American, I'm Canadian."

Sensing a reprimand, Doyle became immediately apologetic, although he wasn't entirely sure of what he'd done wrong. "Sorry," he offered, "I meant no offence, I was just—"

"Why don't ye take the weight off for a wee minute." Bill nodded at a short stool on Doyle's side of the table. Doyle mumbled his thanks and seated himself. Bill tipped his glass in his direction. "Here's all the best,"

"*Sláinte*," said Doyle, taking the obligatory sip.

"It means health, or cheers," Bill explained to Carol. "Isn't that right there…er…," he peered at the name on Doyle's shirt "Marty, is it?"

Doyle nodded and wiped his lips on his shirt sleeve. "Aye," he said, "it does. That's me."

"So, I take it ye're a local lad, Marty?"

"I am," said Doyle. "Born and raised here in Ballycastle." He leaned forward conspiratorially. "Listen, I didn't mean t' eavesdrop, or nothin', but I thought I heard yiz talkin' about Bonamargy a wee bit earlier on…?"

Bill, feeling Carol stiffen, spoke before she could. "Well," he said, "it seems t' me that ye were eavesdroppin', Marty, mate." The "mate" and his smile took any threat out of the statement. "What are ye askin' anyway? Is there somethin' ye want from us?"

Doyle, looking abashed, said, "No, no I don't at all. It's just…well…it's just that I work for the council hereabouts, and I could take yiz there. Show ye round the place, ye know? Give ye its history, like, ye know what I mean?"

Bill guffawed then. "Away on with ye!" he said. "Who d' ye think ye're talkin' to? D' you think we're goin' t' pay ye to give us the guided tour of an oul ruin?"

Doyle raised both hands in a defensive mode. "Not at all," he said, starting to rise. "I was just tryin' to be friendly, that's all. I'm sorry to have bothered ye."

He was about to return to the bar when Carol elbowed Bill in the ribs and said, "Wait, Marty. Hold on a wee minute." *Christ! It's catching!* Turning to Bill, she said, "What's wrong with you, sweetheart? Tell Marty to sit down, for goodness' sake."

Doyle waited until Bill was suitably acquiescent before retaking his seat on the stool. He nodded his gratitude at Carol who, indicating his pint, nudged Bill again. "Let's get you another one of those."

Bill stared at her in disbelief. "Are ye—"

"Yes," said Carol, "another round would be great," and Bill was on his way to the bar, once more shaking his head and smiling, but with little joy.

Upon returning to the table with a drink-laden tray, Bill found Doyle and Carol in animated conversation. Each was smoking— *Carol's* brand, he noticed. Carol looked up at his approach. "Bill, Marty works as a groundskeeper at Bonamargy, and Dunluce, and…and *all* the other places of interest around here! Isn't that great?"

Fuckin' fantastic. Bill slid into his spot on the bench seat. Aloud, he said, "Really! Is that so?"

"Yes," said Carol, ignoring his sardonic tone. "And he says that Julia wasn't murdered by Vikings, or Normans, or anybody like that. Marty says that she was murdered by some men from Ballycastle, and—"

Doyle interjected, "I said it was more than likely that she was—"

"And," continued Carol, dismissing the interruption, "that she had a sister—Julia, I mean—and that she died in Bonamargy too!"

Bill took a long pull on his pint. "Is that a fact," he said. "Well, it's been—"

"And guess what else," said Carol, excitedly. "There's going to be a full moon tonight…" At Bill's confusion, Carol went on hurriedly, "Remember? Her ghost…Julia's ghost, I mean…appears on the night of the full moon! Marty says he can take us to a safe spot where we can watch, isn't that right, Marty?"

Doyle started. "Well, I—"

"Anyway. I think we should go." Carol stubbed out her cigarette in the tin ashtray.

"I said I'd take you there, remember?"

"I know, I know," said Carol, "but Marty knows where we can go to get a good look at her."

Bill leaned forward and looked directly at Doyle. "So," he said, "you've seen her then. You've seen the Black Nun, have ye? With your own eyes?"

Doyle looked discomfited now. "Well," he said, "not personally, no. I—"

"We-ell," said Bill, "thanks, Marty, but I don't—"

"Well, *I* think we should all go to Bonamargy together!" said Carol indignantly, staring at Bill. "Are you coming?"

What's gotten into her? "Now wait a wee—"

A large man appeared behind Doyle. "What about ye, Marty, mate," he said. His voice was low and gruff. "Are ye goin' t' introduce us to yer friends then?" The man was tall and wide at the shoulders. He had a wiry mop of red hair which was mottled with some kind of dust—plaster, or concrete—and he grinned while ogling Carol. Another man, shorter and slighter, hovered to the big man's left.

Doyle half turned on his stool. "Cormac!" he said, "What about ye, big man?" Bill heard a lack of enthusiasm in the smaller man's greeting. "And Tommy! How are ye doin', mate?" Tommy, also staring at Carol's thighs, offered no reply, and Bill, discerning Doyle's uneasiness, was immediately on his guard. *These two are bad news.*

Doyle looked uncomfortable and did not appear to like Cormac MacDonald or Tommy Calhoun either.

Cormac MacDonald looked hard now into Carol's eyes. "Ye don't mind if we join yiz, do ye?" He slipped onto the stool next to Doyle's without waiting for an invitation. Tommy Calhoun, remained standing. "I hear yiz are Americans," said MacDonald. "Is that right?" His head swung from Carol to Bill, but his eyes stayed on Carol's.

"No," she heard herself, say, "I'm Canadian. I live—"

"But *you're* not Canadian," MacDonald rudely interrupted, turning to Bill and meeting his eyes for the first time, "are ye…Bill? Where are you from?"

So, he knows my name. What else does he know? Bill, finding MacDonald's manner and interrogation openly antagonistic, automatically searched for a weapon. His heavy beer mug, still close to full, sat before him on the table. Keeping his eyes on MacDonald's, he wrapped his fingers around its handle. "No," he said, "I'm not Canadian. I'm from Belfast."

"Aye," said MacDonald, keeping his grin, "I thought so." He looked at Bill's hand on the beer mug's handle for a second and allowed his grin to widen further before looking him in the eye once more. "Whereabouts?" he said. "I mean, whereabouts in Belfast are ye from?" He turned to smirk at Calhoun before adding, "I think our Bill here's an Orangeman? Am I right, mate? Are ye a Billy Boy?"

Then all pretend smiles were gone, and Carol sensed open hostility between the two men. "Hey, hey guys," she said, uncrossing her legs, sitting upright, and pulling herself to the edge of her seat. "Hold on here." She put her hand on top of the fist with which Bill clenched the beer mug's handle. "I mean, I thought we were just getting to know each other. What's with all this macho shit, all of a sudden?"

MacDonald, unfamiliar with the term, was thrown momentarily. Turning to Carol, he said, "*Macho?* What's *macho?*" And the dangerous moment passed.

The tension eased further when Carol, giggling girlishly, said, "It doesn't matter." She pulled out a cigarette and put it between her lips. Still smiling, she laughed when MacDonald quickly produced a lighter and flicked a flame. "Oh," she said. "A gentleman too, I see!" She let him light her cigarette then slowly recrossed her legs. "Thank you," she said, and staring at Bill, added, "You don't meet many gentlemen anymore."

"Well, *some* of us still know how to treat a lady." MacDonald ogled her unabashedly for a few seconds, and when it was apparent that no reaction was forthcoming from Bill, he turned his attention to Doyle. "Well, wee man, what have ye been tellin' these folks, eh? And just where are ye thinkin' of takin'…er…Carol, is it?"

Carol decided there and then that she did not like the sound of her name coming from those lips. *Just how long have these two been watching and listening to us.* With more than just a tinge of nervousness, she managed a smile. "Yes, how did you know that?" MacDonald smiled, and Carol noticed that although his bright, blue eyes shone, the smile itself never reached them.

Doyle spoke, and all eyes were drawn to him. "They were askin' about Bonamargy, big lad, Ye know, askin' about the Black Nun and all."

"Ye're not thinking of takin' her to thon place are ye?" MacDonald, looked and sounded shocked at the thought. When Bill shifted in his seat, the big man focused on him. "What do *you* think of that, Bill? I tell ye somethin', *I* wouldn't be takin' *my* wife to thon place *any* time of day, never mind when it's comin' on t' dark!" MacDonald, keeping his eyes fixed on Bill, went on, "What about you, Tommy? Would *you* take the wife there?" Bill had forgotten about the other man. He was still standing behind and to the left of his cohort.

"Fuck, no," he said. His voice seemed to come from his belly, but it was the casual use of the four-letter word that caused the raised eyebrows around the table.

"Jesus, Tommy!" said MacDonald. "Have ye no manners about ye at all? There's a lady present!" Calhoun seemed ready to say something more but thought better of it when he caught MacDonald's look. The big man turned his attention to Carol again. "Now tell me this, why would ye be wantin' to go to Bonamargy, love? It's a bit of a weird place ye know. Marty here says he was tellin' ye about the Black—"

"Yes…" Carol interrupted. The big man frightened her a little, but she did not like the way every man here thought they could call her "love," and the scene playing out now was becoming tiresome. "We know all about the Black Nun, and how she's meant to appear tonight at the spot where she met her untimely demise, and maybe all of you are right, maybe it's not a good idea to go traipsing…"—she glanced at Bill—"…around there, but if I want to go there, I don't think that that's anybody's business but mine." Carol, picking up her purse, started to leave the table. "Now," she said, "excuse me, but I need to find a washroom."

It took a moment for Doyle to realize what she was in "need" of. "Er…the…the *Ladies* is over there." He pointed. "To the left of the bar. D' ye see the sign that says Toilets?" Carol nodded her thanks, slid carefully off the bench seat, and headed in the direction indicated.

MacDonald grinned at Bill, shaking his large, dusty head. "She's a feisty one, isn't she, yer wife I mean."

Bill extracted a cigarette from the packet on the table and took his time lighting it before answering. "We're not married, but ye're right, she *is* a feisty one." Turning to Doyle, he went on, "I think we're done here. So, we're just going to finish our drinks and head back to the B and B. Thanks for the history lesson and all, but as for the guided tour, I don't think so, alright?" He looked from face to face, keeping his expression neutral.

Doyle was the first to react. Rising, he said, "Oh, whatever ye say, mate. No problem. Listen, I didn't mean to…Anyway, listen, I hope there's no hard feelin's." Bill hoped he wasn't going to offer his hand and was glad when he didn't. Doyle turned to MacDonald and his silent partner. "C'mon," he said. "I'll buy yiz a pint at the bar, alright?"

MacDonald lingered for a second, eyeing Bill, seemingly undecided, then he stood too. "I'm yer man, Marty. C'mon Tommy, lad…the pints are on the wee man!" He slapped Doyle heartily on the shoulder. "Lead on, MacDuff!" Looking at Bill, he let his smile fall to the floor. "See and take care of yerself, Billy Boy, alright?"

Bill, keeping his expression noncommittal, simply nodded.

"Oh," said MacDonald, pushing the phony grin back onto his face, "and say 'cheerio' to Carol for me, would ye?"

Doyle, having done as promised, was heading to the toilets when he met Carol on her way back from the Ladies. They exchanged smiles, but Doyle was surprised when, touching him lightly on the arm, she stopped him. "Marty," she said, "are you still willing to take me to Bonamargy later?"

Doyle started to shake his head, but Carol persisted. "Look, don't worry, I'll talk to Bill. I wouldn't go there without him anyway. He *knows* that."

Doyle started, "I don't—"

"You'll have to get rid of that Cormac guy, though." she interrupted "And his friend. Bill didn't like them. *I* didn't like them!" She looked askance at the little man. "I don't think you like them either, do you, Marty?"

"Well, no, I—"

"Well, that's okay then. So, let me talk to Bill, and I'll let you know when we're ready to go, okay?"

She was gone before Doyle had a chance to reply, and in the toilet, facing the wall of the urinal, his mind was performing somersaults. *She'll let me know, she says. How? It doesn't matter anyway—yer man, Bill's, never goin' to go for it.* Back at the bar, he found MacDonald and Calhoun, heads and voices low, deep in conversation over their respective pints.

MacDonald acknowledged Doyle's return. "Well, wee man, me 'n' Tommy's for the off. Things to do, people to see, ye know what I mean?" Lifting his glass, he emptied it in one swallow, then nodding at Carol and Bill's table, he grabbed at his crotch. "She's a fuckin' cracker, isn't she?" he said. "Pity ye can't get shot of her man, eh?" He cast a quick glance Calhoun's way, before adding, "Ye know what? I think she's taken a fancy to ye, Marty." Calhoun chuckled at this, and MacDonald went on, "I think ye're in with a chance there, if ye play yer cards right, know what I mean, mate?" He winked, and slapped Doyle heavily on the shoulder. "All the best, now."

Doyle watched them leave, with great relief. He manoeuvred himself into a position where he could get an unobstructed view of Carol. There he waited…and hoped…and wished…and sipped at his pint.

CHAPTER TEN

1

Falling ever farther behind, Carol finally stopped to remove her "stupid" heeled sandals. They had not waited for her, and when she looked up, Bill and Doyle were smaller shapes, in an ever-darkening landscape, some ways ahead.

Cold now, as well as drunk, and wallowing in self-pity, she looked to the sky. "Where is this fucking full moon anyway?"

Not watching where she was going, she stumbled and fell to her hands and knees in the shifting sand. "FUCK!" she screamed, then taking a big breath, she shouted, "Hey…!"—into the wind and over the sand dunes—"Bill! Wait for me!" But she knew her words died on the tines of the wind even as she spoke them.

Biting back the tears that threatened, she chided herself. "Don't you dare!" she said, aloud, wiping her dripping nose with the back of her hand. "Don't you dare! This is all your own, stupid fault! 'Where's your sense of adventure?' you said, you stupid bitch!" Still, she could not understand why Bill was so mad at her. What was his problem?

Rising with some difficulty, she thrust her hands, and her shoes—one in each hand—into the pockets of her denim jacket, Bill's jacket, and trudged on.

When they left the pub, Bill gave her his jacket when she complained about the cool breeze coming off the sea. He had not bothered to help her on with it, simply held it out to her, hooked on the end of an extended finger.

"ASSHOLE!" she yelled now, after his retreating form.

But, by the time they reached the shoreline, Carol was turtling into the jacket, glad of it when those cool breezes turned into a colder, incessant wind. She would have asked Bill to take her back to the bed and breakfast then and there, but could just imagine the smug look on his face, so…

Another particularly, strong gust lifted her short summer dress and bit hungrily at the flesh of her exposed upper thighs. The dress's skirt flapped about her waist, like a white flag of surrender, and in weary capitulation, Carol let it go unbridled. She was tired of fighting with it; and what was the point anyway? There was no one else stupid enough to be out here among these fucking endless dunes to see her naked ass anyway.

The wind dropped suddenly, and in the ensuing, eerie silence, Carol stopped and stood stock-still. The feeling of someone, or something, being with her on the narrow path was tangible, and fear tightened her chest. She swallowed hard when, just a few yards ahead of her, the figure of a woman materialized upon the path.

The woman, tall and slender, had long, fair hair reaching down to her waist. She wore a tattered white nightie. This flimsy garment was wet and plastered to her form, giving Carol the impression that she had come out of the sea.

The woman held one hand pressed to her abdomen as she staggered over the sand, suggesting that she was injured and in pain. Then she stopped, and turned to look at Carol. She seemed startled and about to say something, when the wind suddenly returned with a vengeance. Carol shielded her eyes momentarily, and when she looked again, the woman was gone. Carol scanned the immediate vicinity for a sign of her, but there was none. Then she realized what it was that was strange about the woman's movements: the sand did not move under her feet; her passing left it undisturbed. Carol was shocked, and rooted by this comprehension. She screamed, "BILL!"

Carol's cry fought its way through the wind to reach them, and this time Bill stopped and looked over his shoulder. He thought he heard panic in the cry.

"You go on ahead," he said to Doyle. "I'll wait for the stupid bitch to catch up." Then, he grinned sheepishly. "Be better if you go on, okay? It'll give me a chance to talk to her, ye know? I mean, I suppose I could've been a wee bit nicer to her, eh?" Shaking his head, he shrugged his shoulders. "Fuckin' women!"

Minutes earlier, when Carol starting having difficulty walking through the sand, Bill had ignored her pleas for help, and stridden on deliberately. Doyle would have helped her—he wanted to—but Bill had told him to leave her be.

"She said that she could look after herself, didn't she?"

Back in the bar, when the three of them were discussing their plans, Bill suggested again that Carol might not be dressed for the expedition to Bonamargy, and that she'd had a few too many drinks. When he said that he didn't want to be responsible for her hurting herself, she snapped at him:

"You're not my father!" she said. "I can take care of myself, don't you worry!" Doyle remained solicitously silent, and in the end, it was decided, without input from him, that they were all going.

The sun was low in the sky, and Doyle knew that twilight was nigh. He did not like the idea of being in Bonamargy after nightfall, and was now thinking to himself that this might not have been one of his better ideas. All he had wanted was to spend as much time near Carol as he could; to watch her as she clambered through the ruins of Bonamargy, wearing that short sundress. He had not considered that Carol and Bill would continue to argue, and that he would spend more time with him than with her. The very fact that Bill could lose his temper with his gorgeous girlfriend was simply implausible to Doyle.

Bill had been seething, but the walk in the dunes, fighting the wind, had dulled his irritation. He started to walk back but thought better of it. His sense of injustice was not diminished that much. He managed to light a cigarette in the gusting wind and waited the few minutes it took for Carol to reach him. When she did, he was pleased that she huddled silently, and gratefully, into his relative warmth. Bill lit another cigarette and he wrapped her in his arms.

After a moment or two, Carol said, "Can I have one of those, please?"

Smiling, Bill took the cigarette from his lips and put it between hers, not wanting to bother lighting another. He began to feel sorry for her and to regret his surly behaviour. Carol was just a wee bit drunker than usual, that was all. They'd go to Bonamargy quickly, take a wee look around and be back at the B and B before dark. *Wee Doyle's, alright too. He's just under Carol's spell—just like everybody else. Just like me!*

Carol detached herself from him and stood back. "Bill I...I think I saw a...a—" Another gust of wind hit them—a gust strong enough to lift Carol's skirt and send it billowing around her waist.

Immediately, Bill's conciliatory thoughts dissipated and his previous annoyance returned "Jesus *Christ*! Will ye at least *try* to keep yerself covered!"

Carol bristled too. "You know what? Fuck you!" Pulling off his jacket, she threw it on the ground at his feet. Remembering her sandals, she retrieved them from the garment, and vehemently threw it to the ground once more. Sliding her feet into her sandals, she straightened, and brushing past him, sashayed along the sandy path towards Bonamargy. For a moment, Bill considered leaving her, and heading back to Ballycastle, then, he followed her.

Doyle was leaning on one of the gateposts, waiting and watching. When Carol came along the path, he pushed himself off the post to stand straighter.

Carol, holding her head held high, swayed her hips with each step. The wind whipped her long, blonde hair about her face and shoulders and tugged insistently at the hem of her dress. Carol retained her modesty by holding one hand, placed strategically, with fingers splayed, at her crotch. Between the first two fingers of the other hand, she held her donated cigarette and with it, she described an arc in the air, in time with her steps.

Martin Michael Doyle felt an unfamiliar ache in his chest as he watched Carol's approach: He had never been in love before.

2

Bill caught up with Carol just as she reached the gate and tried to put a protective arm about her shoulders, but much to Doyle's secret delight, she shrugged it off. She looked at Doyle and nodded at the gate. "Is it locked?"

"No," he said. "At least, it shouldn't be."

"Well…?" said Carol, and Doyle immediately turned his attention to the wrought iron gate, and its latch.

Bill said, "What time is it, Marty?" and Doyle stopped what he was doing to check his wrist. He could not see his watch face in the fading light.

"It's hard to see. It…it looks to be about—"

"It's 9:32," said Carol. Her digital watch could be illuminated by the press of a button. "Why?"

"Well," said Bill, "she's not meant to appear 'til midnight, remember?"

"So?"

Bill kept his tone even. "So, what are we goin' to do till then?"

Carol had not considered that, and vented her frustration on the obvious target—Doyle. "Are you going to open that gate or not?" she snapped.

Doyle refocused on the job at hand. "It's already open," he said, almost to himself.

"What's that? Is there a problem, Marty?"

"No," said Doyle. "I just said that the latch is open. Usually, the gate's left closed, and latched, and I just wondered how—"

Carol's petulant attitude returned. "Is that significant?" she said. "Can you still open it?"

Doyle pushed on the gate and, with some effort, opened it wider. Bowing slightly, he stood aside to let Carol enter first. Suddenly, she was reticent, and turned to look at Bill.

Bill, ignored her and turned to Doyle. "What's worryin' ye about the gate?"

Doyle chuckled self-consciously. "Well, it's nothin' really," he said, "but 'round here, we always make sure that the graveyard gate is closed—and latched—when we enter or leave. And not just here in Bonamargy…we do it at any graveyard…it's just what we do."

"But, why?" asked Carol, curiosity momentarily overcoming trepidation.

Doyle, started to lead them through the gateway. "Well…" he said, looking sheepish, "it's meant to keep the spirits of the dead where they're meant t' be, so that they don't…er…*wander.*" Thinking he might find support, Doyle looked at Bill. "Have ye never heard of that?"

But Carol snorted. "Yeah, right," she said, pointing to the tumbled-down walls around the perimeter of Bonamargy, "like that's gonna make a difference!"

Doyle, peeved, turned and looked at Carol. "Sure, ye can laugh and titter all ye want, but it's believed that since the dead enter through the gate, they can only leave by the gate." Doyle grabbed the gate and shoved it closed with a loud CLANG. "So, we keep the gate closed!"

Carol jumped at the sound. "Jesus Christ!"

Doyle, ignoring her, slipped past her to check the latch, and finding it secure, said, "And latched." His actions having achieved the desired effect, he slipped past the visibly shaken Carol. "Now, shall I lead the way?" He started off in the direction of the gatehouse without waiting for a response.

Carol looked at Bill and was angry to see him grinning at her. "What are you—" She stopped suddenly, and clutched at Bill's arm. "It's her!" she gasped. "Look!" The woman she had seen earlier among the sand dunes was on the path, between them and Doyle, who was nearing the ruin of an old gatehouse. "Hey!" she cried. "Wait, wait a minute."

Doyle turned around. "What now?" he said, irritably. And the woman—the one that Doyle plainly could not see—also turned to look at her for a moment, before disappearing.

Bill was studying Carol when she brought her attention back to him. "You didn't see her, did you?" she said. "She was right there." She pointed. "There, on the path." She looked accusingly at Doyle. "How could you not see her?"

Doyle's only response was a look of bewilderment and a shake of his head. "See who?"

Carol, still searching the grounds with her eyes, said, "It was probably all this talk about wandering spirits and stuff—now *I'm* seeing ghosts." She tried to laugh, but it came out as more of a squeak. A definite sense of unease took root in her belly. "Look, Bill, maybe—"

She was shocked into silence when her boyfriend suddenly crumpled, and collapsed at her feet and someone grabbed her in a bearhug from behind. When the figure of Cormac MacDonald loomed from the shadows brandishing a large rock, Carol let loose a scream borne of fear, revulsion, and frustration.

"Hold onto 'er, Tommy, mate," said MacDonald. "Sure, she can scream all she wants. There's none but us can hear 'er."

3

Bill regained consciousness slowly. He had not yet managed to open his eyes when he heard Doyle's voice:

"Take it easy there, mate," he said. "I was beginning to think thon big bastard had done ye in." Bill's head ached, and a sharp pain stabbed at the back of his eyes when he forced them open. Doyle's voice came from somewhere behind him. "He was goin' to hit ye again ye know, but I stopped 'im, told 'im he'd likely *kill* ye if he did!" Bill turned his head and Doyle's face floated into focus. "They wanted me to go with them," he was saying, "to…ye know…with yer girlfriend, like, but I wouldn't."

Bill managed to push himself onto his hands and knees, then stopped, waiting for the world to stop spinning. "Carol?" he croaked.

"Now, listen to me," Doyle began to babble, "I tried to stop them. I told them that I wanted *no* part of it!"

"Where is she?" said Bill, starting to rise. "What have they done t' her?"

Doyle took a step back, warily, when Bill finally stood. "They took her into the ruins," he said.

Bill's fingers came away bloody when he touched them to the back of his head. "Which way?" he said, staring farther into the ruin of Bonamargy. He was puzzled by the strange purple darkness that lay about the place, not dark enough to be called night, and definitely not day. *It's like a dreamscape. Is this what this is…am I dreaming?* But the pain in his head seemed real enough. Aloud he said, "What the fuck's happening here?"

Doyle backed away from him. "Now, listen," he said, "I swear t' ye…I wasn't in on this. And I didn't do nothin' to yer girlfriend! MacDonald's the one who whacked ye from behind with a big, fuckin' rock!" He cowered when Bill took a step towards him. "Hold on, now," he said, "I told ye, I—"

"I asked ye," said Bill, glowering, "which way did they go?" Doyle's hand shook as he indicated the direction. Bill nodded. "How long a—"

Suddenly, a shriek reverberated in the ruins. Bill, thinking that he might have imagined the sound, glanced questioningly at Doyle. The little man stared back, horror-stricken, and Bill, surmising then that he too had heard the bone-chilling screech, set off at pace in the direction it had come from.

Startled into action, Doyle was about to follow him, then thought better of it. *Get yerself the fuck out of here, son!*

"Mind now," he called after Bill's retreating figure, "I never touched 'er!" Then, he turned, and starting off in the opposite direction, hurried towards the gate. A second, louder screech stopped him in his tracks, and the sound of this one chilled his blood. Now, Doyle had heard that expression before, but he had never, ever, experienced the *actual* sensation; it was one he would never forget.

He was struggling with the latch when he heard the chopping sound of a helicopter overhead, but the sound was unnaturally slow. He looked up, and what he saw brought him to his knees. The air rippled and seethed with a mass of huge black bird-like shapes, all headed into the heart of Bonamargy. Doyle thought they looked like bats, but as quickly as the idea entered his mind, he dismissed it. He did not know what these things were, but they certainly were not bats. He cowered, quaking in the shadow of the gatepost, until yet another piercing screech rent the atmosphere, then Doyle flung the gate open, and ran as he had never run before. The thought of closing the gate behind him didn't enter his mind...

4

Carol slapped, kicked, screamed, and cursed, all to no avail. Tommy Calhoun, locking her arms in his, rendered them ineffective, while MacDonald, parrying her wild kicks, moved in closer.

Carol felt her strength waning under MacDonald's assault. He pulled and tore at her dress, until its remnants were rucked up over her breasts. Tearing at her flimsy bra straps, he ripped that garment from her body. When he stepped back to admire his handiwork, Carol spat in his face.

MacDonald, wiping at the spittle with his left hand, backhanded Carol viciously with the other. Grabbing her by the throat he waggled the finger of his free hand in her face.

"Ye fuckin' *slut!*" he snarled. "Ye do that again and I'll rip yer fuckin' lungs out!" Carol was on the verge of unconsciousness when MacDonald, easing his grip, reached for her sex and whispered into her ear, "I'm really goin' to enjoy this." Stepping back, he started to undo his belt.

Then Calhoun was at her ear. "Wait 'til ye see this," he whispered hoarsely. "The big man's hung like a donkey!" He chuckled and his chest rattled. "I'm tellin' ye, just wait till—" His words caught in his throat when he noticed a shadow, darker than the rest, moving in the arched opening in the wall behind MacDonald. "Hey, Cormac, there's somebody over there, behind ye, hidin' in them arches, watching us."

MacDonald glanced quickly over his shoulder, and seeing nothing untoward, brought his attention back to the woman. "Catch yerself on. Ye're imaginin' things, mate. Keep yer head, for fucksake. Hold 'er tight now." MacDonald ogled Carol while he unbuckled his belt. "Fuck me, Tommy," he said, "she's a fuckin' *cracker*, isn't she?"

Carol attempted a feeble kick, but parrying the blow easily, MacDonald stepped closer, and once again, she felt his calloused hand force its way between her thighs. When he spoke, his breath was foul and hot on her cheek. "Well, *princess*," he said, "ye've been askin' for this and now—"

"Fuck *me!*" said Calhoun. "It's her! It's the fuckin' Black Nun!"

"What the *fuck* are ye talkin' about?" said MacDonald. When he turned to look once more, Carol took his earlobe between her teeth and bit down as hard as she could. MacDonald screamed and pulled away, and Carol spat a mouthful of blood and flesh onto the ground at his feet. "Ye fuckin' *BITCH!*" he roared.

Carol closed her eyes and readied herself for a vengeful assault. But before it came, Calhoun's grasp on her loosened, and his voice held a tinge of fear:

"Cormac," he said, "I'm not kiddin', mate…look…it's her…*look!*" he shouted, staring bug-eyed at the archway. The expression on his mate's face, and the timbre of his voice, stopped MacDonald's imminent assault on Carol. Nursing his wounded ear, he turned and followed Calhoun's haunted gaze. He was stunned to see the black-robed and cowled figure hovering in the archway. He quickly bit back his fear.

"Alright," he called out, "who the fuck are ye?" Getting no response, he went on, "Look, whoever ye are, ye're not foolin' anybody. Now—" An ear-piercing screech pushed the air and his words back into his throat, and reverberated off the walls around them. MacDonald was running before he knew it. Calhoun pushed Carol to the ground and was hard on MacDonald's heels when he heard a strange *whoosh whoosh* sound in the air above his head, and as he started to look up, several large, black-winged shapes came hurtling out of the gloom, and knocked him and his cohort off their feet, leaving them fighting for breath, sprawled on the ground.

Carol lay where she had fallen, and hid in the grass, watching as more and more of the black shapes landed, and the ruins echoed with their whispered hissing. Everything was moving in slow motion, and the world was drained of colour. Some creatures, black against a strange purple background, crawled over MacDonald's and Calhoun's prostrate forms.

Suddenly, one of the men screamed, and Carol decided to make a run for it. She darted from her hiding place but was immediately confronted by one of the creatures who barred her way and hissed at her menacingly. The thing was crouching but was no taller than a child. It wore a black cloak—or robe—with a large hood covering its face. Slowly, it lifted its head, and when Carol saw its face, and found its eyes staring at her balefully, she felt her fear burble in her stomach.

"Oh, dear Christ," she prayed. Those unsettling, deep-set eyes sat on either side of a protuberance that looked like a beak rather than a nose. "Please—" Without warning, the creature straightened, and screeching resoundingly, unfurled and spread what appeared to be huge leathery wings.

Carol stared open-mouthed as the bird thing, flapping those wings, rose slowly into the air to hover a foot or so above the ground. Carol smelt the stomach-turning stench of putrefaction, and fighting to keep the contents of her stomach intact, she backed away slowly. The thing, flapping its wings, rose higher still, and Carol could have sworn it was smiling at her. Then it screeched, and Carol thought she would never breathe again, let alone scream, but she did when she felt arms about her shoulders.

"Carol!" said Bill, turning her around to face him. "It's me. Come on!" Dragging her behind him, he ran along the path. "What the fuck are those things?" he said over his shoulder.

"Just run, Bill," Carol said. "RUN!"

"But what *are* they? They're not *real*, are they?" Just then a putrid odour cloaked Bill's senses, and fighting against a feeling of nausea, he looked up. Just above their heads, two of the monsters hovered, keeping pace with their headlong flight.

"Holy *shit*, I think we're fucked."

Carol, taking the lead, pulled at his arm, urgently. "No, Bill, don't! Don't say that. Don't *look* at them!" Another screech filled the air, and Carol, hearing the familiar *whooshing* sound, screamed, "BILL!"

The sudden crackling explosion of light was blinding white. It only lasted a moment—no more than a pulse—then darkness enveloped the couple who lay inert among the gravestones, bringing with it a complete and uncanny silence.

5

Bill waited, tense, eyes wide open, seeing nothing. "Carol," he whispered into the sudden blackness, "where are you?"

Her voice answered, close by, "Bill? Have they gone? Where are you, Bill? I can't see." Bill reached out and felt her flinch at his touch. Grabbing his hand, she clung to it. "Jesus, Bill," she said. "What's happened? Is it the end of the fucking world, or—"

"It's okay, Carol," he said. "*We're* okay." He pulled her to him and held her, hoping and praying that he was right, that when his sight returned, they would be safe in a world that had resumed its normal state. Moments passed in the unearthly silence before Bill could see Carol, cradled in his arms, and shapes in the landscape around them became more distinguishable. Pushing himself to his knees, he lifted her onto hers. Carol's features were still a blur to him as they got to their feet, but Bill thought she might be smiling. Carol chuckled, which was disconcerting, but he was shocked when the chuckle turned into a maniacal laugh. Then, just as suddenly, she began sobbing.

"We've gotta get out of here," she said. "Jesus, Bill, what the fuck were those things? Did you see them? Did you? Did—" Carol screamed. From the depths of her being, one long, continuous screech spewed unbroken from her mouth.

Bill, his sight improving by the second, grabbed her shoulders and yelled into her face. "Carol! Stop it, Carol!" But Carol just screamed louder, and squirmed in his grasp. Bill yelled. "*CAROL!*" Still, she screamed unabated, until he slapped her face—hard—and amazingly, she went silent. Bill's concerned gaze was met with a detached and vacant stare. "Come on, honey," he said, "let's get ye outta here."

The grounds were devoid of life, for the moment, and he was thankful that Carol offered no resistance when he began to lead her in the direction of the gate. Nervously, Bill searched the darkness behind them for signs of movement. He did not care about what had happened to the other two, however, he did care about another possible encounter with those weird, stinking, flying monsters. He felt Carol's eyes on him and summoned a smile. "Are ye feelin' a wee bit better?" Her eyes had lost that vacant look, and Bill was relieved to see fear and anxiety replace it. a more normal and healthier reaction in his opinion.

"I'm okay, Bill," said Carol. "Just get us out of here."

The gate was open when they reached it, and Bill thought idly about wee Marty, and what might have happened to him as he ushered Carol over the threshold.

"Wait a minute," she said, stopping. "We have to go back. My sandals…where are my sandals?"

"Never mind yer sandals," said Bill, pushing her, but Carol resisted fiercely.

"No, Bill!" she said. "I need to get my sandals!"

"Carol!" said Bill. "Listen t' me. Ye're in shock, d' ye hear me? Come on now, let's just go." But Carol, pulling free of his grasp, tried to make for the path. Bill grabbed her again. "Sorry about this, sweetheart," he said, and picking her up bodily, he threw her over his shoulder and carried her—over her protestations—through the gateway. Bill carried her until they were well away from the gate and her struggles had lessened considerably. "I'm goin' to put ye down now," he said, "okay?"

"Yes," said Carol, "okay." Bill set her on her feet.

Pulling her hair from her face, she said, "I'm okay, Bill. I don't want my sandals any more, but haven't you forgotten something?"

"What?" said Bill, exasperatedly. "What have I forgotten?"

"The gate, Bill," she said. "You didn't shut the gate." Bill, shaking his head dismissively, started to move again, but Carol, grabbing his arm, looked pleadingly into his eyes. "Please, Bill," she said. "You have to listen to me. Remember what Marty said, Bill, remember? You *have* to shut the gate. Shut—the—gate—Bill...*please!*"

Bill, remembering, saw that there was no sense in arguing. Running back, he grabbed the open gate in both hands and shut it with a ringing *CLANG*. He could not stop himself from peering back along the path, through the gatehouse and deeper into the dark confines of Bonamargy. There was no movement; no one was following them, that he could see; no voices, no flying monsters—just the natural sounds of a summer night in Antrim. Night had fallen, but it was a natural darkness that surrounded Bonamargy. The clouds had broken and the full moon shone brightly. Turning from the gates, he jogged back easily to where Carol stood waiting.

He studied her face. "Are ye okay?"

She nodded, and looking back towards the gate, said, "Are *we* okay?"

Bill smiled. "Yes," he said, "we're okay." Then he glanced downward. "What about yer feet?"

Carol smiled. "I think I might need a piggyback."

CHAPTER ELEVEN

Carol took a long drag on the cigarette and passed it back to Bill. The bus was chock-a-block with passengers, and the young couple had been lucky to get two much-coveted seats in the smoking section. Bill also felt they were fortunate to get tickets at all, as only one bus ran the coastal route to Belfast on weekdays. The weekend buses had been fully booked, or else they would have been in Belfast by now: Bill and Carol were done with Ballycastle and its "attractions."

They had passed Saturday and Sunday in Seaview, waiting nervously for the proprietor to tell them that the police were downstairs, wanting them to help with their enquiries. Carol spent a long time in the bath during the early hours of Saturday morning, and more time after she awoke from a troubled sleep on Saturday afternoon. They did not speak of the events of Friday night until after finishing breakfast at the B and B on Sunday morning. Having eaten little all-day Saturday, both awakened that morning feeling ravenous.

When Carol's plate was empty, she sipped a mug of strong hot tea and stared through the window at the harbour below.

"They didn't...didn't...you know..." She tried for words keeping her gaze fixed on the view beyond the window, but turned, and smiled feebly when their waitress appeared at the table holding a large tray under her arm.

"Is that yiz all done and dusted, then?" she said. "Jennifer," according to the badge on her blouse, was a chunky green-eyed teenager, with long, frizzy red hair, noticeably large breasts, and lots of freckles. "So, yiz're off home to Canada tomorrow? I hear it's lovely there..." She hovered momentarily after clearing the table, then quickly moved off when Bill ignored her, and Carol offered nothing more than a monosyllabic response and a feeble smile.

Bill waited a moment after the waitress had gone, but it seemed Carol was not going to continue. "We can still go to the police ye know," he said. "If ye want to." He reached across the table and laid his hand on hers. "I'm sure those two fuckers would be easy enough to track down…thon Marty fella too."

Carol, her brow furrowed, turned to look at him. "I told you…they didn't *do* anything!" Bill looked at the bruise on her cheek, and gave her hand a little squeeze. He had a headache that would not quit, but made no mention of it or the attack he had suffered. "Fuck *them*, anyway!" Carol continued, staring down some of the patrons at nearby tables alerted to her profanity. Slowly, she brought her eyes back to his. "I don't *care* about them; I don't care what happened to them, or what happened to those…those *weird* bastards either—the ones playing *dress up*."

Bill recalled the sinister flying creatures and did not subscribe to the idea that anyone, or any*thing*, that was there that night was playing dress up. Nor did Carol, he surmised:

The mind has a way of dealing with things we'd prefer not to think about.

And he knew Carol was strong; she wasn't going to crack up on him. Shortly, he realized that she was talking again.

"But I *do* care about her!" she was saying. "Who *was* she? She looked hurt, Bill. And she looked so…so *lost*…lost, and in pain, and needing help…and then…then she just disappeared." She stared at Bill, and he was disconcerted by the intensity of her gaze that begged response.

"I don't know," was all he could offer. "I suppose she could've been a…a ghost…or something."

"But then, why didn't you see her?" She made it sound like an accusation. "Why just me? If she were a ghost, wouldn't *everybody* see her?" Fellow guests began to cast glances in their direction—some furtive, some not so much—and Bill was glad when Carol, softening her expression, lowered her voice before continuing. "She was hurt, Bill. I could tell she was in pain." Bill was at a loss to respond, but he recoiled visibly, when she added, "Do you think we should go back there?"

"I really don't think that's a good idea," he said, and seeing Carol gird her loins for an argument, he took her hands in his and lowered his voice to a whisper. "Look," he said. "I don't think anyone in that place on Friday night, was playing dress up." Letting go of her hands, he reached for the open pack of cigarettes on the table but began to shake uncontrollably. He discovered that retrieving a smoke proved difficult, so he stopped trying and clasped his hands together entwining his fingers. "Listen, I don't know what those…those…*things* were, but they were *real,* Carol! I was hoping that when we woke up in the mornin' it would all turn out to be a dream. It felt like one, a nightmare, but don't ye remember the smell? That was real! And the fear, sweetheart, that was real too. I'm the one who carried ye out of there, remember? You were the one screamin'!" He stopped talking and took a deep breath. "Those…*things* were real, Carol. You're the one who got a good look at them—up close—do you think they were just people, playing dress up? That whole, fuckin' *place* is scary. It gives me the creeps, just thinkin' about it; it's weird."

"It's haunted," said Carol.

"Yeah, haunted…*infested*…more like." Bill shivered and rubbed briskly at his bare arms. "Anyway, I don't think we should go back there. I don't think we should ever go back there—*ever*! Okay?"

Calmly and steadily, Carol had pulled two cigarettes from the pack. She placed one between Bill's lips and one between hers, then striking a match, she lit both. Carol inhaled the smoke and exhaled the word, "Okay."

"So, how long does it take to get to Belfast, anyway?" she said now. She was looking out the bus window as it hurtled past the blur of stone walls and hedgerows hugging the impossibly narrow road and obscuring the sea.

Bill smiled, laid his head back on the headrest, and closed his eyes. "We'll be there before ye know it."

Carol, turning to him, laid her head on his chest. "Bill," she said, sleepily, "I wish I hadn't seen her."

"What? Who?"

"Never mind."

***

The nightmares start soon after the incident; they are frequent and unchanging: Carol is walking through the purple, twilit grounds of Bonamargy with Bill. He speaks. "Yer not dressed to go traipsing through graveyards ye know."

Carol is dressed exactly as she was the night of the *actual* nightmare, and the skirt of her white dress is catching on the taller brambles that reach into the path. Bill is tugging at her dress and laughing. Then suddenly, it's not Bill but Cormac MacDonald, and he's leering while ripping her clothing:

"I'm really goin' t' enjoy this!" he says.

The air is filled with the sound of a rushing wind, and the creatures, shrouded in black, come from the shadows, laughing huskily and whispering unintelligibly.

As suddenly as they appear, they, and MacDonald, are gone. Carol is alone, standing in the opening of a *cul-de-sac* of stone walls. She has no recollection of this place. The darkness around her is deepening, and she is assailed by a belly-cramping fear. Her attention is drawn to a small archway in the facing wall that joins the other two, and forms the "box canyon." She sees the ghost lady beckoning to her and, in an instant, Carol is standing in the gloom of a stone stairwell, at the foot of a narrow stone staircase.

The ghost lady is naked, and her body is haloed in a pulsating soft blue glow. Carol thinks she looks more like an angel than a ghost.

Her lips move and she speaks. *"Cuidich leinn."*

Then the darkness outside begins to seep into the stairwell. The ground under her feet and the stairs and the walls start to heave and roll. The stairwell begins to swell with the sound of countless voices whispering and laughing.

Then the ghost lady angel speaks again, more urgently. *"Dúisigh!"* she says, and Carol awakens…

PART THREE

August, 2005

CHAPTER TWELVE

Ballycastle, Friday, August 19, 2005
Bonamargy Friary

Marty Doyle, standing with one hand in the pocket of his official, dark green blazer, was just getting into his stride:

"Now," he said, eyeing the group, "Bonamargy Friary was built 'round about the year 1485—long before there was any sign of a castle hereabouts. The town that would come to be known as Ballycastle, was still known as Port Brittas. Of course, the friary was known by its original, Gaelic name…*Bun-na-Mairge*…which means, 'at the foot of the Margy River.'" Doyle indicated the river running beyond the ruins with his free hand before opening the wrought iron gate and stepping into the grounds.

A gravel pathway beyond the gate wound through a graveyard of half toppled, ancient-looking headstones, buried in the weeds and long grasses growing untended around them. Having ushered the group through the gate, Doyle made a show of closing and latching the gate behind them. "We wouldn't want them spirits wanderin' would we?" he said with a conspiratorial grin. "Now, please be careful, and stay on the path. Them thistles and brambles are wicked, so they are, and ye'll be covered in burrs if ye go anywheres near them. We're always cuttin' them back to try to keep 'em under control, but boys-a-dear, they're tenacious, and they'd cover this wee path here in the blink of an eye, given half the chance." As he spoke, Doyle was watching his footing, careful not to scuff the finish on his recently purchased, brown suede loafers, and determined to keep his own non-iron khaki slacks burr free. After reassembling the group before the tumbled-down stone outer walls of the ruin, he cleared his throat, called for their attention, and continued.

"Now, Rory McQuillan it was who built *Bun-na-Mairge*, and it was him who let Third Order Franciscan monks establish a friary within its walls." Doyle paused, waiting for questions, but there were none, and he was glad, for his knowledge of Bonamargy's earliest beginnings was scant at best.

It was a small group for the time of year, which meant Doyle would be light in the tip department: three middle-aged couples, two of which were friends and travelling together; two young men in their early twenties, also travelling together; and a tall slender woman travelling alone. The woman's features were obscured by a large wide-brimmed sun hat and opaque sunglasses, so Doyle could not accurately determine into which age category she should be placed. A large, eggshell handbag, which matched the colour of her summer dress, dangled carelessly from a shoulder, and a pair of white-heeled sandals completed her ensemble. Although Doyle could not see her eyes, he sensed her staring. Offering her a slight nod of his head, he smiled before continuing with his spiel.

"Now, Rory was the leader, or chieftain, of the McQuillan clan— or *sept*, as clans were also called at the time. He decreed that the primary function of *Bun-na-Mairge* would be to serve him and his family, and he only allowed the Franciscans to have their friary on that condition." Sensing that he was losing his audience, Doyle coughed into his fist and chuckled. "Ye know, our Rory was a bit of a lad. A Scot he was, cut from the same cloth—*tartan*, of course—as yer man, William Wallace…ye know…thon *Braveheart* fella." Winking, he added, "Probably didn't look a bit like Mel Gibson though, but then, he'd 've surely had a better Scottish accent!" Everyone smiled, or tittered politely, and Doyle decided then that it would be better if he simply stuck to his script and kept the Hollywood references to himself.

"Now, the McQuillans ruled in this region of Antrim—which, by the way, was then known as the 'Route and the Glens'—since the beginning of the fifteenth century, so Rory, when he became chieftain, also took onto himself the title of, 'Lord of the Route.'

"The McQuillans also took Dunluce—the castle ruin yiz all just visited a wee while ago—as their family seat." Doyle noticed that the woman was having trouble controlling her frequently-billowing skirt in the gusty coastal breeze. He furtively sought a better vantage-point before continuing his talk.

"Now, clan warfare was rife in sixteenth-century Ulster, and the McQuillans fought continually—and resolutely—to hold onto their lands and titles. And for over a hundred years, hold them they did!

"Then another Scot, this one named James MacDonnell, crossed the Sea of Moyle," Doyle indicated the body of water beyond the cliffs, "and dared to settle his own clan in the Glens of Antrim, during the summer of 1550."

Suddenly, he clapped his hands, which startled his audience out of their apparent torpidity. "The clans clashed!" he said, smiling inwardly at the reaction his clap had evoked in the group, especially from the woman. "They waged a war that lasted ten years! And it ended…here!" He opened his arms to encompass the ruin and its surrounding landscape, which included a golf course. Doyle did not have much going for him in terms of presence, but he could tell a story, and his tour group was listening now.

"Now, in July 1559, the current Lord of the Route, Edward McQuillan, led an ill-fated attack on the MacDonnells at their camp just across the road, there,"—again Doyle pointed—"near the sixteenth hole!" Everyone chuckled as they turned to look. "The attack was repulsed, and the McQuillans were forced to retreat to their camp on the Glenshesk River." Doyle pointed vaguely at the nearby glens, but all eyes followed his finger. "But the MacDonnells, under the leadership of the famous Sorley Boy MacDonnell—who ye might've heard tell of before—pursued them, and they met in a ferocious battle at that river, where both forces suffered heavy losses!" Doyle lowered his eyes and shook his head slowly. "The McQuillans retreated to the 'Mountain of the Ridge'—*Slieve-na-Aura*, in the Irish—and there, at the 'Battle of Aura', as it later came to be known, Edward McQuillan—the last Lord of Dunluce—was slain. The McQuillans suffered a devastating defeat—one from which they never recovered—so that the clan was forever scattered and expelled."

A stronger gust ballooned Doyle's blazer, and his eyes flicked in the direction of the woman. She emitted a small scream when, despite best efforts, her dress billowed and flapped in the swirling wind. Doyle did not *want* to avert his eyes, but he did so—theatrically—keeping his poise.

"Excuse me, madam," he said, turning his head and shielding his eyes dramatically with one hand, "could ye please try to control yerself—and yer…er…wayward skirt. Don't ye know that I'm supposed t' be the centre of attention here?" The woman mouthed an apology while the rest of the tour chuckled.

Benevolently, Doyle continued, "Now, with the constant warfare of that time, *Bun-na-Mairge* changed hands several times over the next twenty years, until it was finally burned and partially destroyed in 1584.

"Ironically, it was the MacDonnells who did this, when they attacked an English garrison bivouacked here. Ye see, when they weren't fightin' amongst themselves, they were fightin' with our friends across the water, who'd come lookin' to pick a fight." Doyle accepted the obligatory snickers before going on.

"*Bun-na-Mairge* was left more or less uninhabitable after that, but again, ironically, the clan MacDonnell adopted it as a family burying place. Sorley Boy himself was interred in the vaults below the chapel when he died in 1590 at the remarkable age of eighty-five!" Arching his eyebrows, he said, "Must have been the sea air, eh?" Everyone smiled or tittered, and Doyle decided that at least they were a friendly bunch. He readied himself for the tour's *pièce de résistance*.

"Now," he said, darkening his demeanour, "in the early part of the seventeenth century, the friary was finally abandoned and left to ruin, and it was fifty years or more before a McQuillan returned to live in *Bun-na-Mairge*. This time it was a woman. Her name was Julia McQuillan. You probably know her better as the Black Nun." Doyle knew that they would all have heard of the Black Nun, and that *that* was why most of them were here. He paused for effect, and when he moved on, everyone followed obediently.

"Now, nobody knows how Julia came to live here, alone, in this God forsaken place," he said, shaking his head at the wonder of it, "but live here, she did, for some ten years, or more. And no one knows why she was called the Black Nun, or even if she was a nun. It's rumoured that she was a prophetess of sorts—and that some of her predictions came true. But one thing she didn't foresee was her own death!"

Turning suddenly, Doyle pointed at an arched opening in a stone wall. "And there's where she met her gruesome end. Murdered! Stabbed! Right there in thon stairwell, on the seventh step of the stone stairway that lies beyond that arch." He looked at the doorway ominously, before turning back to the group. "Now, *Why?*' you ask. Well, the plain answer is that no one knows the answer to that either!" Raising one eyebrow, he pointed at the archway. "Now, who'd like to be first to take a wee look?"

The two young men, raising their hands, stepped forward immediately, but Doyle was secretly delighted when the woman, following suit, came to stand close beside him. The rest of the group, deferring to the woman and the younger men, formed a loose queue behind them.

Doyle went to the doorway and raised his hand. "Now, be careful in here! It's dark and the stairs are worn, and they can be very *slippy—*

as we say here—you'd likely say *slippery!* But no matter how ye say it, mind yer step, especially around the seventh one!" He turned and winked at the queue conspiratorially, and received the programmed smiles and chuckles.

"Now," he said, looking at the young men, "ladies first, I think?" The men nodded in unison. Offering the woman a bow, Doyle said, "After you."

The woman entered the darkened doorway with the young men close behind, and Doyle called out, "I'm right behind ye!" Turning to the others, he said, "Now, just bide here a minute, if ye don't mind. There's not much room and we won't be—" Doyle jumped when there was a sudden *clatter* in the stairwell and he heard the woman scream.

All three came to the opening, and all three struggled to get through the narrow archway at the same time. One of the young men spoke excitedly. "There was this grating noise," he said, "and this…this stone…it just, like…came out of the wall, and like…fell on the steps!" Pointing, he added, "It almost hit her!" The woman had stepped out of the archway and was leaning against the stone wall.

"Are ye alright?" Doyle asked. The woman nodded, and Doyle turned to the others. "Stay here, all of ye!"

He stepped into the gloomy stairwell. Once his eyes adjusted, he saw a large stone lying on the fourth step, but the hairs at the back of Doyle's neck bristled when he heard someone laughing softly within the confines of stairwell. And when he heard several voices whispering together, he quickly stepped back into the sunshine beyond the doorway and forced a chuckle. "Well, oul Julia usually waits 'til dark before she starts playin' her tricks!" He looked at the young man who had spoken. "She must have an eye for young men like yerself."

No one laughed, and the young man in question was evidently not amused. "I think that what just happened here should be reported," he said. "That stairwell's obviously unsafe."

American, thought Doyle, hearing his accent, but the young man's annoyance was plain to see when Doyle reached up and laid a fatherly hand on his shoulder.

"It certainly will be reported, sir," he said. "Now, how would you best explain the incident? What exactly happened in there? I mean, did thon stone just fall out of the wall?"

The man shrugged Doyle's hand off. "What are you saying? Are you implying that…that I might have had something to do with it?" He looked into the faces around him. "I didn't do anything!"

The woman spoke up, and Doyle detected another American accent. "It wasn't him," she said. "It couldn't have been. I went first, and saw it happen! He's right: there was this sort of a scraping sound, and then the stone just…well, it flew out of the wall. It landed on the step, above the one I was standing on." She turned to the men. "But I also heard you two whispering and laughing, and I don't find that funny!"

Both men began to talk angrily at once, and Doyle intervened. "Easy now, gentlemen," he said.

"But it wasn't us laughing!" the first one said, looking at Doyle. "We thought it was you!"

"Well," said Doyle, "it wasn't me!" He heard the whispering and the laughter again in his head, and now, under their scrutiny, felt himself redden. He turned to the others. "There's no need for ye to worry yerselves about this, folks. I'll be putting a report in, just as soon as I get back to the office." He clapped his hands. "Now then, I think it's back to the bus, eh?"

Everyone made their way back to the car park with the bemused tour guide bringing up the rear. Doyle studied the path at his feet as he walked.

Just what the fuck *happened back there?*

The stone falling out of the wall was one thing—strange, but there could be a reasonable explanation, perhaps—but Doyle had never heard that weird, disembodied laughter or those whispering voices before, and it had definitely left him unsettled. He almost collided with someone standing in the middle of the path. It was the woman.

"Sorry," she said. "I didn't mean to startle you."

Doyle composed himself. "I was just daydreaming, I suppose…"—then—"…is everything alright?"

"Does that sort of thing happen often here?"

Doyle was not a tall man—five-foot-six and a half, according to the nurse at his last physical a few years back—and this was a tall woman, at least two, maybe three inches taller than him, so he had to look up into her face, an action made all the more frustrating because he could not see her eyes behind those dark sunglasses.

"Oh, strange things happen around here all the time," he said, planting an agreeable smile on his face. "The old place *is* haunted, ye know." *I wish I could see yer eyes.*

"Yes, you told us. The Black Nun. I've heard of her before. Isn't she supposed to have been buried here too?"

Doyle assumed his professorial persona. "Well, yes," he said. "At least that's the general consensus, but—"

"She asked to be buried at the entrance to the chapel," the woman interrupted, "so that people would walk over her grave when they came to worship." She nodded her head in the direction of an ancient tilted headstone, carved in the shape of a Celtic cross with a hole at its centre. "What do you think?"

"Well," said Doyle, "I—"

"I've been here before you know." she interjected, "years ago. I didn't think you'd remember…?"

After a moment's pause, Doyle realized that the woman was waiting for a response. "I..." he stammered, "...I-I don't—"

The woman's dress danced in the breeze, and Doyle's eyes were drawn to it. The woman noticed. "Oh, don't you just *love* this dress?" she asked. "You know, I bought it just to come here." Leaning closer, she whispered, "I knew *you'd* like it!" And with that, she turned, left Doyle—shaken and bewildered—and walked back to the bus.

CHAPTER THIRTEEN

Carol sat in her room going over that morning in her mind. She had been shocked to see Doyle on the tour bus and could hardly remember their scheduled stop at Dunluce Castle because of it. Her shock gave way to an unaccountable irritation as she watched the little tour guide "working" the group.

She surmised that it was because of her hat and sunglasses that Doyle had not recognized her. He had been more focused on trying to get a look under her skirt, much as he had done thirty-four years ago.

The incident in the stairwell had terrified her, but despite that, she thought she handled her interaction with Doyle well. Carol enjoyed teasing him back in Bonamargy—telling the little man that she bought her dress with him in mind. She smirked at the memory.

Doyle had not changed that much, Carol thought. He had managed to avoid major, middle-age spread on his small frame, so his build was much as it had been three decades ago. The shoulder-length, fair hair Carol remembered was gone, and the short hairstyle he sported now was tinged with grey; it seemed Doyle was fighting a losing battle against male pattern baldness.

The most visible change she noticed was in his once-boyish features: Lines crinkled the corners of his eyes, while more crossed his prominent cheekbones to bury themselves amidst the dimples and laugh lines deeply etched into weathered skin on either side of his generous mouth. Marty Doyle apparently spent a lot of time laughing and smiling.

Or squinting and ogling…

No matter: It was comforting to see someone else who had been there that night. But what exactly would he remember? What had he seen?

Carol found *Seaview, Bed and Breakfast* much the same too. She studied her reflection in the room's dressing table mirror. *Christ, talk about wrinkles!* She dropped her bath towel and looked at herself critically in the full-length mirror attached to the back of the room's door.

Carol Flanagan—she had kept her married name—at fifty-four, was aware that she was still an attractive woman. Thanks to genetics, and perhaps that she had never borne children, Carol did not have to try hard to keep her body in good physical shape. In addition, she was careful with her diet and adhered to a robust exercise regimen. Nevertheless, she found now, that even with the diet, the workouts, and the application of countless creams and lotions, she was still losing her war against the effects of nature and gravity. Carol was aging, but she would be damned if she would do so gracefully!

She donned clean underwear and put on the same dress from that morning. It was A-line in style, short, but not overly so, with three-quarter sleeves; slipping her feet into the same heeled sandals, she assessed her reflection in the door mirror once more. She thought she looked just as she had on that fateful night—as was her intention. Realizing that the replication of her attire was inauthentic, she removed her panties and put them in her handbag. Carol felt ready to go ahead with her plan, such as it was…well, at least she would be, after lunch and a quick drink at the Harbour Bar.

CHAPTER FOURTEEN

1

Stepping into the bar's foyer, Carol was surprised to see the same two doors with their etched signage. She pushed on the one marked *Bar*.

The concept of change was an unwelcome one in Ballycastle, for the interior of the establishment looked pretty much as it was thirty years ago: the low ceilings still swathed in smoke, and the bar's furnishings familiar.

The steady murmur of male voices in conversation muted when she appeared in the doorway. Carol fought to keep a smile from her face as she scanned the dim interior. A buxom, red-haired, green-eyed woman of medium height, loomed out of the smoky gloom.

"Hullo there!" she said. "Welcome to the Harbour Bar. My name's Jen. Now, would ye be lookin' for a bit of lunch?" Nodding over her shoulder at the blatantly gawking, male patrons, she lowered her voice and raised her eyebrows. "Mebbe ye'd find the lounge more to yer likin', if ye catch m' drift?"

"Oh no, it's okay, thanks," said Carol. "I think I'd prefer to stay here. I just love the flagstone floor. And the bar itself is just gorgeous."

"Suit yerself," she said. "It's just that the language in this place can get a wee bit *salty* at times, if ye catch m' drift. But, if ye don't mind the smoke—and a few choice words—there's a nice wee table for ye, over there, besides the window?"

Carol's heart skipped a beat, but she managed to keep her smile. "That would be fine," she said, cooly. It was the same table, in the same place. Only the curved, bench seat's vinyl covering had been replaced with some kind of woven material.

Jen lifted a menu from a nearby stack. "Alright then, if ye'd like to follow me." The low hum of conversation slowly resumed as Carol followed Jen to the table and sat down on the bench seat, facing the bar. "Now," said Jen, "would ye like a wee drink t' get ye started?"

"Yes, please," said Carol. "I think I'll try a pint of Guinness."

"Guinness?" said the barmaid. "Really?"

"Yes," said Carol. "I'd like to try it. I've heard it's delicious!"

"Well," said Jen, "I'd say that it's more of an acquired taste m' self. Mebbe ye should try a wee half pint first?"

"Okay," said Carol, "perhaps that's a better idea. Thanks!"

Jen smiled. "Alright then, a half pint of Guinness comin' up!" As she turned to leave, she hesitated. "I hope ye don't mind the askin', but are ye American, by any chance?"

"No," said Carol, "I'm not. I'm Canadian."

"Here on yer holidays, are ye?"

"Yes," said Carol, without elaborating further, and staring through rather than at the barmaid.

"Just wonderin'," Jen said. "Is this the first time ye've been in here? I mean, here in this pub? It's just that—"

"Yes," said Carol, interrupting the barmaid and breaking eye contact, "this is the first time I've been in Ballycastle."

Seconds passed before Jen replied, "Oh, I'm sorry. Sometimes I'm just a wee bit too nosy for m' own good. I'll be right back with yer drink."

"Oh, no," Carol started, "I only—" But Jen had turned and was already making her way back to the bar.

2

Marty Doyle was in a quandary: He thought the woman was the one who had been at Bonamargy this morning but he wasn't sure. He was doing his best to get a better look without her seeing that he was studying her: the hat and the sunglasses were gone, but unfortunately, silhouetted as she was by the light from the window behind her head, he could not see her eyes clearly, and could not tell exactly where she was looking.

Most of his bar mates had no such inhibitions; they did not care if they were seen ogling or not. Sniggering and nudging one another, they were busy making loud, lewd, and suggestive comments about the alluring, blonde wearing a short skirt and showing a lot of thigh. Now Doyle would have partaken gleefully in these ribald conversations if it hadn't been for this morning's episode. Her words had left the little tour guide bothered and bewildered.

The hubbub subsided during the time that he spent mulling things over, and he chanced another surreptitious glance at her table. The intervening years all but disappeared then, when the woman, her face turned in his direction, quickly flicked the hem of her dress up and down before crossing her long, tanned legs.

Doyle's mind reeled, awash in memories. "Fuck me!" he swore under his breath, but Jen heard him.

"Somethin' wrong. Marty?" she said. "Ye look like ye've seen a ghost." She looked then at the table by the window. "D' ye know her, or somethin'?"

The men at the bar, their interest aroused, guffawed, and one said, "Where the hell would wee Marty get to know the likes of her?"

"Oh, I don't know," said Jen, "still waters an' all, if ye get m' drift."

Doyle, feeling his cheeks redden under the sudden scrutiny, summoned a half-hearted laugh. "Sure ye know I only have eyes for you, Jen, love?"

The barmaid leaned across the bar, purposely flaunting her ample cleavage. Doyle's eyes, and those of the patrons nearby, immediately dropped there.

"Oh yeah, right, Mister Doyle," she laughed, "sure we all know *exactly* what you have eyes for, don't we?" This elicited more chuckles and nudges, and Doyle felt he was off the hook for the time being. Jen nodded at his near-empty glass. "Are ye about ready for another?"

Memories of that long past July evening swirled in Doyle's mind, and a part of him thought that he should just get the hell out of there. He was now certain that this woman was the one who had been in Ballycastle thirty-odd years ago. Doyle had no idea what he would, or could, say to her, if the opportunity presented itself. Making himself scarce might be the better option.

"Marty!" said Jen, bringing him out of his reverie. "D' ye want another pint or not?"

"Well, if ye're going to twist my arm…" Draining his glass, he handed it to the barmaid.

Carol thanked Jen, and waited while she set her drink down on the table. "That man, at the end of the bar, is he a local tour guide?" When she saw that the barmaid, seemed to take umbrage at the question, she continued quickly, "Oh, I only ask because I think he ran the tour at Bonamargy this morning and, if it was him, I'd like to buy him a drink."

Jen's demeanour changed at once. "It would've been him fer sure," she said, smiling. "His name's Marty—Marty Doyle. I'm sure he'd take a pint of Guinness if ye offered to buy him one. Matter of fact, I've just started one for him. I can put it on yer tab if ye'd like."

"That would be great, thank you!"

"Are ye ready to have a wee bite t' eat?"

Carol held up her menu. "Still thinking," she said. "Sorry."

"Sure that's no problem at all. Take yer time."

A sheepish-looking Doyle arrived at her table five minutes later, brandishing his glass. "I'd like to thank ye for this," he said. "Much appreciated."

"Oh, you're welcome," said Carol, indicating the chair across at her table. "Won't you join me?"

"Oh, no, no," Doyle said, awkwardly. "I-I wouldn't want to interrupt yer lunch."

"But I'm not having lunch," said Carol, and nodded again at the empty chair. "Please," she said.

So, Doyle sat facing the woman. "Listen," he said, "this might sound strange, but what ye said this mornin' at Bonamargy, well…um…have we…um…we…I mean…we've met before, haven't we?"

Carol, smiling, uncrossed her legs and leaned towards Doyle, holding out her hand. "My name's Carol."

Doyle shook her hand. "My name's Marty." He kept his eyes on hers. "Marty Doyle." He hoisted his glass. "It's nice of ye to be so generous. I mean…well…after this mornin's goin's on."

Carol sat back and recrossed her legs languorously. "So," she said, "what do you think happened this morning, in the stairwell, I mean?"

"I'm not really sure," said Doyle, wondering where this was going. "It was strange, wasn't it?"

"Didn't you say earlier that strange things happen there all the time, that the place is haunted. Right?" Carol ran the palm of her hand over her dress, smoothing it over her thighs and absently adjusting the lay of its hem across them.

Doyle felt sweat trickling down the small of his back. "I—"

"Have you ever seen the Black Nun?"

"No," Doyle started, "I—"

"Yes," said Carol, continuing to move her palm—and the hem of her dress—up and down her thigh, "we've met before. Don't you remember, Marty?" She leaned forward and picked up her glass. "You took me to Bonamargy one night a long time ago, remember? You told me that you knew a place where we could see the Black Nun when she appeared at midnight." Carol sipped her beer. "There was a full moon that night too, remember?"

Doyle did not like the way the conversation was going. "Look," he said, lifting his glass, pushing his chair back, and rising, "I'm very sorry for what happened that night, believe me, and thanks again for the pint, but I think that mebbe it's time I was goin'."

The other patrons, hearing the scraping of his chair on the flagstone floor and sensing something was going on, began once more to focus their attention on the table by the window.

"Wait, Marty," said Carol. "I'm not going to make a scene. I'd just like for us to talk some more." She indicated his recently vacated seat. "Please, sit down. I have a proposition for you."

Doyle did not retake his seat, but he set his glass down on the table. "Alright," he said, "but just wait a wee minute. I-I'll...I'll be right back."

3

In the men's washroom, Doyle sat in a cubicle, mulling over the situation he found himself in. So, it *was* her! No doubt about that now, and that revelation rekindled memories of the first time he laid eyes on Carol. He remembered how he'd felt; how he would have done anything that day just to be close to her, and how he had managed that.

But why was she here now? Did she want revenge? For what? Maybe she'd gone a wee bit crazy over the years. There was definitely something strange about her; those grey eyes and the way she looked at him with them. Doyle felt intimidated by most women, and this one definitely had the upper hand. Again, he considered leaving—simply walking out the door without as much as a "see ye." What could she do? But in spite of everything, the infatuation he'd felt for this woman thirty years ago was reawakened and his innate curiosity piqued. She had mentioned a proposition...

Carol looked up, when Doyle returned to the table. He did not sit down.

"Listen...um...Carol, like I said, I'm really sorry about what happened that night, okay? Now, I'm thinkin' that ye've probably come back here with some idea of exacting some kind of vengeance or somethin'—and, of course, I can understand that—but I don't know what ye expect me to do about it now."

Carol smiled beatifically. "Listen, why don't you just sit down, Marty?" Doyle hesitated. "Look," she said, "it's okay. I'm not looking for revenge. Would you just sit down for a minute?" Doyle retook his seat submissively, picked up his pint and looked at Carol expectantly.

"Look, Bill told me what happened," she said. "He said that you'd waited till he'd come to, after that big bastard whacked him with a rock, before you took yourself off."

Doyle grimaced at the memory. "Aye," he said, "I did. And ye're right about Cormac MacDonald...he was a big bastard, and a mean one an' all! By the way, how's yer man doin' anyway?"

Carol ignored the question. "*Was?*" she said. Doyle looked questioningly at her, so she added, "You said, *was* his name?"

"Aye," said Doyle. "Well, the general consensus is that he's dead, long dead. Him and his mate Tommy,"—he looked at Carol here—"remember him?"

Carol's look said everything, and Doyle, abashed, coughed into his fist. "Sorry. Of course ye do. Well, apparently Cormac MacDonald and Tommy Calhoun both disappeared that night. I mean the night we all went to Bonamargy, and neither a hide nor hair of either one of them has been seen since. Anyway, both of them were declared legally deceased years ago. The thought is that it was one of the paramilitaries that got them—probably one of the branches of the IRA—but nobody knows for sure." Leaning closer, he added, "Look, love, honest to Christ, I had no idea that they were plannin' to rape ye. I-I—"

Doyle's voice had risen noticeably in his appeal and Carol shushed him, urgently. "Keep your voice down, for Christ's sake!" Once more interested heads at the bar turned in their direction. Carol looked at Doyle as if he was something she had just regurgitated. "As for you..." she continued in a throaty whisper, "...Bill believed you, but *I* think you knew *everything*. I think all of you had it planned from the get-go, and you just chickened out at the last minute!" Carol studied the tabletop and consciously slowed her breathing. When she considered herself calm enough, she went on in a whisper, "Listen, they didn't rape me, okay? Oh, they wanted to, believe me, but they never got the chance." She focused on Doyle. "Did you see those...those *things* too? Did you see that bright flash of lightning, or whatever it was?"

Doyle vividly remembered what he had seen that night above the gates of Bonamargy. Had she seen them too? His hand shook a little as he sipped his pint and collected his thoughts.

"I never got much further than the gate," he said. "And I never saw any bright lights of any kind that night, but let me tell ye this..." He set his glass down on the table. "There was some talk about getting a hold of you and yer man, and bringing yiz back over here, for questionin', like. People had seen all of us in the bar that night, together, talkin'." Doyle looked Carol in the eye. "*Everybody* remembered you! Anyway, the police brought me in, and I told them that I'd been talkin' to you and yer man about Bonamargy, and the Black Nun, and all that, and that we...the *three* of us...had gone off to Bonamargy to see if we could see the old girl, but I told them that *nothin'* happened, and that I'd left yiz there and walked back into town by m' self. I told them that I had no idea where Cormac and Tommy had gone, but that we...us three...never seen them after we left the pub."

Doyle hoisted his glass to his lips. His hand did not shake as much as it had before, and he took a longer draw on his pint before continuing. "Now, listen t' me, for the last time, I swear to *God* that I wasn't in on their plans. Anyway, like I said, the cops were thinkin' of gettin' a hold of you, but I'm thinkin' the fact that me tellin' them that nothin' untoward happened while we were at Bonamargy that night, probably helped. That's why they thought there was no good reason to contact ye."

Carol stared at him from over the rim of her glass. "If you're waiting for an expression of gratitude…"

"No, no, I'm not. Listen, I thought that mebbe they had finished the job on yer man, and mebbe done for you too, and that mebbe I'd be next…ye know…I mean, they'd have to cover their tracks, like. But then I found out that ye were alright, 'cause I saw both of yiz gettin' on the Belfast bus on Monday mornin', so that was alright, y' know?" Doyle finished his drink. "So, that's about it as far as I'm concerned. I really don't know what ye might want from me?"

Doyle's account regarding his involvement that night corresponded with Bill's rationalization, and Carol decided that the little man had actually nothing to do with the assault on her, but she did not soften her expression when she leaned towards him. "I'll tell you what I want from you. I want you to take me back to Bonamargy."

"What? Take ye back to…ye mean now, like?"

"Well, no. I don't mean right this minute. I want to ask you some questions first." She picked up her empty glass. "Maybe I can buy you another drink?"

Doyle's mind was spinning, and he needed time to think. "No," he said, rising and reaching for Carol's glass, "let me get these. Same again…?"

"No," said Carol, smiling, "I don't think I've quite acquired a taste for Guinness. I'll have a glass of the house red, please."

4

Doyle was feeling a lot better about the situation when he came back from the bar bearing their drinks.

A few of the punters had offered their advice as to what he should do with "thon American trollop."

"She sure likes to flash them gams, doesn't she?" said one.

"Aye…and a fair bit more!" added another. This remark opened a debate on whether or not the "trollop" was wearing knickers.

"What d' ye say, wee man? Ye were sittin' right across from her. Did ye see—"

Jen's reappearance behind the bar brought an abrupt halt to the discussion:

"Jesus Christ!" she said. "Ye're just like a bunch of wee schoolboys, aren't yiz? Only schoolboys have more sense!" She turned to Doyle. "Same again, Marty?" Doyle gave her his order, and as she drew his pint, indicating his table with a nod of her head, the barmaid asked him if everything was alright over there. "It's just that ye seemed a wee bit put out at first, ye know, seemed like she was puttin' ye on the spot about somethin' or other, if ye catch m' drift. D' ye know her from somewhere else? I mean other than from this mornin'?"

One of the men interjected, "Like I said before, where the hell else would wee Marty here have met a woman like thon, Jen, love? In his *dreams*, mebbe!" This elicited a round of chuckles and further ribald commentary.

"My God, Gerry," said Jen, with a little more hostility than intended. "Listen t' yerself, would ye? She's just a wumman, for Christ's sake, just like the ones ye see every night in those videos ye watch when yer wife's gone t' bed!" There was outright laughter at this, and to his credit, Gerry joined in heartily.

"And here's me," he said, "thinkin' nobody knew anythin' about that!" Doyle picked up his drinks, and Gerry hoisted his own. "Here's all the best t' ye Marty, lad. She's a cracker! Good luck t' ye, son!"

"Who says Marty needs luck?" said Jen. "Sure, he's a wee cracker himself." There were several vocalizations over this remark, but when Doyle looked at Jen, she was smiling at him. Perhaps this was going to turn out to be better than he had anticipated.

"You look like the cat that got the canary," said Carol, taking the proffered glass of wine. "How come?"

Doyle, dismantling his smile, deflected the question by asking one of his own. "Ye say ye've got some questions?"

Carol hesitated for only a moment. "That night, back in 1971, you say you didn't see a bright flash of light, but did you see anything else strange?"

"Why?" asked Doyle. "What did you see? What were those 'things' ye mentioned?"

Carol did not want to talk about the monk monsters, so she ignored that part of the question. "I saw a woman that night. Or maybe, maybe a ghost. The ghost of a woman, a fair-haired woman, dressed in a white nightie, or something." Carol looked at Doyle imploringly. "I was wondering if you've ever seen her in Bonamargy."

"No," said Doyle, shaking his head. "Sorry, I've never seen anything or anybody like that. Did she do somethin' to ye that night?"

Now Carol was shaking her head. "No," she said, "it's not that. Let me try to explain…"

She began by giving Doyle the details of what she remembered happening on that infamous night, thirty-four years ago. How she first saw the ghost in the dunes, then again in the grounds of Bonamargy, and how no one else saw her. Doyle's eyes widened appreciably when she related the tale of the monk-like creatures' attack on her and her assailants. To his credit, he did not interrupt the flow.

Doyle realized that once Carol started the telling, she could not stop. It was as if she was reliving the events as she spoke, describing every terrifying detail. After recounting how she and Bill escaped, she stopped talking, seemingly spent.

Doyle broke the yawning silence with a cough. "But why would ye want me to take ye back there then, especially after what ye've just told me?"

Carol looked at him enquiringly. Locking her eyes on the tabletop, she began.

"I…I have these recurring dreams. Well, nightmares, I suppose. I've had them, off and on, with different regularity, for the past thirty years. Ever since that night. Sometimes the dream comes every night for a month, then there'll be nothing at all for a couple of months, but they're always about Bonamargy, and usually a stairway is involved."

"Is it the same stairway as the one this morning?" asked Doyle.

"Yes. I think so. Only that stairway seemed to lead into nothing but open air."

"Aye, that's right. There's nothing up there now. They think it used to be the old livin' quarters, ye know, where the monks slept, the dormitories if ye like. But the walls and floors collapsed long ago."

"Well, the stairway in my dreams leads up to a landing. And I think there's a door up there."

"So, is that where your dreams or nightmares start—in the stairwell, I mean?"

Carol, returning her eyes to the tabletop, was shocked to see the once-empty tin ashtray at its centre suddenly full of spent cigarette butts.

Doyle saw her flinch and her eyes widen. "Are ye okay? Somethin' wrong?"

Carol blinked. The ashtray was empty once more. She gave a little giggle. "Oh, everything's fine. It's just that I haven't smoked in twenty years but, all of a sudden, I wanted a cigarette. Isn't that strange?" She moved the ashtray out of her line of sight. "Now, where was I? Oh yes…you were asking where my dreams start out, right?"

Carol went on to describe her nightmare…

She finished with, "I'm at the bottom of the stairs and, and this *blackness* starts to creep into the stairwell and that awful whispering laughter begins."

Doyle's head came up suddenly, and she stared at him.

He shook his head. "It's nothin'. Go on…"

"Well, this morning, in the stairwell, I thought it was those two guys laughing and whispering. Now I'm not so sure."

Doyle, thinking about the blackness Carol mentioned and remembering this morning's whisperings, shuddered involuntarily, coughing into his fist to mask his reaction. "Then what happens?"

"Then," said Carol, "the ghost lady appears at the top of the stairs. She speaks to me. She always says something, and then I wake up with my heart beating a mile a minute."

"What does she say?"

"I can't remember. Isn't that strange? In the dream, I think I know what she's saying, but I can't understand the words when I awaken."

"What d' ye mean ye can't understand the words?"

"I mean that I can hear the words—in my head, you know? But it's a foreign language, and I don't understand the meaning."

"Can ye remember the words now?"

"Yes. I know that that the last thing she says sounds something like, *dushee.*"

"*Dúisigh!*" said Doyle. "Is that what she says?"

"Yes. That's what I said!"

Doyle shook his head. "My Gaelic isn't great, but I think *dúisigh* means awaken or wake up. So, that's what she's sayin' to ye. She's tellin' ye to wake up!"

"Really? Why would she say that?"

"I don't know. What were the other words ye said she says?"

Carol, bowing her head, closed her eyes again in concentration. "Okay, she says, 'Cujick Lane.' That's it…well…that's what it sounds like anyway. Could it be an address, here in Ballycastle?"

Doyle repeated her vocalization a few times, saying the words aloud to himself. Then his eyebrows arched. "*Cuidich leinn!*" he said, speaking louder, and in Gaelic. "Is that what she says?"

"That's it exactly! Do you know what it means?"

"It means 'help me' I think. Or mebbe, 'help us.' I'm not too sure."

"Oh my *God!*" said Carol. "I knew it! I knew she needed help of some sort! That's why she's been haunting my dreams all these years!"

"But, what d' ye think she wants ye t' do?"

"Well, I don't know. I'm only telling you what happens in my dream. Don't ask me to make any sense of it."

Doyle felt chastened and annoyed. "So, ye don't know what yer ghost wants then, is that right?"

Carol sat forward in her seat. "Listen, I want you to take me back there. I'll go alone, if I have to, but I'd rather you came with me. That's my proposition. That's what I'm asking you to do for me."

"But, what for? What d' ye want to *do* there?"

"You want to know what I think? I think that what happened in that stairwell this morning was a sign. I think that this ghost's been trying to reach me for years—decades—and all this time I've been trying to…to exorcize her! She want's me to help her and that's what I want to do."

"But I still don't understand why."

"Well, I'll try to explain. I don't know how she did it, but I believe she saved Bill and me that night. She sent that bright light I told you about—perhaps she *was* that light! She saved us, and I want to help her, and then, maybe these dreams will stop once and for all."

"So ye think ye can go there and…and what? D' ye think ye can summon her, or somethin'? Get her t' tell ye what she wants ye t' do?"

Carol slid back in her seat. "I really don't know what I'll do there, but I'd like to get another look at that stairwell, take a look at that stone and where it came out of the wall. Maybe there'll be some other kind of clue there, you know?" Sliding forward again, she picked up her glass and sipped at her wine. "So, what do you say? Will you take me back there?"

Doyle took a hefty swallow of Guinness. "Just to get a look at that stairwell, and the mysterious stone, right?"

Carol nodded. "Right." She looked beseechingly at the little tour guide.

Doyle scratched at the bald spot on his crown. "Well, first I've got some runnin' around to do this afternoon. Then I've got to go to the yard to pick up some stuff, ye know, before I go back out there to make sure the stairs are safe and all, ye know, so if ye—"

"Yes! Whenever you're ready, I'll be ready to go."

"Alright." Doyle looked at his watch. "I'll be about an hour or so, so where do ye want to—"

Carol interrupted him again. "Can you pick me up at Seaview Bed and Breakfast? I could meet you in the lounge at," she checked her watch, "say, three-thirty. How's that sound?"

"Alright." Doyle drained his glass and stood. "D 'ye need a lift now?"

"No, that's alright, thanks. Maybe I'll do some shopping or something till three, and meet you at the B and B as planned."

"Right," said Doyle. "I'll see you then."

He almost bumped into Jen who was wiping a table near the exit. "Where's the fire, Marty?" Noticing the look of consternation on his face, she asked, "Are ye alright, love? Is somethin' wrong? Is it somethin' to do with thon model of yours?"

"Ach no, love," he said. "Nothin's wrong. It's just that I forgot somethin' back at the yard. Sure, ye know me, I'd forget me own head if it wasn't attached!"

Jen chortled, then, lowering her voice she said, "Tell me this, Marty, love…are ye sure ye don't know that woman at all? Somethin about her's doin' my head in, like mebbe I know her from somewhere…if ye catch m' drift." Doyle shrugged, but said nothing. "Anyway, it'll come to me, or it won't, but listen to me now, are ye sure everythin's alright? Yer lookin' a wee bit, ye know, *ragged,* if ye catch m' drift." Making sure no one was eavesdropping, she went on, "Listen now, I know its none of my beeswax, mind ye, but I've been watchin' yer table, off and on, like, and it looks to me like yer woman might be givin' ye a hard time about somethin'?"

Doyle forced another little laugh. "No, no," he said. "Everything's fine. She's just pickin' my brain about Bonamargy, that's all." He winked. "She's not makin' any improper suggestions or anythin' like that. Don't ye be worryin' yerself about me, now."

Jen laughed and spoke in her normal voice. "Who said anythin' about me bein' worried about ye?" She flicked her cloth at his shoulder, playfully. "On ye go. Will ye be back in later on?"

Doyle laughed too. "Is the pope Catholic?"

Jen brought her receipt to the table while Carol was readying herself to leave. "Are ye stayin' here in Ballycastle then?"

"Yes, at least tonight, and maybe tomorrow. It's…um…it's lovely here."

"Well," said Jen, "I hope ye enjoy yer stay. Mebbe ye'll be back in before ye go?"

"Yes," Carol said, smiling, "I could well be. Well…um…thank you so much. Everything was…um…I really enjoyed everything."

"Oh, yer very welcome," said Jen. "Hope t' see ye again."

The barmaid surveyed the men watching the woman leave as she made her way back behind the bar. "There's something strange about that one," she said to no one in particular. "And I'm almost sure I've seen her somewhere before. I just can't remember when or where."

"Who?" someone said. "Was there a *strange* wumman here?" The laughter burbled along the bar.

"Ye *all* know the one I mean, don't yiz?" said Jen, raising her voice. "The one who thinks she's God's gift t' men, right? The one who didn't mind lettin' yiz all see *everythin'* she's got! And yiz *all* looked, didn't ye?" Softening the edge to her voice with a smile, she let her eyes play over the faces at the bar. "Just look at yerselves, lookin' all innocent, and all. Ye needn't try t' tell me ye weren't lookin'. Sure, ye're nothing but a bunch of perverts—*all* of ye!"

CHAPTER FIFTEEN

1

Ron Harper leaned back and pushed his chair away from his cluttered desk. "What the fuck d' ye mean, it just *fell* out of the wall?" Tipping his white hardhat back, he stared incredulously at Doyle over the top of his computer screen. "Stones just don't *fall* out of walls, fer fuck sakes!"

"Listen," said Doyle, "I'm not makin' this up; I'm just tellin' ye what happened, alright?"

"But *you* didn't actually see it happen, did ye?" Harper, a no-nonsense kind of guy, was the maintenance supervisor, and Doyle liked him, but was beginning to tire of this roundabout discussion.

"Look, I've already told ye what I seen," said Doyle. "It's all there in the report," he indicated the paperwork on the desk, "in *triplicate*, okay? I'm goin' back there now to hang some caution tape and put down a cone or two. What d' ye want me to do with the stone?"

"The stone?" said Harper.

"Yes, Ron," Doyle said patiently and dramatically. "The stone. D' ye want me t' leave it where it is, so that ye can see for yerself where it came from, and where it fell, or what?"

Harper appeared have had enough talking as it was close to quitting time. "Ye can move it wherever the fuck ye like...just make sure nobody's goin' to trip over the fuckin' thing! I'll get a crew over there first thing Monday mornin', alright? Right now I'm going beat my past Tetris score."

"Aye, alright," said Doyle. He was out the door before Harper had repositioned himself behind his desk, and before his computer screen.

Doyle ruminated behind the wheel of the Ford work van as he drove away from the town council's work yard. That spring he began his sixtieth year on this planet and what had he done? He thought that the words of "Nowhere Man" were written with him in mind. Doyle had never aspired to greatness or fame; he was just an ordinary bloke; always had been, and always would be, and really, that was okay. But there was *something* that took him out of the ordinary: Marty Doyle was likely the only sixty-year-old virgin in Ballycastle—if not the world!

Now there's somethin' to brag about!

Doyle had no aversion to women—quite the opposite—but he was an old fashioned, small-town boy who had never travelled outside of Ireland, and he found the fairer sex intimidating. He had never had a sexual relationship with anyone—female, or male, for that matter—no relationship that went beyond the fumbling and petting stage. Marriage therefore, had never been a serious consideration for him, and now he thought it unlikely that it ever would.

A heart attack had taken his father unexpectedly when Doyle was eight-years-old. Martin Doyle, the elder, left his widow to vent the anger and frustration she felt at the unfairness of the world on their only begotten son. For twenty-five years—until she too, shuffled of her mortal coil—Bernice Doyle harangued and bullied her son until Doyle felt nothing but relief at her passing. He was grateful, however, to inherit the neat, semi-detached, two-storey, two-bedroom house that he was born and raised in.

Doyle decided he would stop there before he went to pick up Carol. His pulse quickened at the thought of seeing her again. The chest-tightening infatuation he had felt thirty years ago was not as acute now perhaps, but evidently, there was still something of it there. Doyle thought a quick shower was probably in order.

2

Carol waited impatiently while the librarian finished her phone conversation. The woman and she were probably of an age. "Lorraine," according to the plastic name tag pinned at her breast, had short pixie-cut red hair, and stood behind her desk as she conversed. She was tall and slim, conservatively dressed in a peach-coloured blouse, a brown, knee length, pleated skirt, and brown, low-heeled, "sensible" shoes; a pair of wire-rimmed reading glasses hung from a linked chain, looped around her neck. Finishing her conversation, she beamed a radiant smile in Carol's direction.

"Hello there, how can I help ye?"

"Hi," said Carol, matching the librarian's smile, "I'm a visitor and I was wondering if maybe you'd have some literature regarding places of interest in and around Ballycastle."

"Why, of course we do. Right this way." She led Carol to a low table by the entrance door, and waved a hand over the brochures and glossy pamphlets displayed on top. "We've got quite a few pamphlets and such, as ye can see. Is there anything in particular ye're interested in?"

"Actually, yes," said Carol. "I visited Bonamargy this morning, and found the ruin fascinating." She cast her eyes disparagingly over the tabletop. "I wonder, would you have anything more, more substantial regarding its history?"

"Oh, I see," said Lorraine, "more *substantial*, ye say. I think I know what ye're lookin' for now. This way." Speaking over her shoulder as she walked, she led the way down an aisle of bookshelves. "Seems there's been quite a lot of interest lately in Bonamargy, I don't know why." She stopped in front of a bookcase. "Now, this section here contains *everything* we have on the history of Ballycastle and the surrounding area. I know there are a couple of books about Bonamargy here somewhere." Lorraine settled her glasses on her nose and began to finger through the numerous editions on the shelves. "Ah!" she said, removing two dilapidated booklets from a shelf. "Here's a couple ye might find interesting."

"Thank you," said Carol. "I didn't mean for you to go to any trouble."

"Oh, it's no trouble at all. Unfortunately, ye can't take them out of the library, but there's a wee table over there by the window, where ye can sit and have a wee look through them, if ye like?"

"Thank you," said Carol, smiling. "I won't be long."

"Oh, take all the time ye want. I don't mean to be nosy, but are ye from America or Canada?"

"I'm Canadian."

"Lovely. Well, I hope ye enjoy yer stay in our wee part of the world. Now, as I say, take all the time ye want, and I'll see ye on the way out, alright now?" With that Lorraine turned and made her way back to her station by the door.

Within thirty minutes, Carol had perused both booklets and become more perplexed. Though it seemed that Marty Doyle knew the history of Bonamargy, he had failed to mention something that the authors of both these books discussed at some length. Apparently, Julia McQuillan had a sister!

3

Doyle sat in his favourite armchair, sipping a glass of *Black Bush*, Irish whiskey, trying to get his thoughts in order. He had showered, put on clean underwear and, deciding to doff the work clothes, changed into a tee shirt, jeans, and runners.

Doyle contemplated this trip back to Bonamargy with Carol, and although there was no denying that the thought excited him, his mind kept returning to that night in '71. And what about the "incident" this morning, in the stairwell? What had happened? And what about those whispering, laughing voices?

Doyle had been employed by the Town of Ballycastle since leaving high school at the age of eighteen with five O' Levels, which had secured his position in the town's Works Department in 1963.

His academic prowess didn't help in his new job: In fact, Doyle became a glorified caretaker and handyman for the District of Moyle, looking after the grounds and handling small repairs at all of the Northern Ireland Environmental Agency's (NIEA) State Care Monuments. Bonamargy Friary was one such monument.

In early 2000, after refusing an offer of early retirement, Doyle assumed the extra duties of an official Tour Guide. In all his years, Doyle must have been in and around Bonamargy hundreds—maybe thousands—of times. Although he had never seen the Black Nun— or any other ghost, for that matter—he'd had many experiences that made his skin crawl. This morning's was definitely another one of those.

Doyle had never really tried to understand or explain the strangeness he felt on these occasions, but as he sat there now, he remembered that someone had.

Doyle recalled nicknaming the man the "Professor," at the time, but his actual name was Greenwood. He had not offered a first name, and Doyle did not enquire after it.

Greenwood had been part of his tour. He was a well-dressed, well-heeled, middle-aged Englishman; tall, handsome, and worldly. Doyle thought that the man may have been a writer, or a teacher, or both.

After that morning's tour, Doyle was taking his lunch in the Harbour Bar, washing it down with a pint, when Greenwood approached, asking if he could buy him another pint, and perhaps, "Pick your brain further," on the history of Bonamargy. Doyle accepted the offer readily, and the pair had retired to a small table by the window, away from the bar.

It quickly became obvious that Greenwood's interests lay in the paranormal side of Bonamargy, as his questions focused more on the reported sightings of the legendary Black Nun than on anything else. Obligingly, Doyle laid it on thick, sharing heavily embellished tales of ghostly encounters within and without the boundaries of Bonamargy Friary.

"Have you ever seen her yourself?" Greenwood asked at one point, and Doyle drew the line at making such a claim. The Professor seemed disappointed and Doyle, by way of apology, went on to tell this stranger, things he had told no one else about his experiences in and around the ruin.

"If ye want the truth, it's the place itself that's strangest. Gives me the heebie-jeebies sometimes, I can tell ye. Sometimes, ye don't have to see a ghost to know one's there, d' ye know what I mean? There's times when I'm walkin' through the place, and it's sunny and warm, mind ye, then, all of a sudden, I'll get the feelin' that somebody's just walked over my grave, ye know? That shivery kind of feelin' all over me, like. It doesn't last long, thank Christ, but it's friggin' weird all the same, when it happens." Doyle laughed, apologetically. "Sorry, I didn't mean to go on like that."

But Greenwood did not laugh. He nodded. "Actually, what you've just described, those weird experiences of yours, can probably be explained. Tell me, have you ever heard of Multiverse Theory?" Doyle answered in the negative. Greenwood leaned forward eagerly, placing his elbows on the table before him. "Well, you see, according to Multiverse hypothesis, everything is happening now; past, present and future; it's all happening now, in what we call, parallel dimensions. That's Multiverse Theory."

Greenwood had sat back and smiled, awaiting the questions he knew must come.

Doyle, out of obligation, complied. "So, how does *that* explain the shivery feelin's I get?" Hoisting his pint glass towards his lips, he hoped that the professor would see its meagre contents, and offer to replenish it before continuing. He did not. Instead, Greenwood sat forward once more. "Well, although we—that is, our *corporeal* selves—cannot travel in these alternate dimensions, at least not yet…"—he paused here and threw a knowing smile at Doyle—"…our minds can! The shivery feelings are what happens when your mind frees itself, and travels through time and space to wander in alternate universes."

"Oh," Doyle said, "sort of like when yer dreamin', ye mean?"

"Yes! A very good similitude. Yes, almost like when we dream; our minds can go anywhere, right?"

Doyle nodded compliantly, turning his empty glass with his fingers.

Greenwood went on, oblivious to his listener's actions, "So, let's think of it then as daydreaming. You see, in these daydreams, the mind, freeing itself from its body, undertakes a journey. On these mind journeys, those shivery experiences you've described occur when your mind encounters a fellow mind traveller, someone from the past, or the future, who has inadvertently entered the same space that you, or, your mind, is occupying at that particular time, in that particular dimension." Greenwood sat back triumphantly.

"Interesting," Doyle said. He did find what the Englishman espoused interesting, but he believed it to be a little "over his head," intellectually speaking. "That could explain it, right enough," he added, thoughtfully, tapping his glass on the table.

Greenwood, finally noticing Doyle's glass, said, "Can I get you another, Marty?"

Doyle feigned hesitation. "Well, I—"

"I don't mean to monopolize your time," said Greenwood. "Let me know if I'm keeping you from something, won't you?"

Doyle informed him that he had nothing pressing right then and, accepting Greenwood's kind offer, he got the attention of a nearby waitress by waving his empty glass at her.

"So," he said, "does this theory of yours explain things like ghosts—like the Black Nun—too?"

"You have to understand," said Greenwood, sitting forward in his seat again, "it's not *my* theory, and I'm certainly no expert in the field, but it is a concept that I believe would account for a lot of our paranormal experiences." The Professor waited while the flirtatious waitress delivered the drinks to their table. Returning her smile passively, he thanked her and awaited her chagrined departure, before continuing his dissertation in a conspiratorial tone. "You see, I believe that sometimes—maybe it has something to do with the stars, or how the planets line up, who knows—but *sometimes*, we're allowed glimpses into those parallel dimensions. Perhaps it's only for an instant, or maybe it's for a longer period, and it only seems like an instant, because everything is happening concurrently."

Doyle loosened his features and nodded, as if it was all becoming clearer to him.

The Professor was spurred. "Now let's say, for example, you're going about your day as usual, when suddenly, out of the blue, a memory pops into your mind. You're nine years old, and you're standing under a lamppost at night. You can even smell the cold night air around you."

Greenwood stared at a spot above Doyle's head, as if watching the scene he was describing, reenacted right there. "Snow is falling in silhouette, slowly drifting through the light's corona, and you're looking at it, *staring* at it in wonder." Greenwood fell silent then, leaving an awkward silence, seemingly lost in his memory.

Doyle was sure that what the man had described in such detail *was* Greenwood's memory. It was not an arbitrary example of reminiscence. He chose not to break the silence.

Moments passed before Greenwood, giving his head a shake, cleared his throat. "Well, what if, that for all intents and purposes, you are there? There was no particular reason just then, for you to recall that time and place. It just entered your mind, unbidden, and all of a sudden, in your mind, you're *there* again!"

Doyle nodded, fully aware that there was no part for him in this discussion, and glad of it. Accordingly, he continued to sip his pint, nodding when he thought it appropriate.

"Well," Greenwood went on, "let's just call this event a cerebral arousal, which caused you to think about that particular time and space just then. Say someone or something roused you, awakened your mind when they accidentally collided with your past self…the *then* part of you that's still standing in that time and space, because, remember, everything is happening now. So, as I say, the *then* part of you is disturbed in that space, and perhaps, just for a moment, the parallel dimensions themselves collide and become entangled, so that the *now* part of you, the transcendental part of you, that is, the part of you that needs no form of physical transportation, that part is there too! The collider would then experience your transcendental presence, as that sense of someone being there, or that feeling of someone walking over their grave, even though they could see no one!"

Greenwood had paused, pleased with the manner in which he had presented his hypothesis, and Doyle thought it was incumbent on him then, to play a more active part in their one-sided discussion:

"I—" he started, but was immediately interrupted by Greenwood.

"Yes," the Professor said, "I know. You asked me to explain the existence of ghosts, didn't you?"

Well, not exactly. But Doyle chose to let Greenwood go ahead and hold forth once more, since he seemed to enjoy it so much.

"Well," the Professor started, "back to the subject of the Black Nun. Let's say that someone catches a glimpse her, or her ghost, walking among the ruins of Bonamargy, going about her business. What if the reason they can see her is because they have been cerebrally aroused by her, when their *now* presence collides with her *then* presence. Their dimensions are momentarily entangled, and that person is afforded a fleeting glimpse into her universe, from where, perhaps, *she* sees the *watcher* as an apparition! Or, again perhaps, in her universe, she gets the feeling that she's being watched! And it's all because she and the watcher are both there, in their own universes, parallel to each other, because *everything* is happening *now*! Do you see?"

Now, Doyle could still picture himself, sitting there, nodding sagely, and throwing in the odd, "Hmm" here and there, but he had not *seen* anything. And as for the "*then* you" and the "*now* you" and all those parallel universes, well, he was completely bamboozled. He had done a little reading on the subject since then, and wasn't certain that Greenwood knew too much about what he was talking about either. The Professor had made Doyle think about the theory he was advocating, even though he was no closer to understanding it and did not know how to explain that morning's events.

He looked at his watch, downed the remainder of his whiskey, and grabbed his keys.

CHAPTER SIXTEEN

1

Doyle, momentarily unobserved, watched Carol at her table across the foyer. There was no doubt that she was still a beautiful woman, and he found himself more nervous than he had been on any first date. Taking a deep breath, he stuck a smile on his face and approached her.

A half glass of red wine sat on the low, rectangular, polished wood cocktail table before her, so Doyle deduced that she had not been waiting long. He noticed also that she was wearing the same clothes.

"Oh, hi, Marty," said Carol, smiling. "I thought I'd have a glass of wine while I waited. I hope you don't mind. I didn't realize you'd be so punctual." With her eyes, she indicated an empty chair. Dutifully, Doyle sat. A young waiter approached the table, carrying a pint of Guinness. "Oh, Malcolm, thank you!" said Carol, then looked at Doyle. "I told Malcolm I was expecting a gentleman friend and asked him to bring you a pint of Guinness as soon as he saw you. I hope that's okay?"

Doyle glanced up at the young man and smiled. "That's great," he said.

Malcolm's fair hair looked professionally cut and styled, and he was neatly dressed in a white shirt with black dress pants and shoes; a clip-on black bowtie completed his uniform. He placed the pint on the table. Doyle said, "Thank you."

Malcolm, smiling at Carol, replied, "Yer welcome, sir," and was gone.

Doyle bounced in his armchair. "Oh," he said, "this is a lot nicer than the Harbour, eh?"

"Yeah," said Carol, "but you're probably missing your girlfriend aren't you…*if ye catch m' drift?*"

Doyle, catching *Carol's* drift, looked embarrassed.

"Oh," said Carol, "I didn't mean offence by—"

Doyle put his hand up in a stop sign. "Don't worry yerself. No offence taken at all."

"Have you and…I'm sorry, what was her name?"

"Jen."

"Yes, Jen," said Carol. "Did you and Jen date in the past? It seemed that she and you—"

"Jesus, no!" said Doyle. "It's just that I've known Jen for donkey's years, that's all. Why d' ye ask?"

"Oh, I was just wondering. She seemed friendly, that's all."

"Jen's a very friendly girl."

"And pretty," said Carol. A smirk played at the corners of her mouth. Doyle looked at her questioningly, but before he could speak, Carol said, "Did you get the stuff you need?"

"Stuff…?"

"Yes. You said you were going to pick up some 'stuff' from the yard, remember?"

"Well, aye, I did. I—"

Carol, lifting her glass, said, "Cheers!"

Doyle, caught off guard again, reached for his pint. "*Sláinte!*" he said. "Good luck!"

"No, wait a minute," she clinked her glass against his, "here's to living *with* the past, not *in* it."

They honoured her toast. Doyle saw that Carol seemed to be waiting for him to say something else. After a second or two, he remembered. "Yes, I've got what I need in the van, ready to go."

Carol stared at him contemplatively for a moment, making Doyle squirm in his seat before she spoke again. "Marty, have you heard anything about Julia McQuillan having a sister?"

"Oh aye," said Doyle, feeling relieved. "She was a sinner, so they say. The story goes that she went to see Julia, to ask for forgiveness, or somethin'. But she died, and there was this this blindin' light—" Doyle stopped talking, his feeling of relief a memory, remembering their previous conversation, and looked at Carol who was nodding her head knowingly.

"Yes!" she said. "A *blinding* light, just like the one I saw that night!"

"Jesus! I'd forgotten all about that story."

"Yes, I guess you did, didn't you? And I think that she—the sister—is the ghost I saw that night and in my dreams since!"

Doyle stared at her. "Jesus," he said, picking up his pint and taking a hefty pull from it. "And ye *still* want t' go out there again?"

"Yes!" said Carol. "Even more so, now that I know her story. I'm certain she needs my help; I know she wants to tell me something. That's why she made that stone fly out of the wall this morning—to give me a sign!"

"Who says it was her?" said Doyle ominously. "Mebbe someone, or something else, moved that stone. What d' ye think of that?"

"I…I don't know. What are you trying to say?"

"Well, what if it was those other things ye saw that night? Those monk creatures of yours…?"

"What do you mean, those monk creatures of *mine*? Are you saying that I made them up?"

"No. I—"

"Well, what then?" said Carol, her voice rising. "I mean, why would those…those *things* do that? Why would they want my attention?"

"Easy on there. Lower yer voice and calm down a wee bit, and I'll try t' explain what I'm sayin', okay?"

Carol, arching one eyebrow at him, picked up her wine, sat back, and crossed her legs. "I'm listening," she said.

Doyle sipped at his drink as he tried to collect his thoughts. "Now, I don't suppose ye've ever heard of *Sluagh?*"

She frowned. "No, I haven't heard of *slew-ah,*" she said. "What is it?"

Doyle set his glass down on the table. "*Sluagh*…spelt S-L-U-A-G-H, is the Host, or the Army of the Dead."

Carol guffawed and made to comment, but Doyle, raising his hand, silenced her momentarily. "The full name in Gaelic is *Sluagh na Marbh. Sluagh*—Host, *na*—of, *Marbh*—the dead. Not many people believe in it, or *them*, anymore. To be honest, most people today haven't even heard of them; but legend has it, that *Sluagh* need to harvest human souls to exist. It's believed they—"

"And," Carol interrupted "what has this got to do with me?"

Doyle stared at her stone-faced, then, reaching a decision, he directed his words to the tabletop. "In some parts of the country, certainly around *these* parts, when folks have somebody ailin' in their house—somebody who's near t' death—some people still keep the windows of the houses that face west, tightly closed. The reason bein' that it's supposed t' be the direction *Sluagh* come from to *steal* the souls of the dying. They—" Once again Carol made to interrupt, but Doyle stopped her by raising his hand. "Wait a minute, listen." Carol sat back, and Doyle continued, "It's believed they come like a black cloud, or like a flock of birds, big, black birds, screechin' and whirlin' in the air. Ye see, that's what they say they look like: big, black birds. With big, leathery wings, like huge bats, mebbe. Some say that these wings—when *Sluagh* aren't flyin' and their wings are folded—they say that their wings look like long, black cloaks, or robes."

At these words, Carol sat forward, eyes agog, but she did not speak.

Doyle continued, "Individually, it's said that they have pale, saggy, white or grey skin." He lifted his dark brown eyes to stare into Carol's blue-greys then. "Oh, and another thing, apparently *Sluagh* can't talk too loud—but they can whisper—and they whisper constantly." He picked up his pint. "Now, does that sound familiar t' ye at all?"

"And that's what you're saying those monk things were?"

"Well, it seems t' me that that's what ye were describin' back in the pub, but I don't really know."

"But, how do you know all this?"

Doyle thought for a moment before answering. "Now, listen, I've never told anybody about this, but that night, ye know *that* night?" When Carol nodded, he continued, "Well, when I was tryin' to make my…my getaway, just as I reached the gate, I saw a flock of big, black birds in the sky above me. Huge they were! I thought it was strange because, one, it was nighttime, and two, because they were so big, bigger than any bird I've ever seen.

"Anyway, I was standing there, kind of mesmerized, I suppose, watching them wheelin' in the sky over the ruins., When I heard this screechin', and screamin', and everythin'…well…God forgive me. that's when I ran. I ran for my life!" Doyle stared silently at the woman across the table.

"And…?"

Doyle jumped back on his thought train. "Anyway, after that happened, and when Cormac and Tommy sort of disappeared, I did some research on m' own, ye know, just t' see what those big birds might've been, like. Anyway, off I goes t' the library and got m'self some books and did some readin' and found out about *Sluagh*. And then I talked t' some of the old timers, ye know, asked them about *Sluagh* and a few had their own stories to tell—some stories about Bonamargy—and it was pretty scary stuff, I can tell ye."

Carol did not speak, and Doyle took a few swallows of Guinness before he continued. "So, anyway, what I'm sayin' is this: things happen in and around Bonamargy. I for one, don't like being alone there. Sometimes it feels like the place itself is watchin' me, and to tell ye the truth, that feelin' has been getting' stronger lately, I don't know why. And then this mornin', well…!" Doyle ran a palm over his face. "When I went into thon stairwell, it…it just felt strange, and then I heard the whisperin', and the weird laughin'. Anyway, after that, and after all ye've told me about thon night, I think that what ye saw, and what did for big Cormac MacDonald and Tommy Calhoun must've been—"

"*Sluagh*…?"

Doyle inclined his head and shrugged. "Anyway, if ye're still fixed on goin', I'll take ye back there with me—as long as it's still daylight! Then I'll check out where that stone supposedly fell from, and—"

"What do you mean, *supposedly*? It did fall out of the wall, I saw it. I was there. It was like it was pushed out of the wall. It almost hit me!"

"Alright, alright, I didn't mean anythin' by it, I just meant that we can check the spot it came out of, and I can move the stone to a safer place. Then I'll tape the stairs off, but listen t' me now," he paused, lowered his head and raised his eyebrows to emphasise the point, "that's *all* we're goin' t' do, right? We're not doin' anything else, agreed?"

"Agreed." Carol glanced at Doyle's empty glass. "Should we have one more for the road?"

"Well now," said Doyle, "I don't think that's a bad idea at all."

Carol, glancing over his shoulder in the direction of the bar, caught the barman's eye.

2

Malcolm was at their table seconds later. Doyle watched as Carol drew the young man in, crossing and recrossing her legs, and tossing her hair from her face, smiling radiantly as she asked him if he'd worked there long; if he was from Ballycastle originally, et cetera, before ordering the same again.

"Before you go, Malcolm," she added, "tell me this," she let her eyes catch Doyle's for a second, "have you ever heard of *Sluagh*?"

The waiter looked confused. "Slewah?" he said. "No, I can't say I have. Is it a band or somethin'? Are they from around here?"

Carol laughed coquettishly. "No, I don't think so." She looked triumphantly at Doyle. "Thanks, Malcolm."

Doyle was not angry, but he was irritated by the insinuation that he had fabricated something. "Are ye tryin' t' make a point here? Listen t' me, now, I don't make up stories, okay? I haven't talked to anybody about that night. Now, I don't mind ye sittin' there goin' all *sheela na gig* with thon boy, but I don't appreciate ye gettin' him involved in anythin' I might have told ye, alright?"

Carol was visibly taken aback. "I'm sorry, Marty." "Truly, I am. I was only trying to find out if he knew about *Sluagh*. I have no intention of involving him in anything, honestly."

"Well, it seemed to me that ye were havin' a laugh at my expense." Doyle wasn't completely mollified. "Look, mebbe me takin' ye back there with me isn't such a good idea after all. Mebbe we'd be better leavin' well enough alone, alright?"

Carol leaned forward then. "No, Marty," she said. "Look, please don't be angry with me. I'm really sorry. I didn't mean to slight you in any way. Look, we'll have another drink, and we'll go, okay?" Smiling, she sat back and languidly crossed her legs.

"Here's somethin' else," Doyle hissed, angry again, "I might not be the sharpest tool in the shed, but I'm not a complete idiot. I said I'd take ye back to Bonamargy because I have a feeling that I owe it to ye because…well…because of the part I played that night. So, ye can keep on flashin' yer…yer…private parts at me if ye want to. And let me tell ye, I don't mind if ye do, but ye don't *have* to, that's *not* the reason I'm taggin' along. But for the love of God, will ye stop flashin' everybody else? That's what got ye in trouble the last time ye were here, remember?"

Carol disliked being told off, but she was more irritated than angry. "I'm sorry, Mister Doyle," she said in a deadpan voice. "Please forgive me."

"Aye, go ahead and laugh. I'm just sayin' that it'll probably get ye in trouble again, if ye're not careful." With a puzzled look, he added, "Tell me this, though, why do ye do it?"

"Do what?" she asked, straight-faced.

"Oh, never mind," said Doyle, with a small shake of his head, "it doesn't matter."

The waiter returned then, and once more Carol performed for his benefit as he set their drinks on the tabletop.

"Thank you, Malcolm," she said.

Doyle looked away, but not before he noticed that the young man had the decency to blush.

"Yer…yer welcome, ma'am," he said.

Doyle thought Malcolm was going to bow, before he turned and headed back to the bar.

Carol watched Malcolm go, making sure that Doyle saw her watching. Then she turned to look at the little man and raised her eyebrows enquiringly, "Something you want to say?"

She was momentarily stunned when Doyle replied, "Dreams are funny things, aren't they?"

"What do—"

Doyle smiled at some unspoken memory. "Dreams and ghosts, eh? My oul granny was always tellin' me to curb my imagination: she used to say, 'If ye're expectin' t' see a ghost…then ye'll see a ghost!' In other words, yer mind, yer imagination, will show ye what ye think yer goin' t' see, ye know what I mean?" He shook his head. "I wonder if she believed in *Sluagh*?" Leaning back in his chair, Doyle assumed a more serious mien. "We really don't know what our minds are capable of, do we? What kinds of things we can conjure up in here?" He tapped at his temple with a forefinger. "Now, take you for example. You had a bad experience, and its mebbe because of that, that yer havin' these bad dreams. But mebbe that's all they are, just bad dreams."

"But—"

"Now, some people think that dreams are just the way the mind deals with stuff that it can't deal with rationally, when we're awake, like, in the real world. So any stuff we can't face during the day is manifested in a kind of dream world, ye know, when we go to sleep?"

"A dream world? What exactly do—"

"Have ye ever heard or read anything about Multiverse Theory? Or mebbe, parallel universes?"

"What's your point?" said Carol tersely. "Everyone's read something about parallel universes and multiverses, et cetera, et cetera, but you distinctly mentioned a dream world, and I want to know what you meant by that?"

Doyle looked daggers at her. "Listen, I don't know who ye think yer talkin' to, but I've just about had enough of yer…yer arrogance!"

Carol sat back, surprised at the barely concealed anger in the little man's voice and manner. Doyle calmed himself. "Listen, I'm sorry. Look, mebbe we should just—"

"No, no, *I'm* sorry." She laid a hand on his when he reached for the glass. "I'm…I'm a teacher. I teach history at a high school back home, and I know I can come across as bossy sometimes. I know that."

Doyle smiled then. "A teacher, eh? Well, that explains it. That explains a lot!"

"Did you have a hard time at school?" she asked. "I mean, with your teachers?"

"No. Can't say I did. Got five O levels—one in history, as a matter of fact. No, I just meant that explained the way ye carry yerself, ye know what I mean? Ye've got a *way* about ye, and I couldn't figure out what it was, that's all."

"So, anyway—full disclosure here, obviously—since I've been haunted by these nightmares, I've done some research into dreams. I read Freud and Nietzsche, of course, but their insights and interpretations didn't offer any viable explanations to my personal experiences. And I've done a bit of reading about the multiverse theories. I read about the Dreamworld of the Greeks. Is that what you were referring to?"

Doyle shook his head again, this time in wonder. "I don't know what I was referring to. I've never read anything by Freud, or the other fella."

"Nietzsche."

"Aye, him. And I don't know about Greek dream worlds either, but I read once that when we dream, our souls leave our bodies and travel to other universes…dimensions…ye know?"

Carol sat back. "I think you're describing astral projection. But where are you going with this?"

"Well, like I told ye before, strange things happen all the time in Bonamargy, but there's times when the place seems even stranger than usual, and I get the feelin' that I'm dreamin', ye know? Or…no…it's more that I feel like I'm *in* a dream."

Both sat in contemplation for a moment before Doyle made an attempt at lightening the mood. "Mebbe I'm dreamin' now!"

Carol smiled and lowered her eyes in acceptance of the clumsy compliment. "By the way, what's *sheela na gig*?"

"Oh, look, never mind that. I shouldn't've said anythin'."

"Why? What's wrong? What does it mean? Come on, tell me."

"Alright, alright. I'll tell ye. A *sheela-na-gig* is a stone carving that's found on the walls of some churches and castles, that's all. They're meant t' be apotropaic—supposed to ward off evil—a type of gargoyle, if ye like."

"A gargoyle? Oh, I don't think so, Marty. I know what a gargoyle is, and I don't think they've got anything to do with me doing this." Carol flipped the skirt of her dress up and down.

"I said a type of gargoyle. A *sheela na gig* is a stone carvin' of a woman who's…who's liftin' her skirts to expose her…um…private parts. And she's holding…um…it open, y' know, with her hands, like, with her fingers."

"Jesus!" said Carol. "I—"

Doyle held his hands up then to deflect any admonition that might be coming. "I'm only tellin' ye what I know. Ye asked me to tell ye, so I told ye. But in fact, I should've said *anasyrma,* not *sheela na gig.*"

"Okay, you've got me. What's *anasyrma?*"

"*Anasyrma,*" said Doyle, "describes the act of a woman liftin' her skirts to expose her…ye know…her genitals…her vulva, to ward off evil, or any kind of malevolence, when needed."

"Wait a minute. I read something about this, somewhere, but I've never heard of *Sheela na gigs.*"

"*Sheela-na-gig* carvin's are usually found on, or near the gates of churches and chapels because, in olden days, the…um…the vulva was considered the primordial gate, that mysterious divide between non-life and life." Doyle was slipping into his professorial role again, and beginning to enjoy himself.

"Now, some *sheela na gigs* portray women holding exaggeratedly huge vaginas open with their hands! And in fact, quite a few were removed from churches because they were considered obscene."

"No kidding! But how do you figure that a woman lifting her skirt and flashing her vulva will ward off evil?"

"I don't. I'm just tellin' ye what I read about it. It's believed here, and in other parts of the world, mind ye, that a woman lifting her skirt and exposing her sex will stop anything evil in its tracks." He sat forward in his seat. "In the Balkans, they believed until very recently, that if it rained too much, gettin' their women to expose themselves, would make it stop rainin'! The philosophy behind this, is that a woman, or really her vulva, is the producer of life, so she has the power, in her sexuality, to keep bad luck, and even death, at bay."

"Well, I bet it was the *men* of the Balkans who came up with that philosophy!"

Doyle shrugged. They both looked up, for the waiter cum barman was once again at their table.

"Excuse me," he said. "I was wonderin' if ye'll be wantin' anythin' else? It's just that it's the end of my shift, and—"

"No," said Doyle, "I think we're all done here, aren't we?"

Carol, after pushing her hair back and off her face, crossing her legs, and fixing the fall of her dress, agreed with a smile.

"Alright then," said the now thoroughly flustered Malcolm, "I'll be right back with yer bill. It's all together, is it?"

Carol spoke up then. "Yes, Malcolm," she said, caressing the young man with her eyes, "and could you put in on my account, please. Carol Flanagan, room seven."

"Of course, ma'am. Would you like a copy of the bill?"

"If you wouldn't mind, Malcolm," Carol purred.

"No problem."

Doyle thanked Carol for the drinks and, shaking his head at her burlesque performance, rose from the table. "I have to go see a man about a dog. I'll be right back, then we'll go, alright?" He headed off in the direction of the toilets.

The waiter returned, and Carol accepted the proffered bill. "Thank you, Malcolm." She magically produced a five-pound note. "This is for you."

"Thank you. Are ye…if ye don't mind me askin'…are ye stayin' here long?"

"Just one more night, I'm afraid." Carol crossed her legs calculatingly.

Malcolm looked crestfallen. "Well, I hope ye enjoyed yer stay anyways?"

"Oh, I certainly did."

The waiter reluctantly turned to go and was happy when Carol spoke again. "Tell me, Malcolm," she said, sitting forward in her seat so that her dress rode high on her thighs, "have you ever been to Bonamargy?"

Malcolm Donaldson tried to swallow, but finding no moisture in his mouth, he coughed instead. "Oh aye. Loadsa times. Why? Is that where yiz are off to?"

"Is it scary there?" She plucked at the hem of her dress.

Donaldson did not know where to look. He was beginning to perspire freely. Sweat trickled in his armpits, and his dress shirt stuck to his back. He managed a nonchalant shrug. "Not really. Ye should be alright at this time of day anyway; but I wouldn't go there after it gets dark though, if I were you."

Carol, suddenly serious, sat straighter. "Why's that? Did something happen to you there? Did you see something, the Black Nun, perhaps?"

Donaldson laughed. "No, no, nothin' like that, but…um…well…the last time I was there, somethin' did happen."

"Can you tell me about it?"

Before he could reply, Doyle returned, retaking his chair and picking up his glass, "Ready?"

"Wait a minute, Marty," said Carol, "Malcolm's about to tell us what happened to him the last time he was in Bonamargy. Why don't you sit down, Malcolm?"

The young waiter looked around at the empty lounge. "Well, I'm done at five anyway, and it's five to now, so I guess it'll be alright, at least for a couple of minutes." He sat in the chair next to Doyle's.

"Well…?" said Carol.

"Well," Donaldson began, "it was nothin' really. Me and my mate Alan Price took a couple of girls there one night, a few years back."

3

It had been five years ago. A Sunday evening, late in July, during the summer of Donaldson's sixteenth year. Belinda Quinlan and Geraldine McCracken, nineteen and twenty, respectively, were exiting the Harbour Bar when they bumped into Donaldson, who had just exited the bar's off-licence with a six-pack of beer hooked between his forefinger and thumb.

Donaldson knew Belinda Quinlan. They lived on the same street, but because of their age difference, did not move in the same circles, and rarely, if ever, communicated. Donaldson did not know the other girl's name, but he had seen her with Belinda before, and it was she who spoke.

"Easy there, wanker!" she said. "Where's the fire?" Donaldson did not answer immediately because his attention was drawn to the girl's large breasts, which seemed desperate to escape the confines of her skimpy, red tube top. Before he could think of a reply, Belinda opened.

"Hello, Malcolm," she said, "where're ye off to in such a hurry, eh?" Donaldson was visibly flustered. Two girls, who ordinarily wouldn't give him the time of day, were actually talking to him.

"Oh hi, Belinda," he said, and made to move on, but the other girl blocked his way. Donaldson was once more distracted by her considerable cleavage.

"Mebbe he's lookin' for someone to share those with," she said, indicating the beer, and deepening the boy's consternation. "Maybe, if we're nice to him, he'll give us one each!" She smirked at this, and nudged her friend with her elbow.

"Whaddya say, Mal?" said Belinda, giggling. "Would ye like to give us one?"

Geraldine McCracken bent over laughing. "Oh, don't, Lind, ye'll make me pee m'self!"

Donaldson's eyes were locked on her jiggling breasts, certain they were going to fall out, right there in the street. His cheeks burned a deep crimson when Belinda brought his blatant ogling to her friend's attention.

"Ye'd better stand up straight, Ger," she said, "or ye'll get drool on your tits!" That brought forth gales of laughter from Geraldine, who Donaldson now realized, was more than slightly inebriated.

"So, Mal," Belinda continued, "off to see yer girlfriend, are ye?" Nudging her friend, she added, "But ye thought ye'd buy some panty remover first, eh?"

"Oh, look," said Geraldine, making an effort to control herself, "ye're making him blush. Aw, isn't that cute?"

Alan Price came around the corner with a tube of Pringles crisps in each hand and stopped dead in his tracks. All he could see were breasts and legs. Finally, he found his voice.

"I wondered where ye'd got to," he said to Donaldson. "What's goin' on here?"

"We're tryin' to get yer mate to give us one," said Belinda, which set Geraldine off once more.

"I'd give yiz both one," said Price, smirking, "any time, any where!"

"Better watch yerself, Ger," said Belinda, "we've got a *live* one here!"

From the pocket of his hoody, Price produced two hand-rolled cigarettes and held them out in the palm of his outstretched hand. "You girls lookin' t' have some fun the night?"

"Where'd ye get those?" said Donaldson, unaware that Price had purloined the spliffs from his older brother's stash.

"Never mind that," said Price, dismissively. "Doesn't matter." Refocusing on the girls, he spoke to the shorter one, the one he thought the prettier and more sober one. "Well," he said. "Are ye up for it or not? Me 'n' him were thinkin' of mebbe goin' out to Bonamargy, smokin' some stuff, ye know, have a coupla beers, and—"

"Have a wank," said Belinda, and this time Geraldine screamed with laughter.

Price was undeterred. "Aw, come on, ye aren't scared are ye?"

Belinda snorted. "We're not goin' to Bonamargy with a couple of schoolboys like youse two, are we Ger?"

Geraldine wiped her eyes with the back of her hand. "Nah, nothin' but rocks and rats in thon place." She rubbed her upper arms with her hands. "'Sides, it's getting a wee bit on the cool side."

Donaldson set the beer on the ground at his feet and pulled off his jean jacket. "Here," he said, draping it over Geraldine's shoulders, "this'll keep ye warm."

Belinda giggled. "I was wrong, Ger, *this* is the one ye have to watch! A proper Sir Walter Raleigh, this one." But she smiled at Donaldson, making him wish he had given her his coat.

Geraldine struggled into the denim garment and tried to pull it around and over her breasts. "Well," she said, shaking her breasts from side to side, "it's not going to keep these warm,"

"Sure, ye can leave that up to me!" said Price.

"Well, aren't you quick?" She caught her bottom lip between her teeth before adding, "Oh, I don't know, Lind, mebbe we could go with them. What d' ye think?"

"Aw, come on, girls!" said Price. Unzipping his hoody, he shrugged it off and handed it to Belinda. "Here, ye can put this on ye if ye're cold. Come on," he repeated, tucking his tee shirt into his jeans, "sure, it'll be a lark. Come on, let's go."

"Say, 'please'," said Belinda, laughing.

"Pleeaassse!" said Price.

And so, they had set off, the boys walking in front, while the girls trailed behind, walking arm in arm.

Believing he was out of earshot, Price tilted his head towards Donaldson's. "See the tits on that tall one?"

Donaldson nodded eagerly. "Ger," he said.

"What?"

"Ger. That's 'er name."

"Yeah, whatever, but, did ye see the knockers on her? Almost popped out that time she was laughin'."

"Fuck, yeah! And see them wee skirts they're *nearly* wearing! They don't even have to bend over for ye to see their knickers!" Donaldson glanced over his shoulder. "Which one do you want? I kinda like thon Belinda, but I don't really care, just as long as I get my hole tonight."

"Mebbe we'll each get the chance to fuck *both* of them!" said Price, and the boys laughed. They fell quiet and walked on, each lost in his own thoughts.

Donaldson was a bonafide virgin. So was Alan Price. Although neither would admit it to the other—or anyone else—on pain of death. But both teenagers were nervous that night, and the nearer the tumbled-down walls of Bonamargy loomed, the more nervous they became.

Of course, Donaldson divulged neither the details of his conversation with Price, nor the specifics of his sexual experience, or lack thereof, to Carol and Doyle.

"So, anyway," he continued, "the sun was startin' to go down by the time we got to the gate, and Pricer says—in his idea of a scary voice, 'I wonder if the old girl's home this evenin'.' And then, just as we're goin' through the gate, Belinda stops and says, 'Who's that?' and she's pointin' at the walls. Well, we all looked, but nobody saw anythin', and Pricer laughs and says somethin' about her just trying to scare us, or somethin'. But I was watchin' Belinda, and she wasn't actin' the lig or anythin', as far as I could tell. I mean, I thought she actually saw something over there, in the shadows. Next thing, we all heard these voices whisperin' and laughin'. Well, suddenly Belinda screamed, and then Ger screamed, and next thing ye know, they're out the gate, and me and Pricer are right behind them, all of us hightailin' it back down the Cushendall Road, towards town.

"Anyways, we ended up goin' down onto the beach, but nobody was really in the mood anymore, if ye know what I mean. We tried to have a laugh. We drank the beer and smoked the weed, and ate all the crisps, but I knew nothin' was going to happen, and eventually, the girls made some excuse and left, and me and Pricer just went our separate ways."

Carol was rapt. "Did she tell you what she saw?" She was sitting on the edge of her seat, staring fixedly at him. "What did she see? Didn't she say anything about what she saw?"

"Belinda, ye mean? Oh yeah, she told us alright—unfortunately. We'd drunk a couple of the beers, and Pricer sparked a spliff, and we were just beginnin' to get friendly, y' know? Then that stupid Ger goes and asks Belinda what she thought she'd seen back there at the gates. Belinda goes all quiet, like, says she didn't want to talk about it. But Ger keeps at her, and won't let it go. So finally, Belinda says that she thought she saw a ghost, or somethin', said she saw this woman, said that the woman was wearin' somethin' like a nightie, and that it was all ripped and torn and…" Donaldson squinted in thought for a moment, "oh yeah, and she said she thought it was covered in blood!"

No one spoke. Donaldson, thinking it was his story-telling ability that had them transfixed, continued. "Belinda told us that the woman had really long, fair hair, but it was a mess, and…what else…?" He snapped his fingers. "Oh yeah! She said that she looked sodden and drenched, and that she looked like she'd been dragged through a hedge backwards." Donaldson grinned at the memory of that turn of phrase, but then he noticed the furtively exchanged glances between Doyle and Carol, and the grin quickly left his face. "What?" he said.

"What's wrong? What's goin' on here?" Suddenly, he thought he understood. "*I* know what it is. The ghost woman…ye've seen her too, haven't ye? That's why ye're all goin' there, isn't it?"

So," said Carol, "'ghost woman.' Is that what Belinda called her?"

"You've seen her, haven't ye?"

She ignored the question. "What else did Belinda say about her? I mean did…did she say how she was acting, or anything?"

"Aye. She said that she was sort of staggerin', like, stumblin' about, y' know. And bendin' over, and holdin' her belly, and then, she just disappeared, she said." Donaldson peered at Carol. "Ye *did* see her, didn't ye?"

"I think I may have, yes."

"When? When did you see her?"

"It was over thirty years ago," said Carol, and though there was no need to explain further, there was a compulsion in her to do so. "It was back in July 1971, and I still have dreams about it…about her. Nightmares, I suppose."

"That's weird. Belinda Quinlan told me that she has nightmares about that night too."

Carol was visibly shaken. "*Quinlan?*" she said. "That's your girlfriend's last name? Quinlan. Are you sure?"

Donaldson snorted. "Well, first up, she's not my girlfriend, but of *course*, I'm sure!"

Carol chuckled nervously. "Well," she said, "that's a coincidence, isn't it? Quinlan's *my* name too. My maiden name, I mean."

Doyle nodded. "And this Belinda *Quinlan* saw yer ghost too."

Donaldson looked from one to the other. "Do ye think ye know who the ghost is?"

Carol took the question. "Well, we think she might've been Julia McQuillan's sister."

"Ye mean the Black Nun?"

"Yes, the Black Nun. Now listen, you said your girlfriend told you she has dreams about the ghost woman, right?"

"Well, like I said before, she's not my girlfriend, but yeah, she told me she has nightmares, or she *did*, anyway. I met her in town, about a month ago. We were outside the Harbour Bar and I asked her if she fancied a wee drink, and she said, okay."

"Well, we're sittin' there in the pub, gabbin' away like gangbusters, and after a wee bit, she asks me if I ever had dreams about that night. Well, I told her that I didn't, and she said that she was having these weird, scary dreams, after all those years—nightmares, like. She's in Bonamargy and—"

"But, just a minute, nothing happened to her that night, right?"

"Not as far as I know."

Carol looked confused. "So, what does she dream about that's so frightening? What happens to her in her nightmares?"

"Well, I was about to tell ye that, when ye interrupted me."

"Sorry. Please go on with your story. I won't say another word."

"Well, like I was sayin', she said she dreams that somethin's chasin' her through the ruins, but she doesn't know what it is, and then she comes to a stairway, and there's a woman there, and she says something to her, and then, she just wakes up. Said she wakes up sweatin' buckets!"

Carol, looking stunned, fell back in her seat. "As a matter of interest, Malcolm, what's your last name?"

Donaldson told her.

"Really?" said Doyle, toying with his empty glass. "Now that's interestin'. Did ye know that Donaldson is a derivative of MacDonald?" He turned to Carol. "And Quinlan, is a derivative of McQuillan? And here's a wee bit of trivia for ye. Your families, yer forebears, I should say, fought each other over this part of Ulster for centuries. The MacDonalds and the McQuillans were mortal enemies."

Carol, having regained her composure, smiled and said, "Yes, you told us that—on your very informative, guided tour this morning. You said that it was the MacDonnells, who warred with the McQuillans, not the MacDonalds!"

Doyle smiled wearily at her. "Just an alternate spelling," he said.

"Well," said Carol, turning to the young waiter, "I'd rather we weren't mortal enemies Malcolm, wouldn't you?" Malcolm reddened, and Carol said, "Anyway, I take it you didn't see the ghost woman yourself, then?"

Donaldson found his voice. "No, I didn't. But why d' ye think that it was the Black Nun's sister's ghost. I've never even heard of the Black Nun havin' a sister."

Doyle coughed to get the young man's attention. "Well, there's not too many that have, but it seems that there's a fairly good chance that she did. I—"

"Anyway," Carol interrupted, "it doesn't matter, does it? I think I saw the same ghost your girl…your *friend* described to you," she looked defiantly at Doyle, "*exactly* as I described her to you!"

Donaldson stirred in his seat. "But how come I didn't see her, then? None of us, apart from Belinda, saw her!"

"Well, the fact is," said Doyle, "as far as I know, yer friend, and Carol here, are the *only* ones who've seen her."

"Well, that's kinda weird, isn't it? Nobody else has seen this ghost in all these years. I think—"

Doyle interrupted him. "Well, yes, it is, But I've been thinkin' about that too. Now listen, Carol here, and yer Belinda share the same last name, Quinlan, and, like I said, that name could be a derivative of McQuillan and, if that's the case, they could be distantly related, *kinfolk,* so to speak. And mebbe," Doyle continued, focusing then on the young man, "I think that's the reason Carol and yer girlfriend saw the ghost while others didn't!" Doyle let his statement hang, wondering how he had managed to make that connection. He looked at Carol. "Time's a-tickin' and we should get goin'. Are we ready?"

Everyone rose and moved away from the table, but before she followed Doyle to the exit, Carol caught the young waiter by the sleeve. He flinched, and Carol said, "It's okay, Malcolm, I don't bite. I just want to thank you again, for everything." Smiling, she added, "Maybe I'll see you later, when we get back, I mean."

"A…aye…" Donaldson stammered, "…m…mebbe."

CHAPTER SEVENTEEN

1

Doyle, opened the passenger door of the vehicle and averted his eyes as Carol slid into the seat. "We'll only be a coupla minutes, but ye'd better put on yer seatbelt, okay? Alright then, off we go." He climbed in on the driver's side.

In less than five minutes they disembarked in a small car park at the top of the lane which led to the gates of Bonamargy. Doyle looked at the sun's position in the partially clouded sky, then checked his digital watch: 17:42. From the van's interior, he grabbed two safety cones, a roll of yellow caution tape, and a piece of wooden doweling about a foot long and one inch in diameter, which he put in his back pocket. Hanging the roll of yellow caution tape on the doweling, he picked up the cones. "All set?"

"Do you think it would be okay to leave my bag in the van?" asked Carol. "I don't want to carry it if I don't need it."

"Sure," said Doyle. "It'll be safe there, don't worry." He closed and locked the doors and, a moment later, they were standing before the closed gate. Doyle, setting the cones on the ground, reached for the latch. He was unnerved by a sense of foreboding he did not understand and could not quell, but he tried to be nonchalant about it as he opened the gate and ushered Carol over the threshold. He closed and latched the gate behind them. "The oul place'll be empty, I'm sure. It's tea time in this part of the world."

The grounds were deserted and quiet, but Doyle's misgivings increased when he came to the stone cross with a hole in its top—the cross that supposedly marked the Black Nun's grave—near where he was accosted by Carol that morning. He stopped while snippets of that conversation replayed in his mind.

Carol, coming up behind him, noticed his bemused expression. "Is something wrong?"

"Is this where Cormac and Tommy…?" his voice trailed off.

Carol nodded, indicating a spot a little ahead and to the right of where they were standing. "They let me go and chased me…herded me in here, like, like I was a fucking cow, laughing and whooping the whole time." Carol failed to mention that they were just outside the *cul-de-sac* of her dreams—a courtyard, surrounded on three sides by high, stone walls.

"Whereabouts did those monk things come from?" asked Doyle, looking around nervously. Carol pointed at the arched doorway in the far-left corner—the doorway, she recalled from this morning's visit, that led to the stairwell.

"Tommy," she made a face as she spoke the name, "he was the one holding me while his pal pawed at me. He thought he saw the Black Nun in that archway, but I think it was one of the monk things. I told you how they came at us. They came from everywhere! It seemed they were coming right out of the walls and…and from behind those headstones. They were all around us."

Doyle sensed the fear in her voice. "Mebbe ye'd rather go back to the van while I—"

Carol shook her head vigorously. "No, I'm okay."

"Are ye sure?"

"Positive. Let's go."

Doyle thought that she was far from okay, but he led the way to the arched entranceway and, after he set a cone on either side of it, turned to Carol. "Let me get a wee look first."

Doyle stepped inside, but Carol pushed her way in beside him, despite his protests. "I must've been about halfway up when it came out of the wall. Can you see it?"

Doyle found her proximity intoxicating. Feigning annoyance, he said, "Yes, I can see it, but ye'll have t' give me a wee bit more room."

Carol ignored him. "This is definitely the stairway from my dreams."

Doyle followed her sightline. "But ye can see for yerself, can't ye? There's nothin' at the top of them stairs."

Carol saw that he was right; she saw daylight beyond the curve at the top. Undeterred, she said, "I'd like to see for myself, if you don't mind." She fixed Doyle with her classroom look.

"Alright," he said, "but let me go first. I just want t' make sure it's safe. That there's no more stones about t' come shootin' out of the walls!"

Carol nodded her acquiescence, and Doyle proceeded slowly up the stairs.

The stone in question lay close to the wall opposite the one it came out of, so Doyle presumed that it did not simply tumble out of it. A mixture of dust, sand and gravel lay scattered over the adjacent steps. Doyle picked up the stone. It was the size and shape of a turnip and had a substantial weight to it. Setting it down against the wall, he set about clearing the steps of the detritus left by the incident, using his feet as makeshift brooms. He was peering at the perimeter of the hole when Carol came up behind him:

"Can you see anything?" She put her head alongside his. "Let me take a look, I'm taller than you." Doyle stepped aside obligingly. Carol stood on tiptoe and craned her neck in a vain attempt to see into the cavity. "I can't see anything." When she started to reach her hand into the hole, Doyle grabbed her wrist.

"Hold on! Don't go stickin' yer fingers in there!" He lifted the caution tape off the piece of doweling in his back pocket and set it behind him on the steps, then taking the stick, he reached up and swept the hole with it. Nothing but more dust and gravel issued from the space. "There's nothin' in there." But he jumped when Carol screamed. Someone had entered the stairwell through the archway below.

"Hey!" said Donaldson. "I thought I heard somebody in here.?"

2

"Jesus Christ!" said Carol. "You scared the shit out of me! What are you *doing* here?"

Donaldson, grinning apologetically, stepped further into the stairwell. "Sorry, I didn't mean t' scare ye, I——"

"Did ye follow us?" asked Doyle, noticing that the young man was still in his work clothes. "What are ye up to?"

Donaldson put his hands in the air in the universal gesture of surrender. "Take it easy, mate. I——"

"That's my wallet!" Carol pointed to the object in Donaldson's right hand. "Where did you get it?"

Donaldson said, "That's what I'm tryin' t' tell ye, if ye'd give me a chance."

Carol and Doyle waited.

"I found yer purse after yiz left," said Donaldson, brandishing Carol's red, leather wallet. "It was on the floor, under yer chair. Ye must've dropped it or somethin' when ye were leavin'. Anyway, I knew yiz were comin' here, so…"

Carol wore a puzzled expression. "But I——"

Doyle cut in, ushering the woman down the steps. "Let's step outside for a wee minute."

Donaldson stepped outside first.

Carol turned to Doyle. "I haven't taken my wallet out of my purse once today! How——" She snapped her mouth shut when Donaldson pushed his head back through the arched opening.

"Are yiz comin'?"

Donaldson was standing outside the doorway, smoking a cigarette. His bowtie was gone, but the rest of his attire was the same; the top button of his shirt was undone. "So, what were yiz doin' in there?"

Carol put out her hand. "Can I have that, please?"

"Oh," said Donaldson, "sorry! Here ye go." Carol, took the wallet and opened it immediately, sparking an indignant reaction from the young man. "I didn't take nothin', if that's what ye're worried about."

"I'm not accusing you of anything, Malcolm." Carol produced a five-pound note from one of the wallet's compartments. "I just wanted to give you this to say, 'thank you.'"

Donaldson pushed both hands out in front of his body. "No, no, I don't want that. I didn't—"

Carol pushed the note into his hand. "Please, I insist."

Donaldson, exuding reluctance, closed his fingers around the note. "I really—"

Carol, widened her smile and silenced his protests.

Carol was sure Donaldson had pilfered her wallet, but having no proof, she decided to go along with the charade and see where it led. What did Malcolm want? Did he consider himself a young Lothario, bent on seducing her? More likely, he'd simply enjoyed the "show" back in Seaview's lounge, and had turned up hoping for more of the same, and maybe something else. Either way, Carol was intrigued. She looked at her watch and was irritated that its face was blank. What was wrong with the stupid thing? She reckoned the moon, the full moon, would rise over Bonamargy in another hour. She was exhilarated and frightened by the imminent occurrence.

Although Carol's nightmares had lessened in frequency and intensity since the events of that unforgettable night in 1971, they had never completely ceased. Then sometime in the late nineties, they had returned with a vengeance—as frequent and intense as ever.

She married Bill in Belfast during the summer of 1974, just after her graduation, and they had moved to Canada shortly thereafter, as soon as Bill's application for emigration had been accepted. They settled in Peterborough, Ontario, where Bill secured a teaching position at a local public school. Meanwhile, Carol completed her teaching degree at Trent University and found employment teaching history at a nearby high school. To all intents and purposes, Bill and Carol were a happily married couple.

Familial obligations were the reason for the several trips they made back to Northern Ireland in the intervening years, but they made a point of *not* including Ballycastle in any of their holiday plans. And still, Carol's nightmares persisted.

The "event" in Bonamargy had not affected Bill to the same degree, and although Carol understood why, she was still perplexed by this, even though Bill admitted that he too had recurring dreams about that night.

"My nightmare is that I can't reach you," he told Carol. "You're bein', ye know, attacked, but somethin's stoppin' me from gettin' to ye. Somethin's standin' in my way. Somethin' dark—no, not dark—somethin' *black* and massive and...and it terrifies me! That's what I dream!"

"Do you dream about the moon?" Carol asked once. "There's always a full moon in my nightmares, and, and it seems to lead me, you know, lead me towards that stairway, and a door."

"Door? What door? Where does it lead to?"

"I don't know!"

"Okay, mebbe it's time we talked to somebody?"

But they never did.

Then, sometime in 1998, the frequency of Carol's nightmares became such that she was dreaming of Bonamargy every night. She became obsessed with those dreams, trying to decipher their meaning. Nothing else, including her marriage, seemed to matter. She wouldn't discuss her obsession with her husband, telling him that she had it "under control" and that he had nothing to do with it.

They decided against parenthood early in their marriage. Carol had no maternal instincts whatsoever, and Bill had said that he did not care one way or the other, but she always wondered if, in reality, he did.

And then, in 2002, Bill died suddenly of a brain aneurysm. Standing now amid the ruins of Bonamargy, Carol found herself thinking about the man she had loved; the man who had loved her back despite, or maybe because of, her idiosyncrasies.

Carol came back to the present to find Doyle and the young waiter staring at her. Donaldson wore a smirk while the older man looked concerned.

"I'm sorry," she said, "Did you say something?"

"Are ye feelin' alright?" said Doyle.

"I-I was just thinking about Bill. I didn't tell you, did I? He died three years ago. He was only fifty."

"I'm sorry to hear that," said Doyle. "Was he—"

"Thanks." said Carol dismissively. She didn't want to talk about Bill right now "It was quick. I mean he didn't suffer, so that's good. Now, you were saying?"

Doyle knew enough to drop the subject. "I was just sayin'," he said, clearing his throat, "that if ye're ready, we should get goin'. I can drop ye off at yer B and B if ye like?"

Carol, clearing her mind quickly, brought her thoughts back to the here and now. "But wait a minute, I never got to see the top of the stairway. I'd like to see what's up there."

"But I've already told ye, there's *nothin'* up there!"

"I'd like to go to the top anyway. Is that a problem? If it's too much trouble, I'm sure I can find my own way back to town."

Donaldson stepped forward. "I can—"

"No, no," said Doyle, interrupting him. "It's no trouble at all." Shaking his head, he started in the direction of the archway. "I think I'd better go with ye. Come on."

Donaldson said, "No problem. Mebbe I'll just wait here then?"

"If ye like," Doyle said over his shoulder. "We'll only be a minute or two." He disappeared into the stairwell with Carol close behind.

At the top of the stairway, Doyle stepped out into the light of day, and onto the remains of a thick stone wall topped with weeds and tufts of grass. The ground was twenty feet below his feet. Lending Carol a hand, he helped her out of the opening to stand beside him.

"Careful now, we don't want ye fallin', do we?" Nodding at the nothingness before them, he said, "They think this used to be the livin' quarters, but as ye can see for yerself, the roof's long gone. And the rest of it, floors and all, fell to ruin a long time ago."

"Yes," said Carol, lowering her voice to a whisper, "that's all very interesting, but I'd like to know what Malcolm's up to." She hefted her wallet. "I'm almost sure he stole this. I didn't even take it out of my bag at the lounge."

"Yeah," said Doyle, also whispering, "I was thinkin' there's somethin' not right there, but I've no idea what his game is."

"Nor do I. So, what do we do now?"

"We'll just hafta keep an eye on him. Anyway, no matter what he's up to, we should be gettin' back down now. The sun'll be goin' down soon, and I really don't think we want to be here when that happens."

Carol moved closer. "Thanks, Marty," she said into his confusion, "for bringing me back here. And for letting me see the stairway, and bringing me up here, and—well—I just want to thank you."

Doyle almost fell off the wall, when Carol's lips were suddenly on his. Quickly breaking the innocuous kiss, she pulled him from the precipice and guided him back against the wall of the stairwell:

"Careful now," she mimicked, "we don't want ye fallin', do we?" She silenced any answer he might have had with another kiss, but this time Doyle was ready. He returned the kiss with an ardour she had not expected, and did not welcome, apparently. "Hey!" she protested, breaking contact. "Hold on a minute, here. I only wanted to say thank you. Understand? Nothing else." She recoiled when Doyle reached for her, and would have toppled into the abyss had he not caught hold of the sleeves of her dress and pulled her to safety.

"Careful, now," he said, tonelessly, "we don't want ye fallin', do we?" And with that, he turned and started down the steps. "See ye," he called over his shoulder.

Carol started after him. "Marty, wait! I'm sorry, I—"

Doyle turned around. "Fuck me! How many times a day do you say that word?" He carried on down the stairs, saying, "Like ye said, I'm sure ye can find yer own way back to town."

Doyle was already some yards along the path by the time Carol stepped out of the stairwell. "Marty!" she called after him. Doyle kept walking. "Marty! Please...!"

Carol failed to notice Donaldson lurking amidst the deepening shadows at the foot of the stairs.

3

Watching Carol now, Donaldson could see that she was in a quandary. He remained hidden and silent.

Carol turned and re-entered the stairwell, and stood staring up the stairs:

"Where are you?" she whispered. "Are you there?"

Donaldson almost stepped from the alcove before he realized that Carol was not addressing him. He watched as she crept up the steps. She froze suddenly, and Donaldson's breath caught in his throat when the sound of many voices whispering resounded in the stairwell.

Carol's hand went to her mouth. "Oh my God, no...NO!" she screamed, turning towards the exit, but stumbled and fell backwards onto the steps when Donaldson's form loomed before her in silhouette at the foot of the stairs.

Donaldson, stepping closer, reached out to help her to her feet, but Carol, not knowing it was him, shrieked. Throwing her wallet at his head, she scrambled up the steps and away from him. "NO! Stay away from me! LEAVE ME ALONE!"

Donaldson, trying to calm the woman, was deafened by her screaming and the cacophonous, whispering laughter surrounding him. He failed to hear the sound of movement at his back. It was the sudden, pungent stink that roused his senses. He glanced over his shoulder just as something akin to a hand snaked out and snatched a hold of his shirt. Donaldson tore himself out its awful grasp and bolted up the stairs, carelessly knocking Carol aside in his hunger for escape. She recognized him then.

"Malcolm!" she cried, after his rushing figure. "*Malcolm*! Be careful…the stairs—" She did not know whether he screamed and had no time to wonder if he survived the fall, for her assailants were upon her.

The sudden light was blindingly bright, and the accompanying screech pierced Carol's ears. Then all was black and silent.

4

The walk to the gates cooled Doyle's anger somewhat, and when he looked back, he was disconcerted not to see Carol coming along the path. He wondered if she had stayed in the stairwell and wondered too, if he might have overreacted. He really shouldn't have left her there alone, no matter what she'd done to deserve such treatment. Then Doyle remembered the boy waiter. Where was he? Doyle had seen no sign of him when he exited the stairwell. Maybe he'd been hiding somewhere, waiting to be alone with her. Maybe that's what

Carol had been waiting for too? Then again, maybe not. Sighing, Doyle started back along the path.

The sun was on the horizon and its last rays reflected through the large window arch in the west wall of the ruined chapel. Standing next to Julia McQuillan's supposed grave marker, he cupped his palms around his mouth. "CAROL! WHERE ARE YE?" For several seconds his words echoed around the chapel canyon, and then it went quiet. The fast-approaching twilight lent the atmosphere a dark purple aspect, a strange and somehow unnatural tinge which troubled Doyle, for it was familiar. A full moon was rising in the east, and staring at the shining orb, he realized he had been conned: *Played like a fuckin' violin.* Carol had *known* there was going to be a full moon! She hadn't wanted to leave Bonamargy before it made an appearance, and that was why she lingered; that was the reason she kissed him!

Her sudden screams, issuing from the archway, raised his hackles. Before he could react, his eyes were speared by a bright light which flashed like lightning from the window slit at the top of the stairwell. An accompanying piercing shriek brought his hands to his ears and drove him to the ground in terror. Then, just as suddenly, all was silent, and his blindness was complete.

Seconds passed, and Doyle, on all fours, tried to control his panic, hoping that his blindness, and apparent deafness, were temporary afflictions—fearing that might not be the case. He presumed the whooshing sound was due to the assault on his eardrums, but the perception that it had a definite timed beat, and was growing in volume, caused concern. The realization that this sound too was vaguely familiar to him was slow to materialize, but once it did, Doyle's terror increased. He remembered those big, black "birds" and the *whoosh* of their wingbeats.

Sluagh!

Fortunately, his sight was returning to reveal a world bathed in that weird, purple darkness. Staring into it, he discerned the outline of the archway leading to the stairwell. Staying on his hands and knees, he scurried towards it.

Carol started at the sound of someone, or something, entering the stairwell, but she did not make a sound.

"Carol?" said Doyle. It had to be her sitting on the stairs, about halfway up, but he wanted to be sure. "Is that you?"

"Marty?"

"Are ye alright, love?"

Carol, satisfied that it was indeed Doyle, let go of her emotions all at once. "Oh, Jesus, what have I done?" Rising, she stumbled down the steps towards the little man.

Doyle moved quickly to the foot of the stairs and caught her in his arms. Carol laid her head on his shoulder.

"What's happened?" he asked, "What is it ye've done?"

"Malcolm was here," Carol said, her breath hitching, "and then those…those monk monsters came and tried to grab us, and he…Malcolm…he ran up the stairs, and…" Carol had turned to look at the path of Malcolm's flight, and Doyle felt her stiffen in his grasp. He allowed his gaze to trace hers.

"Fuck me," he said, softly.

"So," Carol whispered, "you can see it too?"

He was staring dumbfounded at the landing that was now at the top of the stairway. To the right of this landing, appeared the faint outline of a door. He and Carol stood, still holding each other in a loose embrace, staring mutely at the incredible sight on the stairhead. A minute, maybe two, passed before the silence was broken when the sound of voices, whispering softly, filled the confines of the stairwell once more. Their embrace tightened and their eyes met momentarily, and each saw the unmitigated fear laid bare in the other's.

Doyle pulled Carol into the archway and together they peered out of the opening into the moonlit courtyard of the ruined chapel. Doyle squeezed Carol's arm, needlessly, for she had already seen the black shapes moving in the shadows under the chapel walls.

Then, a distinct voice—one that sounded like a hundred whispers—rose above the tumult that surrounded them. "COME TO US!"

Doyle, seeing an undulating blackness forming and growing in the darkness of the stairwell, felt his feet grow roots. "NO!" he screamed, then forcing his feet to move, he shouted into Carol's face.

"Come on!" Doyle grabbed her hand and led her up the stairs, hoping the door on the landing was unlocked and praying that a lesser evil lay beyond it.

The door looked old and made from thick wooden planks. There was an iron ringed handle on its right side and a small barred window in the centre. He forced himself to peer through its bars before trying the handle.

"There's a wee room," he shouted over his shoulder, his words suffocating in the raucous laughter. Carol, her hands over her ears, did not hear him. Doyle reached for the door's handle, lifted it, and turned it until the door opened. He hesitated on the threshold, peering into the room beyond. Carol pushed him into the room and quickly followed. The din in the stairwell was muted immediately.

Carol shut the door, and stood with her back against it, wide-eyed, listening to her own heartbeat. Doyle, suspicious of the sudden silence, moved her aside as he frantically searched the door and its frame for a bolt, or some kind of locking mechanism. Finding none, he surveyed the tiny room. A wooden table and chair sat against the wall to his right. Grabbing the chair, he tilted it onto its back legs and jammed it between the door's latch and the wooden planking of the floor, just as he had seen it done in countless movies. He did not know if this idea would stop any intruder, but at least he had done something. He looked around the room more carefully.

An old fashioned rushlight, sitting at the table's centre, was the source of the room's feeble light. A small bed hugged the wall opposite, and Doyle guessed the distance between the two walls to be no more than ten feet. He reckoned it was roughly the same distance between the door and the fireplace on the far wall.

Turning to Carol, he smiled grimly. "Alright then, let's just take a wee breather. We'd—" He broke off when Carol slid down the wall to her haunches, and sat, head in hands, crying pitifully.

"Jesus Christ," she sobbed. "This is all my fault, isn't it? What are we going to do?"

Doyle, still struggling to come to terms with what he saw at the foot of the stairwell and the situation he now found himself in, squatted opposite her and brushed her hair away from her eyes.

"Well," he said, quietly, "cryin's not goin' t' help. Come on now, pull yerself together. We've got some thinkin' t' do." Rising, he looked around the little room again. "Was this wee room in yer dreams too?"

Carol shook her head and snuffled, "No," she said, slowly pushing herself to her feet.

"Are ye sure?"

Indignance flashed in her eyes. "Yes. Yes, Marty, I'm sure."

"Alright then. Thon wee light's not goin' to last much longer." He moved to the table. "There's a couple more rushes here. Hopefully, that'll do us. They only last about a half hour at a time."

Carol stared at him. "Are you serious? We have to get out of here. Now! This is fucked up beyond belief. Aren't you frightened?"

He put his hands on her shoulders. "Easy. Try to calm yerself, okay? Take a deep breath or two and we'll try to figure this out, alright?"

She nodded and did as he suggested., Then she said, "How come you know so much about rushlights?"

"Well, I am an official tour guide for the NIEA!"

Carol smiled at his exaggerated gravity, genuinely grateful for the aplomb with which the little man was handling their situation.

"It's lucky that I happen t' *like* history too."

Carol was still sniffling. Doyle, resting his rump on the table edge, continued, "So, what about you? Do ye like bein' a history teacher?"

Carol smiled and moved to sit on the edge of the bed. "Yes, I like history too." Then, the tears returned. "Thanks, Marty, for…for everything. I shouldn't've asked you to bring me here—wherever *here* is. And I know I've been a bitch, too. I'm so sorry."

Doyle's fear had tightened his chest again, and he could not look at Carol, so he allowed his eyes to roam the surrealistic room. "Mebbe we'll just wake up in a minute or two, and we'll…" Letting the sentence hang unfinished, he laid his hand on the table behind him. He knocked on it and heard its solidity—its realness. Shaking his head in wonder, he closed his eyes and whispered, "*Dúisigh.*" When he opened his eyes, he saw that nothing had changed apart from the fact that Carol was staring at him, a worried frown creasing her brow. "I just wanted to see if it would work," he said. "Thought that mebbe it was a magic word or somethin' and that mebbe I'd, we'd, wake up, and find ourselves…" His left this sentence unfinished too, and hung his head. Marty Doyle had come to the conclusion that *nothin'* was going to be the same ever again.

5

"Marty?" Carol's frightened voice sounded a long way away. "Marty…please, Marty…talk to me."

With some effort, Doyle lifted his head; it felt like he was lifting an anvil with the muscles of his neck.

"Heavy hangs the head." he said to no one.

"What?" said Carol. "What's wrong with your head?"

"It's Shakespeare. 'Heavy hangs the head that wears the crown.'"

"It's 'Uneasy."' said Carol.

"What?"

"It's 'Uneasy lies the head that wears the crown,' It's a common misquote."

"Well, I'm glad you're feelin' more like yer old self again."

Carol smiled crookedly. "*Are* you okay, though? I mean, what made you think of that particular quote? You know you're not responsible for me, or any of this, don't you?"

"Oh, I don't know," said Doyle. "I—"

"'Cause you're not! Now, tell me, why did you scream 'No' downstairs, in the stairwell? What did you see? Was it the *blackness* there, in the corner?"

Doyle nodded. "I think it's the black hole of the world! I've seen it before. That's what's haunted my dreams for years! I had this nightmare, all through my teens, where I'd be in a castle, and there was this portcullis. And there was a really dark corner beside the portcullis, and I'd be drawn to the corner. I could feel something bad—evil— was in the corner. I could hear it breathin', or…or mebbe whisperin' to me. It wanted me to come closer, and I would—I couldn't stop myself. When I was about to step into its blackness, somehow, I'd force myself to wake up. I'd wake with a start, y' know? Like when ye dream yer fallin' and ye wake up just before ye hit the ground."

He stared at her searchingly, and got the affirmative nod he was looking for.

"So, did the nightmares just stop by themselves? Or, do you still have them, now and again?"

"I haven't had that dream in donkey's years," said Doyle. "And I just about shit m' self down there!" He pushed himself off the table. "Listen, love, I don't understand. What were ye expectin' t' happen here? I mean, yer dream frightened ye—I can see that—just like my nightmare scared the hell out of me, and because of that, I've never felt compelled to search for that oul castle with its portcullis. Yet, here you are, searchin' for somethin' that puts the fear of God in ye."

Carol said nothing, and Doyle continued, "Even after we came back, like ye wanted, ye used yer…yer feminine wiles to keep us here. Why did ye lie t' me? Ye know ye played me like—"

Carol stood up quickly. "I know, I know and I apologize for that. Look, I wanted to see her, the ghost, again. I thought if I could only see her again, maybe talk to her, I might be able to ask what she wants from me, ask her why she's haunting my dreams. So, I thought it was important to try to replicate that night back in 1971, and I did my best to do that. I made sure we would be here on a Friday night, and that there would be a full moon. I even did my best to dress exactly the way I was dressed that night." Before Doyle could interject, Carol went on, "And there's *always* a full moon in my dreams so that's why I played you. I *am* sorry, Marty."

Doyle fluffed the apology off. "But the things ye saw on the stairs when Malcolm took off, were those the same monk creature things ye were tellin' me about earlier on in the pub? The ones that attacked ye that night? Had ye forgotten them? What were ye plannin' to do if ye ran into them again?"

"My only plan was to get back here and to see if I could reach the ghost lady. I hadn't forgotten about the monk monster things. How could I? But I didn't think—"

"No. ye didn't, did ye? But it doesn't matter now, does it? So, listen t' me, were those the same monsters, or not?"

Carol furrowed her brow in thought. "I don't think they were," she said. "These ones seemed slower to me. That night, those robed monks moved fast. They could even *fly*. But the stench was the same."

"So, what happened after the blindin' light and thon screech?"

"Well…nothing. The creatures stopped trying to grab me. The light must've frightened them. I was blinded and terrified. I sat where I was, and then you came back."

"But ye didn't see the door at the top of the stairs before I got here?"

"That's right. What are you thinking?"

"I wonder," said Doyle, not believing he was thinking this out loud, "if that light, and that screeching sound is what happens when dimensions crash into each other?"

"A parallel dimension? But I think that would entail some kind of out-of-body experience, wouldn't it?" Carol patted the length of her body with both hands. "I don't know about you, but I think I'm still in my body."

"So, you're sayin' this wee room really exists? But I *know* it doesn't, at least, not in my world, it doesn't."

"But the room's *here*, isn't it?"

"Is it?"

6

They shared silent contemplation for a few minutes before Doyle spoke again. "Okay, listen. Remember me tellin' ye that sometimes, when I'm here in Bonamargy, I get the feelin' that I'm in a dream?"

Carol, still feeling oddly slighted, chose not to answer. Doyle continued, "I'm not getting' that feelin' now."

"So, what kind of feeling are you getting?"

Doyle started to pace the floor between the table and the cot. "It feels like…like I'm *livin'* this, d' ye know what I mean? And that's just not possible, is it?"

Carol took in the room as she pondered. "Okay, I don't get the feeling I'm dreaming either. All my senses are working. I can smell this room, the burning of the lamp, the wooden floor," reaching for the table, she ran her fingers over its top, "and this feels real enough. It wasn't made yesterday either, was it?" Receiving no response, she looked up to see that Doyle was staring at the door. Carol craned her neck to look.

"A firefly!" she exclaimed. "That's strange, isn't it?"

"A *firefly*? What the hell's a firefly?"

Under normal circumstances Carol would have found his reaction comical. "You know, it's a…a…" Her voice trailed off when she realized that she wasn't altogether sure exactly what a firefly was. "Don't tell me you've never seen a firefly before!" But this firefly's light was constant—not pulsing—and it wasn't flying, but hovering at head height, just in front of the door. All at once, the firefly came straight at her face. Falling back onto the chair with a scream, she flapped her hands wildly at the offending insect. After several moments, she sat upright, covering her face with her arms. "Where is it? Has it gone?"

"I don't know where it went. I can't see it. Do those things sting?"

Carol gave no answer.

"Carol, I asked ye, do they sting, or bite, mebbe?"

She did not answer—she *could* not answer. No matter how hard she tried, she could not move a muscle. Doyle's voice seemed to be coming from the other side of a wall. The sense of having been invaded was pervasive: something was *inside* her. Her hands fell heavily to her lap and she could speak. "I think I swallowed it. Oh, Jesus, Marty. I think it's inside me!"

Doyle, though discomfited by the blue glow that surrounded Carol, made to move to her side. But her demeanour changed suddenly, and raising her hands defensively, she spoke, "*Stad!*"—Stay!

Her eyes bored into him and he quailed in her gaze, seeing madness in them. "Jesus Christ, C-Carol? Are ye alright, love?"

7

Carol was aware of an invasive presence, and was terrified to find that she no longer controlled her body. Her mind and thoughts were still her own despite being rendered physically impotent.

The immortal being that once essentialized the corporeal Máiri McQuillan was, through use of Carol's body, experiencing the human condition for the first time in over three hundred years, and was enthralled by it. Carol's power of movement had been usurped, but her senses were intact, to be shared with the otherworldly intruder, so that she identified its sensations apart from her own. Carol felt the spirit's unsuppressed exhilaration as it used her senses to stimulate its own.

It ran Carol's hands all over her body and, as it did, Carol shared in the spirit's wonder at the smoothness of her palms and the texture of her skin, and its warmth! It luxuriated in Carol's perfume, and barked a laugh—a single "Hah"—in pleasure.

Then, with some hesitation, it ran those smooth palms down across Carol's belly and slipped them between her thighs, and ran one finger along the cleft there, touching and probing until Carol's pulse quickened further and her body trembled. Carol distinctly sensed the spirit enjoying her arousal, sharing in Carol's natural carnal response to the sexual caresses that were not her own.

The spirit turned its attention to Doyle who had been a spellbound spectator, not knowing what was expected of him as he watched Carol's provocative performance. Doyle knew that the woman now glaring at him was Carol—she hadn't changed physically—but something had happened to her. She seemed to be as fascinated with her body as he was.

Doyle watched as Carol lifted her dress to her waist. Once again, she laughed that strange-sounding "Hah!", stood and walked towards him, holding the dress at waist height. She stopped in front of him and, letting go of the dress, laid the palms of her hands on Doyle's chest. He flinched when she traced the outline of his nipples through his tee shirt:

"Listen, C-Carol," he said, "I—" Then he was kissed. It was nothing like the kisses they had exchanged on the stairway. It was nothing like any kiss Doyle had ever shared before. In fact, there was no sharing; there was a painful mashing of lips, and Doyle tasted blood on his as he was walked backwards until the backs of his knees made contact with the cot. He sat down, hard. Stunned and motionless he watched as the woman stood over him and, lifting the hem of her dress to her chin, offered him an unobstructed view of her naked body.

"*Nach eil I brèagha?*" she said, in an accented voice.

Doyle, was shocked to realize that, although his knowledge of Gaelic was rudimentary, he completely understood what Carol said! "Isn't she beautiful?" she said, but Doyle was unsure if it were him being addressed, and continued to stare mutely at the brazen woman who was now moving her hands along the curves her body, touching and caressing.

Then she repeated the question. "Is she not beautiful?"

Doyle did not know what to say and did not move when the woman came closer. He forced himself not to flinch when she wet the pad of her thumb with her tongue and wiped the trickle of blood on his lips with it, like a mother would do to her injured child. Then, leaning closer, she put her hands on his shoulders and brought her mouth to his again, this time with more tenderness, gently brushing his lips with hers.

Doyle, feeling a physical response, was in a dilemma. Was he meant to respond? Then Carol, leaning her forehead against his, let her hair fall gently about his face and peered at him through its strands of shimmering gold.

Carol continued to speak in Scottish Gaelic. "Ye love her, don't ye? But ye haven't *loved* her, isn't that right?"

Doyle, looking into the depth of Carol's eyes, found himself mesmerized. He nodded and shook his head in unison under the questioning.

"But, would ye lay down yer life for her, Martin?" she said. "Would ye give yer life so that she might endure? Would ye offer yer soul for hers?"

Tears forming in Carol's eyes were an anomaly to the spirit who had cried little when housed in flesh and bone. It sat beside Doyle on the bed and, looking at the floor, thought-spoke directly into Carol's mind. "*Why are ye cryin'?*" it asked bluntly in Scots-Gaelic.

Carol was surprised too, by the fact that no translation was required—she understood the question perfectly. Unable to give voice, she presumed her answer would be read in her thoughts so, she carefully corralled them and, instead of answering, thought a question of her own. "*Are you the ghost of Julia McQuillan's sister?*" she asked in English.

Carol winced when the answer resounded in her head. "*Hah!*" it spat. "*I am* you, *for as long as I want t' be!*"

"*But I don't understand,*" thought Carol. "*Who, or what are you then? What do you want from me?*"

The reply was softer in tone. "*Ye can think of me as the ghost of Máiri McQuillan, for that's who I once was. I want much from ye.*" It wiped at the tears in Carol's eyes. "*Tell me why ye're cryin'.*"

Carol's tears were a surprise to her also. "*I don't know. I guess I didn't know how Marty…Martin…felt about me before you asked him just now. How could he love someone like me?*"

"*Hah! Sure, who gets to choose who or what ye love?*"

"*But you seemed to be getting ready to ask him to do something— something dangerous, and he's only here because I tricked him into being* here. I don't want him to get hurt. And I'm here only because I want to help you!"

Máiri became irritated again. *"You're here only because I saved yer life—and yer soul—else ye'd've been* Sluagh *a long time since!"*

"Sluagh? I don't—"

"Lineage and Fate brought ye t' me the first time. It was me who saved ye from Sluagh, and it was my light that touched ye, and allowed me to reach ye. Ye and me are kin, and we've a kinswoman in need."

"But I still don't understand. Why have you haunted my dreams for thirty years? Why wouldn't you just appear to me again, or…or simply explain what you wanted me to do in my dreams?"

"Because many demons and spirits keep vigil in the Dream Realm, and some are more potent than I. The Burglar could've captured yer soul while it wandered there had I not wakened ye when I did. What's more, it was necessary for ye t' come back to Bun-na-Mairge of yer own accord. I could only offer the invitation. You had t' accept it, d' ye understand?"

But the mention of a burglar stopped Carol's thought stream momentarily. *"What burglar?"*

Máiri sighed, held her patience and thought-said, *"Let me tell ye quickly about m' sister, Julia."*

8

Doyle, judging Carol's tears and hunched demeanour to signify she needed comforting, placed an arm around her shoulders.

"It'll be alright, love. I'm not sure what the hell's goin' on here, but it'll be alright."

Carol acknowledged neither his arm nor his words, and for some time they sat in a silence Doyle found perplexing. Then, all at once, Carol sat straighter, turned her troubled countenance towards him, and started to talk. "Máiri McQuillan, Julia's sister, is a spirit, and she's inside me. She says she's a soul guide—an *angel!*"

"An *angel!*"

"A soul guide. And that's what she want's me for. She needs my—maybe our—help to rescue Julia's captive soul." Doyle repeated her last two words. Carol, with some impatience, said, "Listen, let me tell you what she told me."

She went on then to tell Doyle about Julia McQuillan, and what had happened to Liam O'Kane. She described the Burglar of Souls as an evil spirit, or demon, who steals the souls of mortals, leaving them as ghoulish revenants held in its thrall.

"That's what attacked Malcolm and me on the stairs!" she said. "They're *not* what attacked me back in 1971. Those were *Sluagh* that night, and they're something completely different. The full moon brings *Sluagh* out, and—" She stopped short because Doyle, with eyes closed, was shaking his head from side to side. "What?" said Carol. "What's with all the head-shaking? You don't believe me?"

Doyle stopped shaking his head but kept his eyes closed. "*Believe* ye!" he said. "What's my believin' ye have to do with anythin'?" He opened his eyes and threw his arms wide. "We're here aren't we? And we're not dreamin', are we? This is a fuckin' nightmare alright, but unfortunately, it's no dream." He rubbed at his knees with his hands. "*Sluagh!*" he said. "Angels! Demons! Christ Almighty!" Then he slapped both knees, hard. "So, anyway, what does this…this…this angel of yours want us t' do?"

Carol's mind wobbled. Doyle's outburst brought home the absurdity of their conversation, and along with their surrealistic surroundings and the undeniable existence of whatever it was inside her body, made it impossible for her to answer his question in any intelligible form. *I think I may be cracking up; I think it would be better if you tell him yourself what you want?*

Doyle was surprised, and found it strange, when the other voice took over again, and the Scots-Gaelic tongue issued once more from Carol's lips so naturally:

"We know that Liam's soul is kept in a bottle," she said. "It's—"

"Wait a wee minute. Before ye go any further: What have ye done with Carol—is she alright?"

Máiri/Carol rose and moved to the table and leaned against it. "Carol's alright, but the sooner yiz do this, the better. D' ye understand?"

"No," said Doyle, "I don't, but I'm guessin' you bein' in there…I mean, in there with her, isn't doin' her any good, right?"

Máiri ignored this. "Listen t' me, now, like I said, Liam's soul is in a bottle. We think it's kept in the altar in the chapel."

Doyle's mind was racing: *There's no altar! There's no chapel anymore!*

"There is *now!*" said Máiri, pushing herself off the table and startling Doyle. "Ye must stop thinkin' about what's real and what's imagined, d' ye hear me? Ye've seen many things this night; things both real and unreal, and no doubt ye'll see many more before the night's out. Ye must trust yer senses. And I think ye'll have t' trust me if ye're wantin' to see the morn."

Doyle, desperately trying to keep his thoughts his own, said, "Alright. What d' ye want me t' do?"

"I want ye t' go the altar and get the bottle and bring it back here. It'll be like a witch bottle; d' ye know what that is?"

"I - I think so. I mean, I've seen pictures, and I know what they're for, but I've never actually seen one, in real life, like."

Doyle knew that witch bottles—much like the *sheela-na-gigs* he had described to Carol earlier that day—were considered apotropaic in nature, meant to keep witches and other evil spirits at bay. Usually, they were buried, or placed inconspicuously in homes, specifically for this purpose. "But what d' ye mean ye think it's in the altar? What if it's not?"

"It'll be there," said Máiri. "When Julia was murdered, the Burglar told her it had always been there. In the very place where, every day, she prayed and suffered for the sake of their souls. Now listen, it won't be big and it might break easy, so be careful. It'll be hidden, mebbe, but it's there, somewhere. Find it and bring it back here t' this room."

Doyle looked at Carol askance, and Máiri read his mind at once. "There are many reasons why I can't do this thing," she said angrily, "and *you* don't have t' know any of them."

A switch clicked inside Doyle. "Ye know what? Fuck this! I don't know what the fuck's goin' on here. Yer doin' my head in with all this stuff about angels and demons and shit. I just want t' get the fuck out of here, d' ye understand? Come on, Carol." He held out his hand and moved towards the door. "Come with me. Once we get out of this place, everything will be alright. Come on!"

Carol stepped forward and took both his hands in hers. And it was Carol who spoke to him. "I think she's what she says she is, Marty, and I want to help her. She saved my life, and I think it's the right thing to do. I can't explain why I think that, I just do."

Doyle squeezed her hands tightly. "Listen, if she's an angel like she says, why can't she just go get the bottle herself?"

"It's *because* she's an angel. That's why she can't. Apparently, although she has the…the…*telekinetic* power to make stones pop out of walls, she couldn't pick that same stone up. Neither she nor Julia can use their hands to physically touch or move anything."

"Julia…?"

"She's here too," said Carol, looking over his shoulder.

When Doyle turned to look at the door, he saw a pale-skinned, raven-haired woman standing there, watching them with interest. The fact that the woman was completely naked did not escape his attention. "Jesus Christ! That's Julia McQuillan? That's the Black Nun? But…but why is she…? I mean…she's…she's…"

Carol drew his eyes back to hers. "Julia appears to us as she was when she died. She has no choice in that. But she did choose to stay here in this place—in this dimension—for the sake of Liam's imprisoned soul. She didn't have to do that. Despite what had happened, Máiri could have guided her to the next plane of existence, but Julia—her soul, that is—chose to remain. Do you know why, Marty?"

Doyle looked towards Julia, who returned his look without expression. "I don't know. Guilt?"

Once again Carol sought and captured his eyes. "Her sin would've been expiated in another existence and her guilt absolved. That's not the reason she's here. She's here because she loves Liam."

Doyle looked towards Julia again. "Why doesn't she say something? I mean, she hasn't moved a muscle, or said a word since I seen her there."

"Máiri says that Julia can't speak to us. She says that Julia can see and be seen, but any other interaction is impossible for her." Carol's grip on Doyle's hand tightened. "Will you help me, Marty? I-I don't think I can do this alone, but I will, if I have to. And I know I've no right to ask you to help me, but—"

"But what can we do? Those *whatchamacallums*…those…those *things* ye saw on the stairs, they have special powers and everythin', don't they? What can we do if they want to stop us?"

"The ones I met on the stairs have no special powers. Máiri says that they're revenants—*zombies*—if you like. They're controlled by the Burglar."

"Oh, well, *that's* alright then, isn't it?"

Carol went on, transmitting Máiri's words as she spoke. "They're slow and cumbersome, she says, and they don't like light, or fire."

Leaving Doyle standing in the centre of the room, she went to the corner beside the fireplace and, with a cry of discovery, produced two long pieces of wood. "Torches!"

"Torches?" said Doyle.

Carol brought them to him. "Yes, torches, see?"

Doyle accepted one. It was a cumbersome, roughly hewn, wooden stake, three feet long, topped with straw dipped in pitch or something like it.

"Wanna try to light it?"

"Just hold on a minute," said Doyle. "What's the plan?"

"Plan?"

"Ask her."

"She wants to know what you mean," said Carol.

"She *knows* what I mean." He hefted his torch. "This might keep those *revenant* things at bay, but what about this Burglar fella—whatever he is—what if he turns up? I bet ye he's not afraid of a wee bit of fire."

Once more, Máiri took control to speak through Carol. "The Burglar knows ye're here. But he's already harvested one soul this night and, with luck, he's sated."

Doyle's thoughts went to the young waiter for a moment, then quickly refocused as Máiri continued "There's a full moon tonight so *Sluagh* have more than likely mustered and are abroad. The Burglar and *Sluagh* have no love for each other; *Sluagh* have no fear of him and would like nothin' better than to try to relieve him of his captive souls. Anyway, with this in mind, I'm hopin' that we won't have to deal with the Burglar."

"We? So, you're comin' with us—I mean, with her?" He nodded at Carol's breasts "I mean…in…in there?"

To her own surprise Carol smiled, and it was she who answered, "Yes. Máiri's coming with us."

"Alright," said Doyle, feeling slightly better, "how do we do this?"

CHAPTER EIGHTEEN

1

Doyle did not find the silence in the stairwell comforting. The disembodied whispering laughter had been disconcerting, but at least it keened the senses and kept you on your toes. Now it felt to him as if something was trying to dull his wits.

Carol/Máiri led the way. Her flickering torch-flame created monstrous misshapen shadows which cavorted on the walls behind them. Doyle had not lit his torch, preferring to keep it in reserve. At the bottom of the steps, Carol lifted hers to peer into the corner. Turning to look at Doyle, she shook her head, indicating there was nothing there. Doyle nodded in response. Carol moved into the archway and waited for Doyle to step beside her. They stared into the space beyond it.

Doyle's mouth opened in awe. "Fuck me! I just can't believe this."

"Incredible," Carol whispered reverently in turn. "Unbelievable!"

They were staring into the interior of a large chapel. The once barred and arched window frame in the east wall, above and to the left of where they stood, held a large stained-glass window. Refracted moonlight passing through it was supplemented by the dying light of day coming from three smaller window openings in the south wall, dimly illuminating the chapel's cavernous interior.

In this fragmented light, the floor looked straw-strewn. Warily Carol searched the deeply shadowed chapel walls for signs of movement before stepping forward. Doyle followed cautiously in her wake.

Carol pointed her torch at a wooden structure ten feet ahead of them, in line with the archway they had just vacated. She started towards it.

Nervously they approached the structure. The edifice looked to be nothing more than an oblong table somewhat higher than average, made of wood. It was six feet long, two feet wide, and reached to Carol's waist. The top was a slab of wood, two inches thick, which overhung its base by a few inches. The base itself was six inches deep and supported by two carved wooden pedestals spaced equidistant from either end. Carol, circled the altar searching the base for drawers or cubby holes.

"See anything?" asked Doyle.

"Nothing obvious."

"Let me light this," said Doyle, kneeling and peering at the underside of the base. He pushed the end of his torch into the flame of Carol's until it caught before bending once more to his task. "I don't see any—"

Carol grabbed his shoulder. "Marty!"

"What's the matter?"

Carol stared past him. "Oh Christ! Marty. Look!"

Doyle turned. The sight of the figure in the archway stopped his words and breath momentarily. He was looking at Malcolm Donaldson. One side of the young man's face was streaked with dried blood, as was the front of his once white shirt. He was having a hard time negotiating the steps leading down to the straw-covered floor.

"Jesus!" Carol cried when she too, recognized him.

Doyle stopped her when she made to go to Donaldson. "Hold on a minute."

Carol protested. "But he's hurt!"

Doyle ignored this and continued to bar her way. "Malcolm!" he said, lifting his torch and peering at Donaldson. "Is that you, son? Are ye alright? We'd just about given up on ye!"

"Marty!" said Carol, "Can't you see he needs help?"

Again, Doyle ignored her. "Why doesn't he say somethin'? Are ye alright, Malcolm? D' ye need a hand?"

Donaldson finally managed to step down onto the floor where he stood for a moment, head lolling unnaturally on his neck, managing to focus on Doyle with a leer as lopsided as his head. When he spoke, Doyle was chilled by his words and the rasping sound of his voice.

"What are yiz lookin' for?" Donaldson said, in a harsh tone and accent that sounded nothing like the young Donaldson's. "Why are yiz dabblin' in things that don't concern ye and ye don't understand?"

Doyle started to panic when he realized it was getting hard to breathe. He turned to Carol, mouth agape, clawing at his throat with his free hand, panic-stricken.

"Marty!" cried Carol. "What's wrong?"

A laugh rattled in Donaldson's throat. "That's love for ye. Sometimes it'll take yer breath away." With a flourish, he displayed a small bottle held between the fingers and thumb of one hand. "Sometimes it'll take yer very soul!"

"The Burglar has come!" said Máiri, and Carol felt her mind and body being usurped once more.

The change in Carol's demeanour did not go unnoticed by Donaldson, but he had difficulty moving his torso to focus on her. Then he spoke. *"Mar sin, that hu air tighinn, aingeal?"*—"So, ye've come, angel."

2

Doyle, still struggling for breath, had dropped his torch and fallen to his knees. He clawed at his throat with both hands. The straw around his discarded flame smouldered. Máiri/Carol laid her hand on his head, and suddenly, he could draw breath. Greedily he gulped air into his starving lungs.

"So," Donaldson chortled, "Ye seek a test of mettle, do ye?"

Doyle felt his airways constrict once more.

"No," said Máiri/Carol, "I don't seek confrontation of any kind. Will ye not treat with me?"

The damaged young man laughed, and Doyle, breathing again, moved behind Carol and out of Donaldson's line of sight. He heard a deep, rumbling growl build in Donaldson's throat, and when it escaped the young man's lips, Doyle saw an ink-black fog enshroud the emitter, leaving only his battered face visible. This time when Donaldson spoke, his voice sounded like the crackling of dead leaves pushed before a soughing wind. "We've already bartered, and yer sister is bound to a pact."

"That was no pact," said Máiri. "She had no choice."

"Ah, but there was a choice," the voice responded. "She negotiated, and her decision was made of her own free will, knowin' right well the consequences of it."

The angel spoke again. "Yer appetite will be yer undoing, Burglar. Ye've already been provided with another life force this night, haven't ye? Aren't we acquitted? Will ye not release the one ye hold?"

"*Provided?*" Thousands of whispered voices crawled out of Donaldson's mouth. "There was no provision. I fed on the spoils of foolishness and fear. Nothin' was provided, it was taken! And even if it had been bestowed, tell me, how would this acquit yer sister—or *ye*—for that matter?"

"I brought the mortal here," said the angel, "and thereby gave ye the chance to take his soul and add to yer power. Sure ye get no benefit from keepin' Liam's soul in a bottle? Ye've held Julia and Liam captive for so long now, and for what? Yer power hasn't been increased by their captivity. Why won't ye let them go?"

"Ye only brought the *woman* here," the Burglar said. "She brought the rest. And as for the whys and wherefores, yer sister made a pact. There was no time limit set in our agreement so far as I know. And as for these mortals…" the Burglar's laugh gurgled in Donaldson's throat "…their souls were forfeit the moment they crossed the threshold. *She* may have come hither at your behest, but they entered this world—my world—of their own volition."

The Burglar's voice assumed a tone of solicitation. "I'll tell ye what, angel, leave them to their fate, and I'll let ye take yer sister and go." Donaldson's face loomed even closer. "Go, angel, while ye yet can. Ye know yer potential is wanin'. Ye can't afford t' waste it helpin' these two. Sure, they're nothin' to ye. Leave them."

Máiri/Carol's raised her lowering chin. "Listen, I'll—"

"You'll *what?*" the Burglar hissed through Donaldson's damaged lips. "Have ye learnt nothin'? Does yer vanity—yer arrogance—know no bounds? Ye're nothin' more than an interloper here! Ye've failed, angel—if angel ye are still!" He held up the glass vial and flaunted it. "This soul is mine, and ye'll do as I say. Ye've no choice!"

Donaldson's head was thrown back, and his mouth opened. Carol/Máiri and Doyle watched, horrified, as the vial was dropped into his maw. Doyle heard his teeth crunch on the glass and swallow—once—twice. Then, what was once young Malcolm Donaldson, smacked his lips and opened his mouth. "Aaaahhhh," he sighed.

"NO!" Carol/Máiri cried, but she watched helplessly as Donaldson's head distended. His face disappeared as the skin, like the chrysalis in a metamorphic cycle, split and was shucked off to reveal a growing black form devoid of features and recognizable shape emerging from the wreckage.

A deathly silence ensued. Then a single cry came from somewhere in the growing mass of seething black matter. That cry of despair echoed as Doyle saw countless faces appear, disappear, and reappear within the inky shroud, as if seeking escape. He cowered behind Carol while the shape expanded and that single voice became the cries of thousands.

Only Carol heard Máiri's voice then *"Without God, all is vanity. May God forgive me mine! I've failed. I'm sorry, but the Burglar's found strength in my lack of humility. Now hear me, there's goin' t' be a bright flash of light and a loud scream, so close yer eyes tight, and keep them closed till ye hear the scream, then run for the gate! Don't look at the Burglar! Don't listen to him! Run! And whatever ye do, don't stop. Don't stop for anything, d' ye understand?"*

"No," Carol thought-spoke. *"I don't understand! Can't you just get us out of here? Aren't you an angel of God?"*

"Yes," said Máiri. *"I remember that now. There's no time t' explain. Look t' yerself, cousin. May God bless and keep ye. Mind now, close yer eyes, and wait for the scream, then run!"*

3

She was gone. Carol felt the angel leave her body. She closed her eyes—squeezed them shut. But Doyle didn't. Standing behind Carol, his eyes locked on the rippling black shroud and the faces outlined within it. Then Carol's ghost lady suddenly appeared—exactly as described—to stand between them and the monstrosity. Doyle had no doubt that he was looking at an angel.

"Jesus fuckin' Christ!" he said, laying a hand on Carol's shoulder.

Carol suddenly remembered he was there. "Marty. Close—"

The screech was terrifying and the light blindingly white. Doyle ducked his head and covered his ears. Carol opened her eyes to see the straw floor aflame—all of it. She remembered to avert her eyes when the Burglar spoke with his voice of thousands. "Come to us! Come to us! COME TO US!"

"Marty!" Carol grabbed a handful of Doyle's tee shirt. "Come on, we have to run!"

"I can't see! I can't see a fuckin' thing!"

Carol pulled his hand to her hip and held it with her free hand. "Hold on to me." Turning and brandishing her torch, she added, "Let's go!"

But Doyle resisted. The darkness he found himself buried in had begun to thrum…like a plugged-in amplifier awaiting a call to action. Widening his eyes, he strained for sight as the humming filled his ears. He was relieved when objects around him started to take shape. But his relief vanished when the familiar portcullis slowly materialized to loom before him. This was his nightmare incarnate, only this time, the beguiling core of darkness lay not in the corner, but beyond the gate, and, when the portcullis slowly began to rise, Doyle felt himself drawn towards the abyss behind its teeth.

"Come to us!" the throbbing blackness said, and Doyle started to obey.

Carol grabbed his shirt again and pulled. "Marty! Stop! What are you doing?"

Doyle ignored her. She felt the heel of one of her sandals break in the struggle to stop him. "Marty! Stop, for Christ's sake!" Then, sensing a presence at her rear, she released her hold on him and spun, swinging her torch simultaneously to strike the encroaching ghoul full in the face with it. Soundlessly, it backed off, but Carol was horrified to see several more of its ilk issuing from the darker confines of the chapel.

"*MARTY!*" she screamed, tugging at his shirt. But Doyle, transfixed, was bent on moving towards the monstrous mass. Carol stepped in front of him and slapped his face with her free hand, but Doyle's only reaction was to push her away forcefully. Already off balance because of her damaged footwear, Carol emitted a cry of pain and fell to the ground at his feet.

All at once, the disembodied cries ceased, and the little man was roused from his trance. He faltered as his nightmare landscape vanished. Although the deep black shroud still hovered, it had withdrawn and diminished. Doyle sensed something had changed. He was still trying to figure out what exactly, when Carol slapped his leg to grab attention.

"Help me!" she cried. "It's my ankle, I…I can't get up!" As she writhed, Doyle saw that her once white summer dress, now dirt-smudged and rumpled, rode high on her hips, covering little to nothing of her lower body. She grimaced and clutched at her injured ankle, ignoring her immodesty. "I think it might be broken," she groaned. Then she took note of his inaction. "Marty! Help me up!"

But Doyle was now watching the Burglar. It continued to shrink and retreat, and Doyle thought he knew why. Then it stopped. Looking down, he saw that Carol had fixed her clothing and covered herself.

"Wait!" Doyle whispered, grabbing her shoulder while keeping his eyes on the entity. "Quick, lift up yer skirt again!"

"What? Have you—" Then, she understood. "*Anasyrma?*"

Doyle squeezed her shoulder. "Aye, I think so. *Sheela na gig.* Somethin' stopped it, didn't it? and that's the only thing I can think of."

The Burglar, once more bloating grotesquely, was starting to encroach.

"Well," Doyle said, shaking Carol's shoulder, "what d' ye think?"

The straw carpet smouldered, sputtered, and flamed sporadically in the space between them and the monster and macabre shadows danced on the chapel walls. The scene reminded Carol of a medieval artist's depiction of Hell.

"I think that maybe this Burglar thing is some version of the Devil."

Doyle massaged her shoulder. "Mebbe he is, mebbe he is."

"Well," said Carol, resignedly, rubbing a hand over her injured ankle, "I can't run anymore, can I?" The cries coming from the black mass were growing, and she was horrified anew when she recognized the silhouetted, tortured face, now front and center, among the countless others. "Jesus! *NO!*" She turned her head to hide her face in Doyle's thighs. "NO—NO—*NO!*"

Doyle crouched over and held her head against his inner thigh. "What's wrong?"

"It's Bill! Christ, Marty! I saw *Bill!*"

The Burglar's laugh was loud and harsh, rising above a cacophony of other sounds. "*COME, JOIN US!*"

Carol jerked her head out of Doyle's grasp and turned to face her tormentor. "It couldn't be Bill. Bill's an angel—he was an angel before he died! That…that *thing* is just fucking with me, fucking with my mind, and I think I know why." Biting her bottom lip and eating her pain, she pushed her back into Doyle's legs, bracing herself so that she could raise her knees and lift her bottom off the ground. Then Carol lifted her skirt, parted her thighs, and flashed the devil.

The reaction was immediate. The Burglar blenched and the discordant choir of tortured voices was simultaneously muted.

"Fuck me!" Doyle gasped. The monster retreated, shrinking visibly as it began to disappear into a world that was quickly lightening.

"It worked. Jesus Christ, Carol, it worked! Everything's goin' t' be alright, love; he's gone." His elation was dampened when Carol's shoulders drooped and fell under his hands, and he realized that she was crying. "It's okay, love. Ye did it. He's gone!" Releasing her shoulders he spread his arms and opened his hands. "Look, it's *all* gone."

The brightening sky was visible overhead, and the chapel was once again the ruin that Doyle had always known. "See? Everything's alright, love, we're—"

Carol snorted through her tears. "Alright? *Alright?* No, Marty, everything's not alright. Nothing will ever be alright again!"

Doyle dropped his hands back on her trembling shoulders and gently massaged them. "There now, there," he said, not knowing what else to say or do.

Once more he surveyed the ruin. Doyle tried to bringing to mind the previous night's events, but it was becoming difficult—memory was fading. "Unbelievable!" he whispered.

"What is? What's unbelievable?"

"C-could I," Doyle stammered "I-I mean, c-could *we* have…I mean…," he looked into Carol's tearstained eyes, "could it…was it all…ye know…a dream?"

Carol was touched by his childish naivety. She knew that Doyle wanted—needed—her to share his doubt; he wanted to be told that they could have dreamt the whole thing. That the thing they'd confronted in the darkness didn't really exist. But her memory was vivid and her charity limited.

"No. It wasn't a dream. I know it and you know it. That *thing* was…*is*…as real as you and I are right now. And it's still here, somewhere, we just can't see it. Because of me, we blundered into its world." Carol gifted the little man a smile. "And thanks to you, we managed to blunder out of it." She winged her arms, elbows bent. "Help me up."

Doyle hooked his hands under her armpits and helped her to her feet. He put his hands on her waist when she teetered. "Carol…um…ye can pull yer skirt down now, love."

"Oops!" said Carol.

Doyle averted his eyes politely, while she fixed her attire. The awkwardness of the moment was broken when Carol planted a kiss on his turned cheek. "Thank you," she said, and Doyle was further surprised when she immediately wrapped him in a bear hug. "I mean it. Thank you, Marty!"

"Me?" said Doyle. "Sure, what did *I* do?"

"You didn't abandon me when you could have—and probably *should* have. I'll never forget that. And thank you for *sheela na gig!*"

That memory lingered, and Doyle reddened. "Oh, sure yer alright, love. Ye just wanted yer nightmares to stop, and ye asked me t' help. I didn't do much." He looked at the walls of Bonamargy, bathed now in the morning's sunlight, and still found himself thinking that the whole thing could have been just another nightmare. He shook his head. "Anyway, I hope it worked—I hope yer nightmares are gone for good."

"Well, we'll know tomorrow morning, won't we?"

Doyle looked confused, then blushed even more profusely when she added, "When we wake up."

Carol allowed the smile to leave her face, leaned towards him, and kissed him, tenderly, on the lips. "That is," she said, more seriously, "if that's okay with you? Will you stay with me?"

Doyle tried to control his emotions in his inimitable way. "Well," he said, raising his eyebrows and inclining his head, "technically speaking, love, it's already tomorrow mornin'."

"Well, in that case, we'll just have to wait till the *morn's morn,* won't we...love?" She made to slap his shoulder and stumbled under the effort.

"Okay," said Doyle, putting his hands on her hips, steadying her. "I think we should get ye the hell out of here. So, d' ye think ye can walk?" He watched as she tried to stand on her injured ankle. "Looks t' me like ye might need a piggyback."

Tears welled at these words and the memory they evoked, but Carol managed a smile. "Yes, I think you're right."

***

Julia McQuillan's faith in God had been tested many times, but never more so than with the destruction of Liam O'Kane's soul, and she balked now at her erstwhile sister's pleas that she be allowed her to help Julia's soul continue on its existential path.

"I don't understand," said Julia. "Why did God abandon Liam? Why has He abandoned us?"

"He hasn't abandoned us. He—"

"He let the Burglar *eat* Liam's soul, Máiri. Why? Was it merely t' teach you a lesson in humility?"

"I'm His emissary, Julia," said the angel. "I'd forgotten that. I'm merely a conduit to God and He decided t' remind me of my station."

"At what cost, Máiri? What did Liam O'Kane do t' deserve such a fate? His soul languished, imprisoned by an evil spirit, through no fault of his!"

"How d' ye know that?" said Máiri, her temper rising. "You don't know what faults Liam O'Kane had, or what sins he committed. He had his path and you have yours, and—"

"He loved me." cried Julia.

"Aye. and that wasn't his fault either, was it? Love is just another burglar of souls, don't ye see that?"

Julia was silent.

"Listen, Julia, I can guide ye, and move ye closer to God. Let me help ye."

"Why would I want to move closer to God?"

"Julia!"

"I don't understand God, Máiri. Seems t' me that there's not that much difference between God and the Burglar."

"But God *loves* ye. He gave ye life."

"Why?"

Máiri made to answer and simply hung her head. Julia, softening her tone and demeanour, went on. "Sure ye've done yer best, love, and I thank ye for it, but don't ye think it's best we both try to renew our faith in God now? I don't believe God loves me, and I know I don't love Him right now, so I think I should bide here and let these burglars decide what t' do with my soul."

"D' ye believe that *I* love ye, Julia?"

"Aye. I do."

"Then won't ye change yer mind and let me help ye?"

"No, m' wee darlin', I won't. I'll bide here."

"Then may God bless ye and keep ye, Julia. I pray that He'll continue t' allow me t' protect ye whenever I can. I must leave ye now, love, but I'll return when I can."

So saying, the soul guide diminished and disappeared.

And so, Julia McQuillan, ethereal and alone, lingered in Bonamargy. She had no fear and did not despair. Julia presumed that either the Devil—as manifested in that ancient being calling itself the Burglar of Souls—or God, would take her soul, and as far as she was concerned, her fate was in their hands.

Julia had been born, lived, loved, and died, and none of it was her fault; and neither, she believed, was her fate. Julia did not understand Fate and put it in the same category as Love. Julia thought both were something over which a human being had absolutely no control.

When yer alive it doesn't matter if ye believe in God, or the divil, or fate and ye don't know where yer soul's goin' t' end up when ye die; but Love, now…Love will rob ye of yer soul while yer still drawin' breath…

***

The Burglar neither understood nor pondered on *anasyrma*. Having no concept of good or evil, the spirit was unaware of the act's apotropaic effect and its reaction was elemental. The woman, through the act of simply lifting her skirt, had effectively rescued the mortals' souls from its thrall. The Burglar did not know how or why.

The humans would leave now, unmolested—the Burglar's minions were toothless under the morning sun and could not hinder their escape—but they might return, mortals often did; their need for justification, and their innate curiosity was often their bane. And of course, there was always conscience, and atonement. One of their number had died and lost his soul in Bonamargy, and that would prick.

And certainly, the mortals would dream, and when they dreamt, their souls, awakened and vulnerable, could wander into the Burglar's domain. There were portcullises and stairways aplenty here.

And as for the wraith, she had not moved on with her soul guide. She had chosen to remain in limbo, and the Burglar *did* ponder on that. What were her intentions, if any? No matter, sooner or later, she would falter in her resolve, whatever that might be, and the Burglar could wait; *Borgaire anama* had no concept of time either...

END

ACKNOWLEDGEMENTS

I would like to thank my editor, Shane Joseph, for his advice and support.

Thanks also to Joseph Patrick (Joe) Ryan for his assistance with my use of the Gaelic language in this book. Any misuse is mine and no fault of his.

AUTHOR'S BIO

Brian Ferris is a Canadian who was born and raised in Belfast, Northern Ireland. He emigrated to Ontario in 1977 where he still resides. ***Burglar of Souls*** is his first novel.